PRAISE FOR THE AUTHORS

LARA ADRIAN

"Action-packed, sexy and enticing…Lara Adrian's wild imagination and creativity is amazing."
–Reading Divas

"With an Adrian novel, readers are assured of plenty of dangerous thrills and passionate chills."
–RT Book Reviews

"Ms. Adrian has a gift for drawing her readers deeper and deeper into the amazing world she creates."
–Fresh Fiction

"Folsom's stories and ￼ ￼y are beautiful, sexy and passionate…"
–Aobibliosphere

"Intensely affectionate and blazingly hot."
– Joyfully Reviewed

"Tina Folsom's super sexy romances will be your favorite guilty pleasure!"
–Stephanie Bond, New York Times bestselling author

Other Books by Lara Adrian

Midnight Breed Series
A Touch of Midnight (prequel novella)
Kiss of Midnight
Kiss of Crimson
Midnight Awakening
Midnight Rising
Veil of Midnight
Ashes of Midnight
Shades of Midnight
Taken by Midnight
Deeper Than Midnight
A Taste of Midnight (ebook novella)
Darker After Midnight
The Midnight Breed Series Companion
Edge of Dawn
Marked by Midnight (novella)
Crave the Night
Tempted by Midnight (novella)
Bound to Darkness (Summer 2015)
Stroke of Midnight (novella, October 2015)

Masters of Seduction Series
Merciless: House of Gravori (novella)

LARA ADRIAN writing as TINA ST. JOHN

Dragon Chalice Series
Warrior Trilogy
Lord of Vengeance

Other Books by Tina Folsom

Scanguards Vampires Series
Samson's Lovely Mortal
Amaury's Hellion
Gabriel's Mate
Yvette's Haven
Zane's Redemption
Quinn's Undying Rose
Oliver's Hunger
Thomas's Choice
Silent Bite (novella)
Cain's Identity

Out of Olympus Series
A Touch of Greek
A Scent of Greek
A Taste of Greek

Eternal Bachelors Club
Lawful Escort
Lawful Lover
Lawful Wife
One Foolish Night

Lover Uncloaked (Stealth Guardians, Book 1)

Venice Vampyr (Novellas 1 – 4)

PHOENIX CODE
Novels

Cut and Run

Hide and Seek *(forthcoming)*

CUT AND RUN

PHOENIX CODE SERIES
Books 1 & 2

NEW YORK TIMES BESTSELLING AUTHORS
LARA ADRIAN
TINA FOLSOM

ISBN: 1941761011
ISBN-13: 978-1941761014

PHOENIX CODE SERIES
© 2014 by In Media Res Publishing, LLC
Cover design © 2014 by CrocoDesigns

CUT (Phoenix Code Series: Book 1)
© 2014 by Lara Adrian, LLC

RUN (Phoenix Code Series: Book 2)
© 2014 by Tina Folsom

FT
Pbk

www.PhoenixCodeSeries.com

Available in ebook and print. Unabridged audiobook edition forthcoming.

CONTENTS

CUT

Lara Adrian

1

Portland, Maine
Three years ago

When he got out of bed that late-February morning, Ethan Jones had no idea his life was about to end.

Standing barefoot in just a pair of jeans at the kitchen window of his girlfriend's small bungalow, he palmed a mug of fresh-brewed black coffee as he watched the sun rise. He'd been up for about an hour, leaving Tori to sleep in a while before she had to get ready for her nursing shift downtown at the medical center ER.

It was snowing again. Fine white crystals ticked against the windowpane as a gust blew through the tree-lined, working class neighborhood.

When he'd first moved to the Northeast from New Mexico, he'd hated the winters. Hard to imagine two years into his teaching stint at the local community college, he was actually growing accustomed to the snow and cold.

He was growing accustomed to a lot of things lately.

Getting too comfortable.

He recognized that fact for the risk it was, but it didn't keep him from registering genuine warmth as Tori Connors shuffled sleepily into the kitchen.

She was wearing his white button-down from last night and nothing else, her pale blond hair a messy tangle around her shoulders. The hem of the shirt fell halfway down her slender thighs, a single button fastened between her pert breasts.

"Mmm, it smells good in here," she murmured, drawing closer. "Fresh coffee and a hot man. Two of my favorite things."

As he took down a mug for her and filled it, she walked over and wrapped her arms around him from behind. Her cheek rested warmly against the center of his bare back. "Why didn't you wake me when you got up?"

"Because if you'd been awake, we'd still be in bed, doing everything but sleeping."

Her little moan vibrated through him. "That sounds like a great idea to me. Let's call in sick," she murmured, dropping kisses along the groove of his spine. Desire ignited through him with each soft press of her mouth on his skin. "Or we can say we're snowed in, trapped by a freak blizzard that only hit the East End. We can play hooky and spend the whole day in bed together."

He groaned, closing his eyes as his pulse hammered into a heavy throb. Spending the day in bed with Tori was never a bad idea. God knew, he'd been doing enough of it lately. And despite the fact that his cock responded with enthusiastic agreement, Ethan broke out of her loose hold and pivoted to put the mug of coffee in her hands.

"It's a test day for my eight o'clock class. Before that I've got an advisory meeting with a student who wants to drop Comparative Lit." He bent his head to give her a brief kiss, tasting the faint mint of toothpaste on her tongue. "I can't blow off the day, no matter how tempting you make it."

She gave him an arch look. "Apparently not tempting enough to make you jeopardize your perfect attendance, Professor Jones." She smiled, but her smart, denim-blue eyes were studying him over the rim of the steaming mug. "You're a strange one, you know that? I swear, sometimes I just can't figure you out."

"What's to figure out? I don't think I'm that complicated." His tone was calm, even amused, despite the prickling of his instincts.

As for complicated? She had no idea.

And he meant to keep it that way.

He might have gotten too comfortable with Tori in the months they'd been together, but he was never careless.

He was too well trained to let any part of his cover slip, even with her.

Ethan casually strode to the refrigerator and took out a carton of eggs and a bowl of fruit he'd chopped up earlier. "You want french toast or pancakes for breakfast?"

"Surprise me. You know I love whatever you put on the menu. Besides, after last night, I'm ravenous."

Pivoting to lean her back against the counter, she grabbed a strawberry from the bowl and bit into it, watching him gather a few more things from the fridge and cabinets. "Why do I get the feeling you want to change the subject? The way you always seem to do whenever that subject is you."

He shrugged. "I guess I don't find myself all that interesting."

She blew out a soft laugh. "Trust me, Ethan, you're

interesting. You're also charming, athletic, and ridiculously gorgeous. On top of all that, your mind is like some kind of encyclopedia. I don't think there's a book in existence you haven't read, and you can talk about any subject as if you've studied it all your life. Not to mention, you cook like a dream and…do a lot of other things like a dream too. You're actually freakishly perfect."

He set a quart of milk on the granite countertop and met her gaze. "Careful or you're gonna give me a big head."

"And then you'll definitely be late for your class," she said teasingly, her pretty mouth curved in a grin. A mouth that he wanted to taste all over again this morning.

He couldn't resist pulling her into his arms. She went willingly, her soft curves pressing against him as he reached under the cotton shirt to caress her naked breast.

"Do you ever think you should be doing something else with your life, Ethan?"

He smirked. "I hadn't before, but now that you point it out, gigolo chef doesn't sound half bad."

Tori laughed as he kissed her, but when he drew back and met her eyes there was a seriousness in their blue depths. "You never think that maybe you made a mistake coming here to Portland, instead of somewhere else? You don't think you'll get bored here eventually?"

"What makes you say that?"

She gave a vague shake of her head. "I don't know. It's just…something I wonder about sometimes. I know you're devoted to what you do. But you're too smart to settle for Associate Professor. Maybe you should aim for something higher than that."

She thought he lacked ambition or drive? The thought made his brows rise. He wasn't defensive; more privately amused. "I like my job." He grinned. "I'm not trying to save the world or anything."

She rolled her eyes. "I know that. But you're too exacting and meticulous to be teaching liberal studies for the undeclared, don't you think? I mean, I know you're dedicated to your students. If you ask me, you're the best thing that ever happened to that school. But I've known you for almost a year now. I've watched you, Ethan. You're Ivy League brilliant and then some. Yet here you are, hiding out at a small-town community college."

Her choice of words nearly made him choke.

Fuck.

Was it even remotely possible that she suspected something?

He wanted to reassure himself it was only coincidence, merely conversation, but his conditioning was too ingrained for him to tread with anything less than caution.

Tori Connors was a small town girl. She'd been born and raised in rural Maine. She didn't have the same mileage on her that he did, nor the years of training in concealment and subterfuge, but she was a sharp, observant woman with a keen intelligence. It was part of what attracted him to her, aside from her girl-next-door beauty and earthy authenticity.

So far, Tori knew only what he'd allowed her to know about him—most of it sticking close to his carefully constructed cover.

She knew nothing about who he truly was, or his work as a precognitive agent in one of the CIA's most covert programs. If he cared about her—and he did, more than he ever should have dared—then he had to make sure Tori never got close to that other part of his life.

Ethan drew her further into his embrace and kissed her with an affection, and a desire, that belonged entirely to her, not to his training or his need to ascertain a potential breach in his cover.

He felt more for Tori in a handful of months than he had for anyone else in all of his thirty-one years of life.

That fact alone should probably have told him it was time to break things off and move on, but damned if he'd been able to find the will to do it.

"Hey," he said gently, smoothing a sleep-tousled blond strand from her face. "Tell me what this is about. What's on your mind, babe?"

"I've just been thinking about things." She pressed her lips together as she looked up at him, hesitation in her dark blue eyes. "It's going to be March soon. Which means Saint Patrick's Day is coming up…"

At Ethan's stare, she gave an awkward shrug. "So, in a few weeks, it'll be a year for us."

Shit. A year already? His track record with previous women he'd known had been measured in days and weeks. Yet he'd been with Tori for almost twelve easy, pretty fucking fabulous months.

Tori searched his gaze. "You didn't remember?"

"I remember everything about that night," Ethan said. And he did.

He hadn't been looking for a date that Saint Patty's night in Portland. Alone, he'd been enjoying a pint of Guinness at a decent Irish pub off the main drag that wasn't stuffed to the rafters with tourists.

Just about the time he was thinking of heading home to his rented studio apartment, his eye had been drawn to a pretty, petite blond who'd come in with a gaggle of girlfriends.

He'd debated with himself for half an hour about going over to talk to her. And then things started getting rowdy in the pub. Ethan's senses had prickled with the realization that Tori was in the direct path of an oncoming brawl.

Minutes before the full weight of a three-hundred-pound drunk could plow into the stool she occupied at the bar, Ethan strode over and asked her to dance.

When the fight eventually broke out exactly as he'd seen it happen in his mind, he was watching Tori swivel and sway in front of him while he sported a raging hard-on and U2 sang about "Mysterious Ways."

Before the song was over, Ethan had asked for Tori's number. Instead, she'd taken him home to her bungalow for a night of unforgettable sex.

He hadn't looked at another woman since.

He gazed at her now, and dropped a kiss on her parted lips. "That was a very good night."

"It's been a very good year, don't you think?"

"The best," he said, bending lower to nuzzle her soft neck.

"I'm glad you think so too." She drew back from him with a smile, but there was a deeper question in her eyes. "I guess I've been thinking that since you spend almost every night here anyway, maybe we should make things a bit more official. I've been thinking that maybe you should let your apartment go and move in with me."

His lungs seized up. He had a hundred excuses for

why that was a terrible idea—an impossible one—but nothing came out of his mouth.

Tori rolled her eyes and smacked her palm against his bare chest. "Don't look so shell-shocked. I'm not asking you to marry me, I just thought we could live in sin for a while." She tilted her head and gave a sweet little shrug. "Or maybe for longer than a while."

God, he was a jackass. She looked so earnest, so open and vulnerable. So trusting.

He should never have let things go this far, this long. "Tori, I don't think—"

"You don't have to give me an answer now," she blurted. "I know you like your space, and I know you don't make impulsive decisions. So, just take some time and consider it, okay?"

She leaned into him as she spoke, and before he realized what she was doing, she'd slipped her hand down from his chest to inside the loose waistband of his jeans. She homed in on his cock and held him in her warm grasp, stroking him just the way he liked it.

A hissed curse leaked out of him as his flesh turned to granite under her touch.

She kissed him full and deep on the mouth, then drew back with a sultry smile. "We can talk some more over breakfast. In the meantime, I'll be in the shower, in case you'd like to discuss my offer in greater detail right now."

She unfastened the single button that held his shirt together over her naked body. Then she shrugged out of it and let it drop to the kitchen floor as she pivoted and began an unrushed walk away from him.

Damn, but the sight of her made him hot. He groaned as he watched her rounded bare ass retreat toward the bungalow's bathroom.

"Ah, fuck the french toast," he muttered, primed to leap after her in hungered pursuit.

But as he moved, his arm caught the egg carton on the countertop and sent it crashing to the floor. Yellow yolks leaked out onto the tiles.

Ethan swore and grabbed for the roll of paper towels, tearing off a few to clean up the mess.

Then he froze.

Because at that same instant, a voice speared into his mind. The psychic call delivered a single, unmistakable message...

Phoenix down.

Ethan stood there, his blood running cold, his brain snapped into immediate and total focus.

He'd known this moment could arrive at any time. He knew it, dreaded it.

Believed in some naive corner of his existence that it might never come.

But the signal was irrefutable.

Phoenix down.

It meant one thing. The program he belonged to was compromised. Its director and possibly any number of Ethan's fellow Phoenix agents were dead, or soon to be.

And so was he, if he didn't act now.

Henry Sheppard's instructions had been plain enough, should he ever have to issue the distress call to the untold number of men who belonged to the secret government ESP program.

Assume the worst.

Cut all ties.

Trust no one.

Leave everything behind and run.

Ethan's life—the cover he'd been living for the past two years—was over. That man was dead now.

As for his time with Tori, it was over too. Right here and now. No explanations. No goodbyes.

He could afford neither, and she would be safer knowing nothing.

She would be safer hating him for what he was about to do.

Ethan stared down at the broken eggs at his feet. From the other end of the hallway, the shower hissed softly behind the sweet, off-key tune of Tori's singing as she waited for him to join her.

Regret put a raw ache in his chest, but the agent Ethan had been trained to be pushed the emotion aside. There was no time for it. There was a good chance he and the others like him were already being hunted.

He dropped the paper towels on the counter, then reached down to retrieve his shirt from where Tori had let it fall. He put it on, inhaling the scent of her on the white cotton as he buttoned it up.

It was the last breath he'd take of her. The last moment he would know as her lover.

Grabbing his boots and coat from the kitchen's back door, he quickly slipped them on.

Then he walked out of the house and into the light flurry of morning snowfall without a single backward glance, leaving Ethan Jones and everything that man cared about behind him.

2

Seattle, Washington
Present day

Ethan had picked up a tail about a block away from the hostel where he was staying since he'd arrived in the city less than two weeks ago.

Dressed in dark jeans and a black T-shirt, lug-soled boots and a navy blue windbreaker, the man shadowing him didn't exactly blend in with the summer crowd of tourists and hipsters down near the waterfront.

He didn't seem concerned with blending in. His balding scalp was shaved close to the knobby block of his skull, and behind the dark sunglasses that hid his eyes, the assassin's focus was rooted entirely on Ethan.

Blatantly, he followed Ethan into a packed restaurant on Western Avenue, not far from the bustling Pike Place Market.

The noontime crowd was thick and noisy, the air inside Etta's aromatic with the smell of grilled seafood, interesting spices and hoppy microbrews.

While Ethan was shown to the last open booth in the dining room to the right of the door, his pursuer parked on a stool at the end of the long bar counter at the opposite side of the restaurant. Ethan didn't miss the subtle glance in his direction as the man was greeted by the bartender and handed a menu.

This wasn't the first time Ethan had been hunted in the three years following the demise of the Phoenix program. Another assassin had found him last summer in Kansas City, where Ethan had taken a job with a landscaping firm.

It was an inconvenient quirk of his ESP ability that his premonitions never told him when he was in harm's way.

The day the sniper had him in his sights in the affluent suburban neighborhood in Missouri, Ethan hadn't even realized he was in danger until he bent to clear a jam on his weed whacker and a bullet zipped over his head, missing him by a fraction of an inch.

He'd dropped everything then and there, and started running. He'd cut an uneven path across the country in the year since, never staying put for more than a few weeks at a time.

Cash and carry. No questions asked, and no truths given. That was his mode of operation now.

No strings, no complications. And definitely no emotions. He'd learned that lesson in spades the morning he walked away from Tori Connors.

There were days—and nights—his regret still felt raw.

But he'd had no choice where she was concerned. A reality that was hammered home in cold, inescapable fact when he considered the hired killer waiting for him across the restaurant.

Ethan lived off-grid as much as possible, and made a habit of not letting the grass grow under his feet. It had served him well so far, probably the only thing keeping him alive.

He glanced up with a vague smile as a middle-aged waitress came over to greet him.

"How you doin' today?" she murmured without pausing for a reply. "What can I get for ya?"

"Tell me about the crab cakes. Any good?" he asked, well aware they were the restaurant's claim to fame.

As his server described the special seasoning and cooking method, Ethan pretended to listen, while in his peripheral vision he studied every physical nuance of the man who'd been tailing him. "Sounds great. I'd like two, please. And a cup of black coffee."

"Coming right up."

Ethan settled into the booth, watching as the other man murmured his order and leaned his elbows on the bar. He was trying to appear casual now, watching people stroll past the window. The bartender poured him a beer, but it sat untouched in front of the man.

As Ethan's server delivered his coffee, he wondered what type of weapon the assassin concealed inside his jacket.

Would it be a gun from this one too, or something more personal, something hand-to-hand? No doubt he wouldn't be left to wonder for long.

He should have already been gone from Seattle. Usually, he figured it was time enough to move on once he started seeing Tori's face in his dreams—dreams that woke him with a start, made him wish he was someone else. It happened more often than he cared to admit.

But better that he see Tori in his dreams than the recurring nightmare of fire and destruction that had begun haunting his sleep ever since the Phoenix program went dark.

The flames and melting heat were a premonition; that much was certain.

But a premonition of what?

He hadn't had contact with any other agents in all this time. There had been no other messages—psychic or otherwise—from Henry Sheppard.

Ethan knew the program was no more. He just didn't know who was responsible, or who had betrayed and murdered the program's creator.

Whether the hired gun across the room knew anything useful remained to be seen, but Ethan intended to do what he could to find out. He needed information, answers that might help him understand who he was running from and how far his unknown enemies might be willing to go to find him or the other members of Phoenix. His survival depended on it.

And yes, there was a part of him that wanted something more than that. He wanted to inflict pain. He wanted justice.

He wanted vengeance, not only for the demise of the program, but for all that had been yanked from his own fingers.

When the man at the bar glanced his way again, Ethan decided to put the wheels in motion. Digging out cash enough for his pending lunch order and a tip, he left the money on the table and slid out of the booth.

His pursuer had just picked up his twenty-dollar burger and was about to take a bite when Ethan strode out of the place.

There was no need to look back to check if the man in the windbreaker and dark shades was going to follow him. As he stepped outside, Ethan felt the assassin's eyes on him from the other side of the restaurant's large front windows.

Ethan hung a left on the wide sidewalk, heading for the corner of Western and Virginia. Better to take the steep side street, away from the waterfront and its milling crowds, than risk leading his pursuer into the heart of the tourist zone on busy Pike Place.

He walked briskly up the incline on Virginia, certain the assassin would be rounding the corner not far behind him.

Ethan picked up his pace, ducking into the alcove for an underground parking lot. He positioned himself at the very edge of the concrete wall, waiting for his opportunity to strike.

In a moment, he heard the swift approach of someone on the sidewalk. As soon as Ethan spotted the sunglasses and shaved head of his pursuer, he lunged out, driving his elbow into the man's throat.

The guy gasped at the impact. He staggered, wheezing a sharp breath. Then he lowered his head like a bull on the charge and barreled into Ethan.

The man was a tank, driving him back against the cement wall. Ethan's breath coughed out of him, his head snapping back, cracking sharply on the wall.

He felt the gun a second later. Cold metal came out of the assassin's windbreaker pocket to jam against Ethan's gut. He twisted, grabbing his attacker's wrist in both hands and wrenching it hard, until he heard the pop of breaking bones.

The gun went off as the man lost his grip, dropping it to the ground in a clatter. As it hit, a bullet shot wildly into the alcove, echoing like a clap of thunder.

Shit.

There wasn't a lot of time now. The noise was going

to attract plenty of attention.

Neither Ethan nor his assailant would want to see their faces caught on cell phone cameras, let alone the local news.

Calling on his years of training in hand-to-hand combat and self-defense at the CIA's Farm, Ethan repositioned, twisting the assassin's arm around to his back. He jammed it high, teeth bared in a snarl as his attacker gurgled a curse, face contorted in pain. "Who sent you?" Ethan demanded.

The man groaned, but didn't answer. He struggled, still in fight mode even though Ethan must have broken his wrist and was halfway to dislocating his shoulder as a bonus.

"Who do you work for? Answer, goddamn it."

"Don't know, don't fucking care," the would-be killer finally wheezed out. "I work for my paycheck."

The man heaved his weight as he spoke those last words, a sudden burst of adrenaline working in his favor. He managed to break out of Ethan's hold. With his right hand disabled, it was his left one that came at Ethan now.

A hard punch connected with Ethan's upper chest before he could react.

The blow took him aback...then he realized it hadn't been the guy's fist that hit him.

It was the short blade the attacker held in his curled grasp.

Ethan glanced down at his right pectoral, saw a dark bloodstain growing.

Fuck.

The man made another tight jab, but this time Ethan dodged it. He came back with a fierce uppercut to his assailant's jaw.

The guy fell back on his ass on the pavement. He didn't stay down for more than a second.

Scrambling up in a hurry, the would-be assassin took off running. Not up the quieter side street, but down toward the waterfront.

Toward the madhouse of tourists and locals that jammed the popular Pike Place Market.

Goddamn it.

Ethan retrieved the gun, watching the man beat feet. He had no choice but to follow.

He wasn't about to let this son of a bitch survive to come after him another day.

3

Walking alongside her friend Hoshiko in the bustling midway of Pike Place Market, Tori let her gaze drift over the endless produce and fruit stands.

Everywhere she looked was a sensory kaleidoscope of colors and textures and smells. The crowd inside moved slowly, a shoulder-to-shoulder mass of people from all walks of life.

In the fifteen minutes since they'd arrived, Tori had heard no less than half a dozen different languages spoken near her, not counting the assorted drawls and dialects representing just about every corner of the United States as well.

"What do you think?" Hoshi asked her as they paused to sample some Asian soup at one of the many stalls that lined the central walkway of the market.

She said something in fluent Japanese to the elderly woman behind the counter. The two women chatted animatedly for a few moments, then Hoshi handed a paper cup and plastic spoon to Tori. "Be careful, she says this one has a kick to it."

Tori sipped the citrusy, spice-laced fish and noodle broth and moaned in delight. It tingled on her tongue, exploding with exotic flavors. "Oh, my God. Is this salmon?"

Hoshi nodded as she spooned some into her mouth too. "Didn't I tell you this place was amazing?"

"It's incredible," Tori said, handing back her empty cup and soaking it all in as she followed her friend from vendor to vendor, grazing on one delicious offering after another.

Seattle was so different from anything she'd seen back home in Maine. The energy of the city was vibrant, pulsing, intoxicating. Even a bit overwhelming.

Then again, she'd only been in town for a few days. She was flying home tomorrow morning, but if everything went well, she'd be returning to Seattle in a few weeks as the newest member of the ER staff at Harborview Medical Center, where Hoshi worked.

Tori hadn't come to visit her old nursing school friend with the intent to interview for a new job, but when Hoshi mentioned the opening in her department, Tori had found herself wondering aloud if she ought to apply. A phone call and a couple of emailed resumes later, Tori had a face-to-face meeting with the ER's chief of staff.

The job was hers if she wanted it. The only problem was, she didn't know if pulling up stakes and moving out west was going to be any different from her life back in Maine. Long hours and graveyard shifts as part of a trauma unit would keep her busy, no matter where she did her work. Though she had to admit the idea of a scenery change after living her whole life in the same place was tempting.

Not to mention the fact that her current home held three years' worth of confusion and heartache for Tori that hadn't fully healed.

Three years since Ethan had vanished from her life

without a word of explanation or goodbye.

He'd taken his coat and boots from their spot near her back door, but left everything else behind. His apartment, his belongings, his job at the college and everything else he had and knew in Portland—he'd abandoned it all. As though none of it had mattered to him.

As if she hadn't mattered to him either.

The weight of that realization still crushed her. The pain was still raw when she thought about the moment she'd discovered he was gone.

For weeks afterward, she'd tried to find him. Waited months for him to call or respond to her emails. She'd even scoured police logs and intake records at every morgue in a two-hundred-mile radius.

Nothing. Ethan had simply ceased to exist.

She had so many unanswered questions, even now.

Had she somehow pushed him into leaving? Ethan wasn't the kind of man to spook over anything, but maybe asking him to move in with her had forced him to admit to himself that he wasn't ready to take that step.

At least, not with her.

Maybe she'd woken him up when she pointed out that he seemed to be wasting his time at the community college. Maybe it had been all he needed to decide he didn't want to stay there after all.

There were other times Tori's wondering took much darker turns. Had Ethan been in trouble in some way?

Did he owe someone money, or did he have some hidden problem he couldn't bring himself to share with her? Was he in danger somewhere, somehow prevented from getting in touch with her?

Or the worst scenario of all, could Ethan possibly be

dead?

For a long time, Tori had mourned him as if he *had* been killed. She had seen enough shell-shocked loved ones during her nights in the ER to know the hurt she felt at Ethan's leaving was like the aftermath of a sudden, fatal accident.

He was simply there one moment and gone the next. And she had been left to pick up the pieces of her broken heart and carry on without him.

She'd done her best to do just that, throwing herself into her work and telling herself to forget him. After all, she was a born survivor, a fighter. She'd been taking care of herself from the time she was a kid.

She'd had to, being the only child of a single mom who'd been sick with cancer most of Tori's childhood. From fifteen on, after her mother died, Tori had supported herself. She'd leaned on no one.

She had never allowed herself to need anyone, but damn Ethan Jones for coming into her life and changing all that. He'd been her best friend and lover, her most trusted confidant. He'd been *the one*...or so she'd thought. She'd let herself fall hard for him, and he'd walked right over her on his way out the door.

The best thing she could do for herself was move on, start fresh in a place that didn't carry so many reminders of what she foolishly thought she had with him.

If only she could convince her heart that's all it would take to forget him.

As she and Hoshiko strolled deeper into the market building, Tori realized a crowd had begun to gather around one of the fish stands up ahead. Crabs, shellfish, and a vast array of other seafood was displayed on heaping mounds of crushed ice in stands flanking the walkway.

Tall glass cases stood behind the ice bins, and at the counter, two men in stained white vinyl aprons hawked to passersby. Another man in orange overalls and rubber boots had taken up a position across the midway.

As they worked, they started chanting to each other in unison. "Ayy, oh! Ayy-oh!"

"What's going on?" Tori asked as her friend brought her toward the commotion.

"You'll see." Hoshi grinned. "Just keep your head down."

"What do you mean, keep my—oh!" A large salmon was chucked across the market by one of the guys behind the counter, to the delight of the crowd.

The man in the overalls intercepted, cradling the fish and chanting at his coworker before sending the salmon back over the heads of Tori, Hoshiko and the rest of the laughing spectators. The fishmongers put on quite a show, drawing an even bigger throng around their storefront.

Between the singsong calls of the men at the fish stand and the laughter and applause from the cluster of onlookers, it wasn't immediately apparent that some kind of disturbance was taking place toward the rear of the long market building.

Not until a woman let out a shriek, followed by the crash of a produce stand.

Alarmed, Tori glanced over her shoulder. Something—or rather, someone—was pushing their way through the market.

She spied the sheen of a balding head and the glint of light off dark sunglasses. She saw bullish, bulky shoulders clothed in a light windbreaker, as the man wearing it violently shoved people out of his path. He rolled forward without stopping, throwing down obstacles in his wake.

Screams and curses punctuated his progress as he tore through the thick lunchtime throng like a cyclone.

What the hell is wrong with him?

More than one person shouted at him to slow down, watch where he was going, but the man kept barreling forward with total disregard.

He burst through the edge of the crowd where Tori and Hoshi were standing, cradling his right hand and running at full speed. Hoshi couldn't get out of his way fast enough and he slammed into her, knocking her into one of the fish displays as he passed. Clams and crab legs clattered to the concrete as Hoshi staggered into a spill along with them.

"Asshole!" Tori hissed at him as she rushed to her friend.

The man tore out of the market to the street.

And then the reason for his flight—a second man, obviously in pursuit of the bald guy in sunglasses— emerged from the crowd behind Tori.

She threw an angry glance at him, ready to rip into him for his part in the chaos too. But suddenly her mouth wouldn't work.

The man was younger than the one he chased, probably by an easy decade. Dressed in a tan T-shirt sporting a local microbrewery logo, graphite gray cargo shorts and leather sandals, his clothes would have made him blend in with the rest of the tourists and locals downtown.

But his expression was fierce, deadly. And below his right shoulder, a growing bloodstain bloomed.

All the breath in Tori's lungs seemed to dry up as her gaze lifted to his.

Her mind lurched to a halt as she stared into a pair of hazel eyes she'd know anywhere and a beard-stubbled, handsome face that had been emblazoned on her heart for the past four years.

4

If he thought running into an assassin with a kill order on him was fucked up enough, it was nothing compared to the surprise—and the dread—Ethan felt when he found himself staring at Tori Connors in the middle of Pike Place Market.

And if he wanted to hope that the three years and thousands of miles between them might have dampened her recognition of him, he couldn't have been more wrong.

She knew him instantly, even if she seemed unable to say so at first.

"Oh, my God," she finally managed to gasp. "Ethan?"

He wasn't about to stop and chat.

Without a second's hesitation—without giving her even so much as a blink of acknowledgment—he bolted after his quarry, leaving Tori to gape behind him.

He couldn't afford the delay. Had no time for explanations or apologies, even if she deserved both.

For her own safety, he couldn't let on for a moment that he knew her or that she might know anything about him, even his name.

He was the hunted now. Already in the crosshairs of powerful enemies who had demonstrated twice so far that they were capable of finding him, no matter where he ran or for how long he kept moving.

He'd be damned before he would let that target settle on Tori's back too.

Ethan dodged outside the market building, squinting through the hazy glare as he searched for his assailant. *Where the hell did he go?*

"Ethan." Tori's voice sounded several paces behind him, filled with confusion and disbelief.

He didn't turn around. Not even when it killed him inside to treat her with such coldness.

There was no other way. Seeing her here and now was the worst thing that could've happened. If he was lucky, she'd either chalk him up as an illusion or as a black-hearted bastard who didn't deserve the time of day.

But that wasn't how Tori Connors rolled. Indefatigable, unshakable, he could practically feel her determination like a current in the air as her eyes bore into him from behind. "Ethan, talk to me."

He moved deeper into the crowd, needing to lose Tori as he continued to look for the assassin among the clots of people arriving and departing from the market square.

He heard a sharp scream off to his right and swiveled his head in that direction. There—he spotted the bald man near the head of the street. He was hauling an old woman out of a compact car that idled at the curb.

Light footsteps sounded at his back and he knew Tori was following him.

"Ethan Jones!" Her shout drew several gazes toward her. Toward both of them.

Including the gaze of the assassin.

Ethan's gut tightened when the bald head pivoted toward him, the eyes hidden by dark shades zeroing in on Tori as she caught up to Ethan in the crowd.

"Get away," he growled without looking at her. "For fuck's sake, woman, get out of here and leave me alone."

Too late. The hit man paused as though cataloging her face, as if noting her apparent familiarity with Ethan.

A brief smile played over his lips. *Until next time,* that thin smirk seemed to taunt.

The assassin ducked into the old woman's car and slammed the driver's side door.

He peeled away from the curb with a screech of spinning tires, then rounded the corner out of sight.

Goddamn it.

Ethan wheeled around on Tori's confused, questioning face. She was oblivious to the danger she'd just stepped into, but he felt it with a dread he could hardly contain.

He wanted to roar at her—at himself too—but there was another part of him that ached to do nothing more than drag Tori into his arms right then and there.

Instead, he did neither. Just stood in place, frozen by the sight of her after so long apart.

She'd cut her blond hair much shorter than she used to wear it before. The spiky, pixie style made her dark blue eyes seem even larger, as deep as sapphire pools.

Summer had left her skin tanned a golden hue, and her simple white tank and olive shorts bared a whole lot of that soft skin to Ethan's roving gaze.

His mouth watered despite the fury and fear hammering through him at this very inconvenient, unwanted reunion.

"I told you to stay away from me," he muttered.

"Jesus Christ. What the hell are you doing in Seattle?"

"I'm visiting a friend," she scoffed. "And I could ask you the same thing. Is this where you've been all these years?"

"You don't need to know where I've been. And I'm not staying."

It took all of his will to pivot and take the first few steps away from her.

He heard her breath catch behind him. Heard her sandals clip swiftly over the pavement as she came after him.

"Ethan, wait." She grabbed him by the arm. "You're bleeding."

Her touch electrified him, even after all this time. In the years since he'd left Maine, he'd almost convinced himself that he was over her.

Now, he felt all those lame rationalizations disintegrate around him as every cell in his body responded to the warmth of her fingers clasped onto his arm.

He scowled and pulled out of her grasp. "Don't worry about me. I'll live."

"What's wrong with you?" She stared up at him, her blond brows furrowing at his harsh tone. "Why are you acting like this, like you don't even know me?"

That's exactly what it was—an act. It was all he could do to make sure anyone who might be watching their exchange wouldn't think Tori meant anything to him.

With every cold glare and disregarding word, he prayed like hell that his act might keep her safe.

But she was a tenacious one, always had been. She hiked up her chin and he knew she wasn't about to let him dismiss her so easily. "Ethan, tell me what's going on. That man—who is he? Did he…Jesus, that's a stab wound. Did that man try to mug you or something?"

"Or something," he murmured. "Like I said, I'll live. Now, do us both a favor and forget you saw me."

He saw her gaze shutter as if she'd been physically struck. "That's it? Are you fucking kidding me?" Her voice rose, taking on an uneven edge, full of hurt and outrage. "All this time, after everything you put me through, and this is all you can give me?"

Ethan glanced around the market square as she railed at him, trying to discern if there were any eyes on them with something more than passing curiosity. It didn't seem so, and although his security training told him to extricate as quickly and cleanly as possible, he couldn't disengage from the look of betrayal on Tori's pretty face.

"I can't do this with you, Tori. I don't expect anything I tell you right now would make it any clearer for you, anyway."

"Try me."

He gave a tight shake of his head. "It's too dangerous."

"You're not making any sense. What's too dangerous?" She looked at his bleeding wound again, her gaze sober. "You need medical attention, Ethan."

He wanted to deny it, but he could hardly argue that Tori was wrong. Pain lanced him where the knife had pierced his pectoral. A numbness had begun to seep into his upper arm as the blood leaked out of him.

He needed to get somewhere safe where he could clean up and stitch his injury, if nothing else.

"My friend has a car parked in the public lot down the street," Tori told him. "I'll go back in and get her, then we're going to take you to the hospital before you lose any more blood. You need to go to the police—"

"No," he said, all but cutting her off. "No hospitals. No police reports. That will only make things worse."

She stared at him for a long moment. "You're serious, aren't you. Jesus, Ethan…what kind of trouble are you in?"

His feet itched to bolt, but the rest of him refused to cooperate. And the throb of his chest wound was intensifying by the second.

He was growing weak the longer he stood there. Too much blood loss and his body was starting to sink into shock.

"This friend of yours who you're staying with," he murmured. "Do you trust her?"

"Of course. I've known Hoshi since nursing school." Tori stared at him, her dark blue eyes concerned, but also suspicious. "I trust her a hell of a lot more than I can say for some other people."

Ethan grunted, knowing he'd more than deserved that dig. "I need to take care of this wound, but I can't risk going to a hospital and I can't go back to where I've been staying in the city the past two weeks."

The hostel had been compromised the instant he'd spotted the assassin tailing him today. There was nothing of value there anyway. Ethan traveled light, and took precautions in case he needed to escape any given location in a hurry.

He planned on doing just that, once he was patched up and rested, and ready to hit the ground running again.

"I can't be seen in a public place, Tori. Not now. And not with you."

"Okay." She listened soberly, then gave him a tight nod. "Hoshi's got an apartment on the other side of town. We can take you there. No doctors. No police. I'll have a look at your wound. Then you're going to give me the truth, Ethan. I think you owe me that much."

Yeah, he did. But even though he gave her a nod of agreement, Tori was asking him for the one thing he could never give her.

5

Even after making the drive across town with Ethan in the backseat of Hoshi's Subaru, Tori could still hardly believe it was really him.

After all this time, here he was again. In the flesh.

In the injured and bleeding flesh.

And he was slipping into a paler shade of gray with each passing moment.

Tori held a bunched-up beach towel against the wound to try to stanch the blood flow until she could go to work on him. It helped, but by the time they reached Hoshi's place, Ethan's lids were drifting closed more than they stayed open.

Lethargically, as if he had no choice, he followed Tori's orders to hold on to her as she and Hoshi extricated his big body from the car and helped him shuffle into the building.

The one-bedroom flat on the first floor was cozy but cramped, especially with the sudden presence of a six-foot, semi-conscious man in it.

Tori's unease worsened when her hand brushed the cold metal grip of a pistol tucked into the back waistband of Ethan's cargo shorts.

"Wait," she told her friend.

Hoshi's eyes narrowed as Tori carefully removed the

gun and set it down gently on the kitchen table just inside the apartment.

"Jesus Christ," Hoshi whispered. "Are you sure this is a good idea? What the hell do you really know about this guy?"

Tori shook her head, unable to answer that at the moment. "Let's put him on the sofa, okay?"

They guided Ethan over to the pull-out that had been her bed during her visit. He slumped down onto the cushions as Tori and her friend snapped into nurse mode.

Tori had assessed in the car that his airway was clear and that the blade had luckily missed his lung. Now, she carefully removed his blood-stained T-shirt while Hoshi disappeared into the bathroom down the short hallway and began rummaging in the cabinet under the sink.

Ethan roused at the noise in the other room. His head lifted, and his eyelids dragged open. "Have to get up," he murmured thickly. "Gotta get moving...before he comes after me again."

Tori put her palm on his good shoulder and held him down with surprisingly little effort. "You're not going anywhere right now. Be still and let me get to work."

He quieted, but as he settled back his brow remained furrowed, his sensual mouth held in a tight, grim line.

He'd sunk back into a drowse by the time Hoshi returned with an armful of things they would need: surgical gloves, antiseptic, bulky bandages and medical tape, nylon thread, packaged needles and syringes, and a small bottle of topical anesthetic.

They cleaned and prepped, then went to work immediately, tending Ethan's knife wound, then stitching it up while he faded in and out of awareness on the sofa.

As Hoshi tied off the final suture, her dark eyes flicked over to Tori. "So, this is him, huh? The guy who tore your heart out?"

"Yeah, this is him. This is Ethan."

Hoshi knew all about what happened back in Portland. She'd been a true friend through Tori's pain, so it didn't come as any surprise that Ethan wasn't exactly a welcome guest in her home. Particularly in the disturbing condition in which he and Tori had just reunited.

Tori couldn't keep from looking at him as he rested.

She could hardly keep from stealing a caress of his peaceful, handsome face.

Then again, she also wanted to slap him.

"Thank you for helping us, Hoshi."

"Us?" Her friend shook her head. "I'm doing this for you, not him. If I'd known who he was back at the market square, I would've let him bleed out on the pavement."

Tori frowned. Even she had her doubts about Ethan. In fact, doubt was all she had where he was concerned.

It was obvious enough that his stabbing hadn't been random violence. The man he chased through the market had attacked him for some reason, a reason Ethan refused to share.

And while he had always been elusive when it came to answering even the most innocuous questions about himself, the dodging and full-out refusal to be straight with her today was something far more troubling.

She didn't believe anything he'd said today.

She couldn't turn her back on him as easily as he'd been able to do to her three years ago, but looking at him now, Tori realized she didn't really know him at all. Maybe she never had.

For the first time since she'd known Ethan Jones, she didn't trust him.

The rectangular outline of a cell phone sat in the side pocket of his cargo shorts. Tori hesitated all but a second before carefully reaching in to retrieve it.

She powered it up, noting that it was one of the prepaid kind. There were no contacts stored in the device. The call log was empty too.

As if its owner wanted to leave no trace of his activity.

Tori set the phone down on the floor beside her, then reached over to search the other pocket of Ethan's shorts. Her fingers curled around a worn leather wallet, bulging with folded cash. She pulled it out, flipped it open.

A lot of small bills fell onto her lap, more than just a few hundred dollars' worth, from the look of it.

"What the hell?" she whispered, an odd sense of dread washing over her.

Ethan had no credit cards. Not even a gas card or any other piece of plastic that most normal people carried on them as a matter of habit, if not necessity. But there was one form of ID inside the wallet.

An out of state driver's license.

She stared down at the heavy beard and unkempt hair in the photo, and the familiar, all-too-gorgeous face that couldn't be fully obscured even under the careless, rumpled appearance.

Tori glanced at the South Dakota address. She didn't know it. Then again, she didn't know the name listed on the license either.

Not Ethan Jones, but a different name.

One that clearly didn't belong to him.

Everything she'd seen today, everything she'd heard from Ethan in the past couple of hours—or rather, everything she *hadn't* heard from him, namely anything resembling the truth—put a sick feeling in her stomach as she looked at him now.

Hoshi had paused in the collecting of their used medical supplies and was staring at her. "What is it, Tori? What's wrong?"

She didn't know what to say.

What was wrong?

Everything.

Hoshi came over and looked at the ID in Tori's hand and the fat wad of cash scattered in her lap. "I thought you said his name was Ethan."

Tori didn't answer. She glanced at him as he slept, uncertain of anything right now.

She felt as though she'd been punched.

What had happened to the straitlaced liberal studies professor she'd known and loved?

Then again, she might have thought she loved him, but it was becoming clearer by the second that she didn't really know him at all.

Maybe she never had.

6

I'm not going to make it in time.

The thought hammered through Ethan's head— through every screaming cell in his body—as his legs pumped across the desert sand and his heart felt ready to explode in his chest.

It was the dream again.

He knew that, in some dim corner of his sleep-encumbered mind.

The premonition that only came to him as a nightmare, whereas his other visions had always played out when he was awake.

Ethan ran and ran, but his feet felt leaden, not moving fast enough to make it.

I'm not going to be able to stop it from happening...

Even though he knew what was coming, the dread of it, the horror of what he was about to see, gripped him in a stranglehold.

No. I can't let it happen.

He ran as hard and as fast as he could, until his lungs were on the verge of bursting. Yet he made little progress on his way toward the building in the distance.

I have to get inside.

Someone has to be warned...

But who? Warned of what?

He didn't know. Those answers were never shown to him.

He only saw the building in front of him—close enough that he always believed this time he would reach it. This time, the nightmare would be different, and he would find a way to thwart the annihilation to come.

Yet it never happened that way.

Ethan ran and ran, but never got close enough.

Already, the rolling cloud of yellow sand was churning in the distance.

Just like every other time he had this nightmare premonition, the caravan of black SUVs slowly came into view on the far desert road. They sped toward him, nine gleaming ebony vehicles with diplomatic plates.

"Stop!" he shouted in the dream. "Go back!"

But the cars kept coming.

They always did.

Ethan counted them as he dragged his leaden feet through the deep sand. *One. Two. Three. Four...*

As soon as the ninth SUV rolled past him on the stretch of desert sand, it was too late to do anything more. The detonation boomed in his ears.

The sonic blast knocked him backward, flat on his ass.

The heat was unbearable.

Hellish.

Relentless.

It seared his face and eyes, drew hot flames up into his nose.

When his skin began to melt and fall away, Ethan roared in agony. He sat bolt upright on a curse before he had fully awakened.

A hand came down gently on his good shoulder and

Ethan swung to grab it. He twisted the delicate wrist and heard a shriek.

Tori was draped across him where he had been resting on the sofa in what he now recalled was her friend's apartment. The heat of her closeness, the scent of her, filled his senses with a new, and not at all unpleasant warmth.

"Shit," he muttered savagely and released her at once.

He could hardly summon his voice for anything more. Sitting there while Tori stared at him, Ethan panted in abject horror as he tried to blink away the images and reassure himself that he was unscathed.

He was alive.

The nightmare vision wasn't real.

Not yet, anyway.

He had to get moving. If the run-in with the assassin wasn't omen enough to tell him he needed to go, then the recurrence of the dream he'd been having with more and more frequency in the three years since Phoenix went dark sure as hell was. He needed to bail, head to ground as soon as he was able.

Ethan moved to a better sitting position so he could drop his feet off the sofa, but a sharp tug of pain in his shoulder slowed him down.

"Careful," Tori admonished him. "You'll tear the sutures. You need to sit still for a while."

He glanced at the bandages taped loosely over his wound. His chest was bare. "Where's my shirt?"

"You can't wear it. It's soaked in blood." Tori said it like an accusation. "What's really going on with you, Ethan? Or should I call you Daniel Gonzalez?"

How the fuck did she know that name? A pivot of

his head and he saw his wallet and cell phone lying on the table at the other end of the sofa.

The pistol he'd retrieved from his assailant was there too. Someone had emptied the rounds from it and set the bullets on the table with the rest of his belongings. "You went through my things?"

She scoffed. "I'm not sure whose things they are. Maybe you want to tell me why your photo is on someone else's ID? Is the gun his too?"

Ethan ground out a curse and heaved himself up to his feet. His vision spun, dizziness pouring over him. He pushed past it and pinned Tori in a glower. "Where's your friend?"

"She went to get takeout a few minutes ago. We didn't get a chance to bring anything home from the market for dinner." Tori crossed her arms over her breasts. "Don't change the subject. Why are you walking around with a loaded gun, more than two thousand dollars in cash and a burner phone? Who is Daniel Gonzalez?"

"I don't know," Ethan muttered. "Just the name the fake ID came with."

Tori gaped at him warily, disgust in every nuance of her pretty face. "Are you dealing drugs?"

"Christ, no."

"Why else would you be skulking around like this, telling me lie after lie, getting stabbed and refusing to go to a hospital or the police? You're acting like a criminal, Ethan." She shook her head, her lips turned down, eyes shadowed with mistrust. "You're acting paranoid, like you're on something. Or like you're having some out of control anxiety issues that are far from normal. Either way, you're acting to me like someone who needs professional help."

"For fuck's sake, Tori. I'm not crazy. I'm not some paranoid crackhead either, if that's what you think." He blew out a sharp sigh. "I'm not a criminal, and I'm not dealing drugs or anything remotely like that."

"Then what? Talk to me, damn you! Explain what's really going on, so I can understand."

He considered the hired gun who'd come after him today, and the threat that man still posed as long as Ethan allowed him to keep breathing.

That would-be killer had seen Tori too. Ethan knew it in his gut, in the chill that seeped into his bones at the thought of his enemies ever getting close enough to touch her.

He couldn't let that happen.

As for the fiery vision, he was determined to prevent that too…if he could stay alive long enough to figure out what it meant.

"The less you know, the better, Tori." He stepped past her. "I have to go now. Being around me is only putting you in danger. It might be too late already, but I'm not going to risk it."

He walked over and began picking up his things. He slid the wallet into his shorts pocket, then put the phone in another cargo compartment before gathering up the rounds and the emptied pistol. His blood-stained T-shirt was draped over the back of a kitchen chair.

When he headed for it, Tori hurried around the sofa and got there first. She held the shirt in a tight fist, shaking it at him as she spoke. "You're in no shape to go anywhere, and I'm not letting you leave this apartment until you give me the truth."

Ethan stalked closer to her, saying nothing. He took

one end of the wheat-colored cotton and gave it a slow tug. Tori didn't let go.

As he pulled, inch by inch, she drew toward him, still clutching determinedly to this final piece of him.

"You have every right to hate me," he murmured. "You could've left me out there today. You should have, Tori. Instead, you're killing me with your tenderness. With your kindness."

She didn't speak, just swallowed hard as she stared up at him. Ethan closed the distance between them even more, until only a breath of space remained.

A storm of conflicting emotion roiled in her indigo eyes.

Confusion.

Anger.

Mistrust.

But there was affection there as well. Something even deeper than that.

She still cared for him, and now that they were standing together, gazes locked in a hold that no lies could penetrate, Ethan could not deny that he still felt something for her too.

He felt it as if no time had passed since that morning in her bungalow kitchen back in Portland.

He reached up, tenderly stroked her cheek.

"Ethan…" His name was a whisper on her parted lips, a sigh. Her gaze darkened, her breathing picking up tempo as he indulged in the feel of her velvet skin. "I wish I could hate you. But I've missed you…"

A low groan curled up from the back of his throat at her soft admission. He'd missed her too. He had to touch her, wanted to do so much more.

He hadn't realized how powerful that yearning was

until now, when he was standing before her with nothing but silence and three years of lies and heartache between them.

Ethan wrapped his hand around her bare nape, smoothing the callused pad of his thumb along the side of her delicate neck. "Damn you, Tori. I never thought I'd touch you again. I thought we'd never see each other after I left. It would've been the best thing for both of us."

He lowered his head and took her mouth in a crushing kiss.

Tori's gasp at the moment of contact seeped out of her an instant later on a slow exhalation.

She melted into his kiss, their lips and tongues joining with a familiarity—a rightness—that rocked Ethan to the core. He'd never known this kind of fierce connection with a woman before.

And it didn't exactly reassure him to realize his feelings for Tori Connors hadn't faded in the least since the last time he'd held her in his arms.

Heat poured through him with each delicious thrust and sweep of her tongue against his. Need coiled in him, rendering him stiff and ready to bury himself inside her. Ethan dragged her deeper into his embrace, bruising her mouth with the force of his desire.

He couldn't help it. His body's reaction to her was too intense and too demanding to be denied.

All the years he'd been kept from her burned away under the ferocity of their kiss, and it was all he could do not to tear her clothes off right where she stood.

"Oh, my God, Ethan," Tori rasped.

Her shivery response skated over his mouth as he pulled back and bent to kiss her throat. She moaned when he caressed her small breasts. Gasped when he let his hand drift lower, to the heated juncture of her thighs.

He cupped her mound over the fabric of her shorts, wringing a shaky sigh from her and a shudder that raced over her from head to toe. She dropped her head against his good shoulder as he indulged in the growing inferno between her legs.

Her mouth fastened onto his skin, her teeth biting down on a cry as he worked one finger inside her panties. Silky wetness slicked her cleft.

"Ah, fuck," he uttered hoarsely. "You're so soft, Tori. Always so ready for me when I touch you."

He could have lost himself in her body's sweet response.

Hell, he'd been more than halfway there before he picked up the sound of someone approaching the apartment door. A key jiggled in the deadbolt.

Ethan reacted on pure instinct. Letting go of Tori, he swept her behind him in less than a second, prepared to protect her with his body and his life.

But as the door swung open, it was her friend, Hoshi, who stood there. She had a carry-out bag gripped in one hand, the key still held in her other.

Her dark, almond-shaped eyes slid to Tori in question, then to him in blatant disapproval. "Is everything all right in here?"

Ethan cleared his throat. He didn't have to look at Tori to know her cheeks were likely flushed with color and her lips moist and kiss-swollen.

As for himself, Ethan couldn't even try to hide his rampant erection.

"Let me help you with dinner," Tori blurted as she ducked around him. She shot him a meaningful look over her shoulder. "We're not finished here. And don't think I'm going to let you dodge my questions after a kiss like that."

He didn't have the words to deny her. Still weathering the need that had slammed into him like a hurricane, he wanted nothing more than to haul Tori back into his arms and do what she threatened—to finish what they had started.

As she pivoted around to follow her friend into the small kitchen, Ethan considered that this would be an ideal opportunity for him to walk out the door as he'd planned, before things got any more complicated with Tori.

Hell. Things had been nothing but complicated with her, starting from the moment he first laid eyes on her that St. Patrick's night four years ago.

And like it or not, the fact that his assailant saw Tori with him earlier today meant it might already be too late to shelter her from the secret, dangerous life he'd been hiding from her all this time.

He might have no choice but to trust her with that secret, and hope he could convince her to get as far away from him as she possibly could.

7

Tori pulled Ethan's T-shirt out of the dryer and tried to shake out the wrinkles.

Not that a few creases were going to get any notice next to the frayed knife hole and the rusty ghost of a bloodstain that still clung to the light-colored cotton after it had twice gone through the cold water wash. Better than nothing, and since Hoshi was even more petite than Tori, Ethan's current replacement clothing options were essentially nil.

Walking back up the short hallway of Hoshi's apartment, Tori heard Ethan running water in the bathroom. The door was cracked open a bit, just enough that she could see him standing at the sink, rinsing his face and hair at the tap.

He took her breath away, just like that. Just the sight of him, standing bare-chested, almost in arm's reach, doing something as mundane as scrubbing a hand over his face and scalp, left her immobile. Mesmerized. Afraid to move a muscle for fear it might shatter the illusion and he would be gone again.

As though he were still nothing more than a figment of her desperate, far too forgiving imagination.

Their kiss had been real enough.

Tori's senses still vibrated from the intensity of it.

She licked her lips, recalling the hungry way Ethan claimed her mouth.

And just thinking about that made her also relive in vivid detail the way he'd touched her, with strong, masterful fingers that still knew exactly how to stroke her into a frenzied state of need.

That need simmered within her even now, banked embers that surged with new heat as she watched Ethan reach for a towel on the hooks behind the door.

His gray cargo shorts hung low on his athletic form, baring the lean cut of muscle and hip bones she used to enjoy following with her tongue. Ethan had become leaner than she remembered, wilder looking in many ways.

His sandy brown hair was shaggier than he'd ever worn it. The squared line of his jaw and the angled slope of his cheeks were shadowed with dark stubble.

As for his body, that seemed leaner and wilder too. His abdomen had always been delectably firm and muscled. Now he was rock-solid everywhere she looked, his chest and arms corded with planes of firm sinew that flexed and bunched in fascinating combination as he moved.

She'd stared too long, too blatantly. Ethan's hazel gaze spotted her through the wedge of space.

Tori's cheeks fired, but it was much too late to feign disinterest. She approached the door as he slowly opened it all the way. "I washed your shirt. The blood's there to stay, unfortunately."

He shrugged and took the shirt out of her loose grasp. "Thanks."

She gave him a nod, then gestured toward his wound. "Doing all right?"

"I've come through worse." His sensual mouth quirked into the small smile that had always done bad things to her self-control. "Couldn't have asked for better field medics."

She didn't want to return his smile, dammit. She didn't want to feel the heat or the concern that coursed through her as they faced off in the open doorway of the small bathroom.

She stifled all of those unwanted impulses as best she could, and gave his wound a quick visual assessment instead. "Those bandages have been on there long enough now. The sutures need to breathe for a while." She pointed to the closed toilet seat. "Sit down. Let me have a look."

Ethan did as she asked while Tori washed her hands. He parted his legs to allow her space as she moved in close to inspect the injury. Carefully, she peeled away the tape and gauze and uncovered his wound.

"The puncture was deep, but it could've been much worse." She wet a fresh washcloth and dabbed gingerly around the area, knowing it still had to be very painful. She was satisfied to find only the expected inflammation and fluid leakage along the seam. "If you take care of it, you should heal up just fine."

Ethan didn't say anything. He watched her intently, his muscled chest rising and falling in a slow but heavy rhythm.

As she stood between his spread thighs, Tori was suddenly acutely aware of the intimate position they were in. Against her will, her heart began to gallop, all of her senses tuned to this man she should not want, but could not seem to deny.

She felt, more than saw, his hand lift toward her.

Before he could make contact, she abruptly withdrew, moving out of his reach. Despite her desire, she was still angry and suspicious of him. Still hurt.

She tossed the used tape and bandages in the nearby waste can, then rinsed out the cloth and folded it over the edge of the sink. Without looking at him now, she cranked the hot water and viciously scrubbed her hands.

Ethan rose, and came up close behind her as she cut the tap and picked up the hand towel.

God, she couldn't think with him so near.

All she could hear was the drumming of her pulse in her ears. All she could feel was the heat of his bare chest behind her, the warmth of his breath against her nape.

"Hoshi thinks I was crazy to let you kiss me today. She says I'm crazy to be anywhere near you." She lifted her gaze to meet his reflection in the medicine cabinet mirror. "Maybe she's right."

Ethan took her shoulders in his strong grasp and slowly turned her around to face him. "Did it feel crazy to you when you were kissing me?"

Tori arched a brow at him. "You kissed me, as I recall it. And no, it didn't feel crazy."

It felt electric, intoxicating. It felt like taking her first breath of air after three years of waiting to exhale.

Ethan's gaze bore into hers, intense, too powerful to break. "There has never been anyone who's affected me the way you do. No one."

She huffed a short sigh and shook her head. "Too bad you didn't feel that way when you left my house that morning without any explanation." Once the words slipped out of her mouth, she couldn't stop the rest. "How could you do that to me, Ethan? Do you know how that wrecked me? Do you even care? I didn't know what happened to you, or where you'd gone. Were you dead? If you were alive, were you stricken with some awful condition that made you forget where you belonged?"

He let her rail, gave her time and silence enough to get it all out. She'd held that anger and fear—the ache—inside her for so long, it left her trembling and breathless to have finally let it out.

"You were gone, and all I had were questions. No scenario I imagined for what you did made any kind of sense. I look at you now, Ethan, and I have more questions than ever. Then you go and kiss me like you did today—as if you still have the right to touch me, to be inside me..." She shook her head and whispered a harsh curse. "I gave you my heart, Ethan. My whole heart. You've given me nothing but lies and pain."

"I never wanted anything bad to happen to you," he said, his deep voice more solemn than she'd ever heard it. "I hate that I hurt you the way I left. There was no other way. I couldn't give you the truth then, for many reasons. Not the least of which was out of concern for you. From the moment I saw you in the pub that first night we met, I've wanted only to keep you safe. To protect you, Tori."

She scoffed quietly. "I never needed your protection. I've been taking care of myself for a long time."

"Yes, but that doesn't mean I care any less." His gaze searched hers, a flicker of uncertainty in his typically unflinching confidence. "Do you remember the brawl that happened while we were dancing that night at the pub?"

"I think so." She'd been more focused on the attractive stranger who'd been staring at her for half an hour before he finally strode over to talk to her.

"I wasn't looking for a relationship," he murmured. "Damn, Tori, you were so pretty. And then you smiled at me. That smile killed me. Still does. But I might not have made my move that night at the bar, if it wasn't for the fight that broke out."

She recalled the way the evening had played out, but Ethan's timing seemed off, to hear him tell it now. "No, that's not right. You came over to me before then. We were already dancing when the fight happened."

"Yes," Ethan replied slowly, carefully. "I asked you to dance because I needed to get you out of the path of the drunk who was going to crash into the bar, directly where you'd been sitting."

Tori frowned. "I don't understand. You couldn't have known that would happen."

"Yet I did," he said. "I saw the fight play out exactly the way it happened."

"You *saw* it."

"In my mind, Tori." Ethan reached over and closed the bathroom door now. His eyes held hers, grave and earnest. "Just before I went over to ask you to dance, in my mind I saw the drunk being shoved back into you at the bar. I couldn't let it happen."

"What are you trying to say?"

"I have an unusual ability. A gift for precognition."

"Precognition? As in ESP?" She cocked her head, pushing out an incredulous laugh. "Come on, Ethan. You don't believe in that unscientific, new age bullshit any more than I do."

"You wanted the truth, Tori, and I'm trying to give it to you. I need you to trust me—"

"Trust you? All you've done since I saw you today is

feed me one lie after another." She crossed her arms over her breasts, incensed that he would think she'd buy this as anything close to the truth. "I'm not an idiot, and just because you might've had a hunch about a fight breaking out in a bar, that doesn't make you a psychic. And none of this explains or excuses the way you walked out on me—on us, damn you—without ever looking back. As far as I'm concerned, the man I thought I knew might as well have never existed."

That stung him. She could see the regret in his expression.

It edged his deep voice too. "I had no choice but to leave like I did. I was part of something secret, Tori. Something I couldn't share with you." He muttered a curse, low under his breath. "I wanted to protect you from what I was doing, but now my secret could get you killed."

Tori stared at him. He believed every word he was saying; that much was clear. But the pieces still hadn't clicked into place for her.

"I don't understand, Ethan. What exactly are you saying?"

"I was part of a classified CIA program that utilized precognitives like me as counter-intelligence operatives. We predicted terrorist activity, averted all manner of disasters. In a few cases—more frequently than anyone would care to know—the program's agents thwarted global war."

"You were working for the CIA?" God it sounded outrageous even saying it out loud. "So, you did this kind of work down in New Mexico, before you took the job at the college?"

He gave a vague nod. "Before I began teaching in

Portland, yes. And during. I would still be part of it now, but the program was betrayed. I don't know by whom, but I need to find out."

"You were an agent in the CIA," Tori said again, needing to repeat it in order for it to truly sink in. "An agent with psychic abilities."

"Only precognition."

"Oh, well. Only that," she replied, unable to curb the biting sarcasm in her tone. She studied him with a suspicion that put an odd ache in her chest. "How long were you in that program before I met you?"

He seemed to think back for a moment. "They recruited me soon after my first deployment overseas with the Army. My CO noticed my intuition skills were off-the-charts accurate. When they realized what I could do, they yanked me from my combat unit and I found myself being interviewed and tested at The Farm."

Tori listened, then gaped when another revelation sank in. "Wait—you were in the Army too? You never mentioned that in all the time we were together either."

"Because at the time, you didn't need to know," he said flatly. "I enlisted when I was seventeen. I wanted to save the world. I suppose I still do—if I don't wind up on a slab first."

Tori didn't even want to consider that possibility.

She couldn't deny that what she was hearing—if it really was the truth—did little to put her mind at ease about Ethan or the relationship they'd shared before he left. He'd still deceived her from the start, even if he wanted her to believe it was out of care and concern for her.

He'd lied about who he was, about his past, about everything.

And now he wanted her to accept that he had a special gift for telling the future?

"If you know what's going to happen before it does, then why didn't you know you were going to be stabbed today? Why keep running and hiding if you have the power to avoid any danger before it happens?"

He shook his head. "The gift doesn't work like that. I don't see things that are going to happen to me. And there are things I never see at all."

"Show me."

"What?"

She spread her arms. "Prove it to me. Tell me something you see, right now. How about you give me the winning lottery numbers so I can cash in before I have to fly home to Maine tomorrow? For that matter, why not use your super powers to amass a fortune for yourself? Then you can build a super-spy fortress and not worry about anyone being able to find you."

Shadows dimmed his serious, hazel eyes. There was a glimmer of anger there too. "It's a skill that requires concentration, respect. It's not a crystal ball, Tori. I can't just wave my hands and conjure up a vision for you. It's not something I need to prove. Not to anyone."

She nodded slowly, letting her arms relax back down at her sides. "Okay," she said. "You're right, you don't need to prove anything to me. I mean, who am I to ask anyway, right? I'm just the woman you practically lived with for a year. The woman you lied to every time you opened your mouth. The woman you fucked and walked away from without a second thought. I'm nothing to you, and I probably never was."

She pivoted to grab the knob on the door.

"Hoshi has the tea kettle on in the kitchen," Ethan

murmured. "It's going to boil in three, two, one—"

From elsewhere in the apartment, the whistle on Hoshi's Hello Kitty teapot began to howl.

Tori whirled around to face Ethan. "You could have heard her out there. You could've known she was making a cup of tea…"

Ethan's expression was grim. Ruthlessly so. "She's not paying attention. The cup is going to slip off the counter—"

His words were punctuated by a sharp clatter and crash in the kitchen.

"Shit!" Hoshi cried. "That was my favorite china teacup!"

Tori gaped at Ethan. "Oh, my God. Everything you said…"

He didn't look smug or triumphant, merely stared at her with sober acceptance. He reached past her and opened the door, expectation in his inscrutable gaze.

Tori moved away from him, stepping out into the hallway.

Ethan said nothing, just slowly closed the door between them.

8

Ethan cursed as he struggled into his T-shirt. His movements were impatient, agitated. Too hasty, when the stitched wound in his chest screamed with even the slightest tension.

The pain wasn't the cause of his anger.

He was furious with himself.

He had fucked things up badly enough when he deserted Tori three years ago. In truth, his fuckup had started earlier than that—when he'd first allowed her to get under his skin. To get into his heart.

He couldn't call that mistake back. And he couldn't change the hurt he'd caused her either.

But what he was doing to her now was even worse.

This unexpected reunion had entwined their lives like never before. Now, Tori was helping him, sheltering him—touching and kissing him, for crissake—in spite of all the things she'd found out about him today.

Not the least of which being his most dangerous secret.

The one that could get both of them killed.

He'd rehearsed in his mind half a dozen ways he could have explained to Tori about his ESP ability and his role in the Phoenix program. It wasn't easy to swallow; he knew that.

He should've known a woman like her—someone with a mind grounded in science, and sensibilities honed by good old-fashioned Yankee pragmatism—would need to see his gift to have any faith in it.

To say nothing of the fact that he couldn't actually expect her to have a lot of faith in him at face-value either.

Instead of easing her into this part of who he truly was, he'd pissed her off, then got defensive when she doubted his word.

Way to go, asshole.

The parlor game demonstration of his gift had been real smooth too.

He hated squandering his ability like that. Over time, he'd learned to be careful with his gift, using it only in the line of duty as a Phoenix member. He rarely forced it to rouse, and then, only in cases of extreme emergency.

When opened on command, his precognitive skills functioned something like a spigot with a faulty washer ring. Visions dripped into his consciousness, abrupt and uncontrolled.

Vague splashes of a premonition danced at the edges of his mind's eye now, as he stood at the sink and smoothed his T-shirt down over his abdomen.

At first, he wasn't sure what he was seeing.

When it became clearer, Ethan's blood ran cold.

He stalked out of the bathroom and found Tori in the kitchen, sweeping broken shards of china into the garbage while Hoshi mopped up the spilled tea on the floor.

"We have to leave. All of us. Right now."

Tori gaped at him. "What's wrong?"

Ethan didn't have time to explain. "The GPS chip

on your phone. Is it turned off?"

"I don't know. I—"

"Give it to me. Now, Tori." She retrieved it from her purse and handed it to him. He disabled the locator and glanced up at her. "Get your things. You too, Hoshi. The apartment's not safe."

Tori's face blanched. "You saw something."

"Yes." Even now, the premonition flashed through his mind's eye. The darkened apartment. Deadbolt breached. A killer stepping over the threshold. Nowhere for any of them to run.

Tori gave Ethan a small nod. Hoshi pinned Ethan with a suspicious scowl. "I'm not going anywhere. And neither is my friend—not with you, anyway. And what do you mean, you saw that my apartment isn't safe? Not safe from what?"

"Hoshi," Tori said softly, urgently. "If Ethan says we need to leave, then we need to believe him."

"Why should we?"

"Because your life depends on it," Ethan replied grimly. "The man who stabbed me today will be coming here, looking to finish the job. I don't know when exactly. Could be tomorrow or the next night. Maybe in the next few minutes. But soon. Trust me when I say that you don't want to be here when that happens."

Tori took her friend's hand in a firm grasp. "Please. We should do what Ethan says."

Some of Hoshi's steam seemed to ebb. Ethan could see the young woman considering his grave warning. She was stubborn, perhaps even more so than Tori, if that was possible.

But she was smart like Tori too, and where Hoshi didn't fully trust the stranger standing in her kitchen, predicting bad things to come, she did trust her friend's judgment where he was concerned.

"Where?" Hoshi murmured. "And for how long?"

"The farther you can get from Seattle, the better," he said. "As for how long, a few days."

She eyed him hesitantly, then gave a faint nod. "My parents live a couple of hours north, in Surrey. I could call them—"

"Don't call. Just get there," Ethan said.

Tori glanced to him, frowning. "What about me?"

He recalled what she'd told him earlier. "You said you were flying home to Maine tomorrow?"

"In the morning. Ten twenty."

"Good. I'm going to personally make sure you get on that flight safely. Then I'm going to take care of the situation back here."

"Take care of it?" Dread dulled her anxious gaze. She eyed him as if she was looking at a stranger. Someone she didn't know and might have even feared in that moment. "You're going to kill that man, aren't you?"

He didn't answer the question, but hell yes, that was precisely what he intended to do. Neither Tori nor he would be safe until the assassin was dealt with and eliminated.

Until then, he would keep her close.

He would protect her with every skill he had and every breath in his body.

First, he had to find someplace for them to go until he could put Tori on her plane home. It had to be somewhere secure. Very public, if at all possible.

For the man who'd spent three years living like a nomad and a pauper, now the most secure place for Tori and him to hide was somewhere they'd be surrounded by people.

"Collect your things," he told the women. "Only the essentials. Nothing you can't carry on your person. And make it fast. We're leaving right now."

9

"Let us out at the corner of Ninth and Pine," Ethan said from the darkness in the backseat, after Hoshi, on his instructions, had driven Tori and him across town from her apartment.

Tori looked out the passenger side window at the busy nighttime boulevard and the tall glass and brick buildings that lined the street and crossroad.

At the corner Ethan indicated was an old theater, its vintage sign and marquee glowing with bright lights. A crowd of people waited outside, lined up to purchase tickets.

Tori slanted him a wry glance as Hoshi slowed to stop at the curb outside. "You're taking me to the movies?"

"Just a pit stop." His mouth quirked, and the fact that he was able to smile in the midst of what they were doing gave her an odd sense of reassurance. "We shouldn't linger."

When Ethan got out of the car, Hoshi reached over to clasp her hand. "Are you sure about this? Are you sure about him?"

Tori nodded, even though her heart was racing with the uncertainty of what awaited her in Ethan's company now. "I'll be fine. Ethan won't let anything happen to me. I know it. And I...trust him."

"Oh, shit," Hoshi whispered. "It's even worse than that, isn't it? You still love him."

Did I ever stop? She knew the answer to that, even if she wasn't prepared to admit her likely foolishness. She leaned over and pulled her friend into a tight hug. "I'm going to be okay. I'll call you as soon as I can, let you know I'm safe."

"You better." Hoshi gave her a stern look as she let her go. "Someday you're going to tell me what's really going on with this guy, right?"

"I have to go," Tori said, a less than artful dodge. Christ, she was getting as cagey as Ethan. But this was life or death stakes, and if keeping him safe meant keeping his secrets, she was prepared to take all of them to her grave.

Though hopefully not anytime soon.

Tori climbed out of the vehicle and met Ethan on the curb as Hoshi pulled back out onto the street and drove away.

"Come on," he said, and led her into the theater.

The place was packed for the evening show, a grim art house film that had brought out about a hundred sullen teenagers. Ethan laced his fingers through Tori's and brought her past the crowds, toward the restrooms in back.

"Go into the ladies' room and wait five minutes," he said. "I'll meet you right here."

She wasn't sure what this little excursion was about, but she did as he asked.

When she came out, he was already standing where he'd left her. Fortunately in the dimmed lights of the theater lobby, amid the hipsters and Goths, the bloodstain and knife hole on his shirt looked like some kind of grunge detail.

"You were fast," she said as she approached him.

He pulled her into a kiss that left her breathless. "I have what I came for."

And with that, they were off again. Now, Ethan took her across the avenue and then down another side street. Up ahead was a large bus station. They entered, and he made a beeline for a bank of lockers inside.

He walked down to one of the last rows and took a sealed plastic bag out of his cargo pants pocket. It wasn't anything Tori had found when she'd searched his clothes back at Hoshi's place. The bag was crisscrossed with silver duct tape, still wet from where he'd retrieved it.

Inside was a folded up paper towel, and inside the paper was a tarnished locker key.

Tori arched a brow at him. "Don't tell me you hid that in a public toilet."

He grinned and discreetly opened one of the lockers.

A battered old backpack sat inside. Ethan rifled through the zippered compartments. Tori saw a change of clothing and a pair of shoes, more plastic bags that appeared to contain assorted toiletries, cash and credit cards.

As he took a quick inventory of his stash, she couldn't help noticing he also had a pistol and three different passports in the pack, only one of them sporting the navy blue and gold colors of the United States.

He closed the locker and slung the pack up onto his good shoulder. "Ready?"

She could hardly stifle her astonishment. "Ready for what—a secret agent initiation ceremony, or the witness protection program?"

Ethan chuckled, but when he spoke, there was gravity in his low voice. "This is what I never wanted to expose you to, Tori. The secrets, the subterfuge. The danger. This is part of who I really am."

"What about my bookish, slightly nerdy liberal studies professor?"

"*Associate* professor," he corrected on a smile. "And what the hell do you mean, nerdy? I got skills. I'm a military-grade, government-certified badass, babe."

"Yeah, you are," she agreed. "And I have to admit it's more than a little hot."

"Yeah?"

She nodded. "Seeing you like this, so cool and capable in a situation that would have other men pissing their Dockers…let's just say I'm glad you're not hiding this side of you from me anymore."

He moved in close, his hazel eyes darkening with interest. "I don't want to hide anything from you right now, Tori. Not tonight."

Because tomorrow will be the end.

He didn't say it, but he didn't have to either.

He would be putting her on a plane to Portland in the morning, and then he would go back to the life he'd been living these past three years. A life that didn't have a place for her.

Ethan stroked her cheek, tenderly, heartbreakingly.

Then he reached down and took her hand in his. "Come with me. Tonight, all the rest of this shit doesn't matter. It doesn't exist. Tonight, it's just you and me."

10

Twenty minutes later, freshly showered and wrapped in a sumptuous white terrycloth robe, Tori stepped out of the bathroom of the five-star hotel's penthouse suite to look for Ethan.

She wasn't sure how much cash and charm he'd had to use in his private meeting with the manager of the property in order to get them into the massive, two-thousand square foot sanctuary on the fourteenth floor. But then, Ethan was full of mysteries and surprises that she was only beginning to see in action.

He had another surprise waiting for her outside the open double doors of the bedroom. She walked into the living area of the penthouse and found the formal dining table arranged with an elaborate room service dinner for two.

Gleaming ivory china. Elegant silverware and glittering crystal glasses. A centerpiece of thick candles glowing warmly against the city lights and moonlit water of the bay far below the floor-to-ceiling window.

Silver domes concealed half a dozen intriguing dishes, the aroma of spiced-rubbed, roasted meat and grilled vegetables making her mouth water instantly.

Next to all of this decadence, a tall, ice-filled bucket held an opened bottle of pricey-looking French champagne that probably cost more than Tori's monthly rent on her bungalow back home.

She couldn't help but be impressed by all of the finery and extravagance, but the real reason for the sudden spike in her heart rate was the sight of Ethan strolling over to meet her, wearing the mate to her white robe. His was untied and open. All he wore beneath it was a pair of black boxers.

She smiled, appreciating every flex of smooth muscle as he walked toward her. "So, this is why you wanted me to shower by myself ahead of you. You've been busy. I have to admit, I wondered if I was going to come out here and find you gone…like the last time."

He gave a slow shake of his head. "I'm sorry for what I did to you, Tori. For everything. I never got the chance to tell you that. I never got the chance to tell you a lot of things."

He picked up a couple of slender crystal glasses from the table and poured some of the champagne into them.

The bubbles sparkled like diamonds as he handed one of the flutes to her. She took a sip of the crisp champagne, practically tasting the expense in its effervescent dance over her tongue.

"You didn't have to do all of this, Ethan. This room and meal…I've never been anywhere so romantic or special."

His mouth pursed slightly, his brows lowering over his intense eyes. "I never got the chance to give you anything like this the first time around. I want you to have it now."

She soaked it all in, the opulence of the table setting, the beautiful suite that made her feel as though she were in a fairy tale. "It must be costing you a fortune."

He let out a quiet curse. "I don't care about that. I can make more money. We'll only have this night once."

His fingers came up to stroke her cheek, his thumb brushing gently over her bottom lip.

Then he bent his head and kissed her, taking her mouth with a passion that was both tender and demanding.

"I should've made you go with your friend," he murmured against her parted lips. "You'd have been just as safe at her parents' with her. I just...ah, fuck. I just wasn't ready to let you go. I wanted more time."

"Me too," she whispered. "There's nowhere else I want to go. I want to be with you, Ethan. I'm not afraid of what you do, or who you are."

"I know, babe." He dropped his gaze then and didn't lift it. It took him a long moment before he spoke. "When you get on that flight to Maine tomorrow, you'll never see me again. I don't want to let you think...or hope. I don't want any more half-truths or lies between us, Tori. No misunderstandings."

She knew, of course. As much as she wanted to imagine otherwise, or pretend the fantasy he'd created for them tonight up here above the city—above the real world—might not unravel in the light of day, Tori knew this was just Ethan's way of finally telling her goodbye.

But she didn't want to hear it.

Not if they were measuring their time left together in hours.

She set her glass down on the table and reached out to him. His cheeks were warm and bristly against her fingertips, his jaw held rigid, unwavering.

She slowly shook her head. "Let's not talk about what happens tomorrow. It doesn't exist right now, remember? Tonight, it's just us. If you want to give me something, then please, Ethan…give me that."

He didn't answer, but the molten look in his eyes spoke volumes. He put his champagne glass down next to hers. Then he caught her face in his palms and descended on her mouth in another blistering, breath-stealing kiss.

He reached between them to unfasten her robe. Then his hands were on her bare skin, squeezing her breasts, rolling the tight buds of her nipples, rounding her back to palm her ass, dragging her toward him, into the hard ridge of his arousal.

He moaned as he ground against her, his breath coming hard and fast. One hand sought the wet heat of her core, his fingers slipping between her folds, teasing the tight bundle of nerves nestled there.

"Ah, Christ, Tori," he uttered hoarsely. "I could come just from touching you like this."

So could she. Her body wept for him, sensation lighting up her every nerve ending. He stroked her more boldly, and his kiss became wilder, deeper, filled with raw desire.

Tori felt that same rising desperation too. She was aching for him already, well beyond pretending that she had any control where this man was concerned.

She ran her palms over his chest, delighting in the velvety strength of his pecs and abdomen, the muscles that twitched and quivered under her roving touch.

Careful only as she neared his stitched wound, she broke away from his kiss to push the thick terry robe off his shoulders and down over his strong biceps and arms. When she reached for his boxers, Ethan was already there, helping her shove them down. His cock sprang free, jutting firm and thick and long.

She gripped him, stroked him from root to tip, reveling in the heat and strength of him.

He sucked in a sharp breath, letting it back out on a hiss as she pumped him in a slow, sure tempo. "Fuck, yes. Damn, that feels good."

"I know you taste good too," she murmured, then sank down in front of him and took him into her mouth.

His strangled cry was all the encouragement she needed. She suckled him with more intensity, until he dragged her off him on a roar.

With one arm circled around her, and his other hand steering her backward, he guided her to the empty end of the long dining table. He kicked the chair out of his way, then spread her down onto the cool wood surface.

He kissed her hard, a possessive claiming that made her writhe and whimper beneath him. "My turn to taste you now," he said.

Then his mouth began a slow, torturous path down her throat and onto each breast, before heading lower, to her stomach and hip bones.

When he reached the trimmed patch of curls between her thighs, he glanced up wickedly. "Who needs dinner when I have something this sweet to devour?"

Tori gasped at the first contact of his mouth on her sex. He kissed and suckled, nibbled and teased. Her spine arched with each delicious torment, and she could do nothing to hold back her pleasured scream when he tongued her from cleft to clit.

They'd always had intense passion together. Tonight it was a need that eclipsed everything they'd known before.

"Please," she murmured, uncertain what she asking

for, other than more of him. Tonight, she wanted as much as he could give her. "Oh, God…Ethan."

He came up and took her mouth in a hot, ferocious kiss. "Are you on anything?"

Dully, she blinked up at him. "What?"

"The pill. Are you still taking it?"

"Oh. No. Not for a while now." She hadn't needed it, hadn't seen the point.

"Shit," he said, panting, as if it took all his self-control to be the logical, cautious one in that moment. He backed off her on another curse. "Stay right there."

She came up onto her elbows. "Where would I go?"

He was already in the other room. "Don't move."

He came back holding a wrapped condom. Grinning, he wagged the packet then tore it open with his teeth. "Had this in my bag from the bus station. Did I mention I was a Boy Scout too?"

Tori arched a brow at him. "I don't know whether to be impressed or pissed off. Have you needed to be prepared with that kind of supply very often?"

His look was cryptic, unreadable. "Less often than you'd think. I've been carrying this around for a while now. Hope it holds up."

Tori sat up and reached for him. "Let me help you with it."

As he stood between her parted legs, she rolled the condom down his length. Their eyes met, and Ethan caught her face in his hands and kissed her sweetly, reverently.

Then he slid her off the edge of the table and onto his shaft.

"Ohh," Tori sighed as she sheathed him to the hilt inside her.

"Oh, God...I've missed this," he uttered raggedly. "I've missed you, babe. So fucking much."

He rocked into her, supporting her body weight as he drove in and withdrew, finding a rhythm that left them both panting and clutching at each other in urgent need.

Tori was on the verge of climax in moments, overwhelmed by the feel of him filling her, stretching her around his cock with each devastating thrust.

He lifted one of her thighs, hooking her knee over his arm and driving harder, faster. Tori could only hang on to him, lost to the pounding force of his body and the tiny detonations deep inside her that were swelling toward release.

"That's it, babe. That's my girl. Let it go."

She was so close now. The pleasure was building, just beginning to crest...

As he coaxed her higher, she noticed his wound had begun to bleed a bit. "Oh, shit. Ethan, your stitches. Slow down, we have to be more careful."

"Fuck careful," he growled, still pumping ruthlessly. No mercy whatsoever. "You won't break me, so don't you worry about that. I want to see you come now. I want to hear it, Tori."

She couldn't have stopped it if she tried.

Her climax exploded and she screamed Ethan's name. Tremors shook her from the deepest core of her being, left her senses splintering into a rain of glittering shards.

She dropped her forehead down on his chest as the spasms rolled over her, one delicious aftershock then another. Ethan was still moving inside her, giving her little time to come down before his merciless tempo renewed her need.

"That was incredible," she murmured. "I needed this so badly. I didn't know how much until right now."

He grunted. "I probably don't have any right to be jealous of anyone else who's touched you, but feeling you wrapped around me so tight and hot and sweet—" He rocked deeper, a slow, silky thrust that made both of them groan with pleasure. "Feeling you in my arms again, Tori, I think I could kill any other man who's known this."

Tori smiled against his warm skin, then lifted her head to meet his desire-swamped gaze.

"There hasn't been anyone else. Not one, Ethan. All this time, there's only been you."

11

Tori's confession registered like a sucker punch to his gut.

No one since me?

It struck him stupid for a second as he tried to process. No easy thing, when his blood was racing so feverishly, most of it departed from his brain and migrated due south.

He stilled within Tori's satin heat and stared at her mutely.

No one else in all this time.

Had he hurt her that deeply, that she couldn't let herself get close to anyone else since he'd been gone?

But Tori's dark blue eyes were tender on him, not accusing. They were so honest and loving, he could hardly breathe under their regard.

She swallowed quietly, but her voice was steady, hiding nothing from him. "After you, there was never anyone who measured up."

"Three years?" he muttered thickly, then cursed in a rough whisper.

He couldn't keep himself from moving inside her again. Picking up a slower, less furious pace than before, he gave a mild shake of his head.

"Jesus, Tori. It's one thing for me to be living like a

damned monk since I left. Not like I've had time or interest in anyone when I'm not in one place more than a couple of weeks at a time. But you…"

She gaped at him. "You mean, you haven't—"

"No one," he said.

And while he might've wanted to fool himself into thinking he'd abstained only due to lack of time or opportunity, the truth was, he'd been holding out for something special too.

Something he'd only found with her.

He grinned at Tori as he thrust long and deep and smooth. "That condom's shelf life was about up. Good thing I finally got the chance to show it a little action."

She laughed—really laughed—and it was a sound he hadn't heard in far too long.

Then she reached down and grabbed his ass in both her hands. She pulled him deeper, grinding into him as if to show him his patient strokes were no longer cutting it for her. He loved her hunger, and the fact that she wasn't too shy to show it.

A sly smile played at the edges of her pretty mouth. "How many more condoms do you have in your secret agent kit?"

His cock leapt at the suggestion. "Not nearly enough."

He kissed her, then he drove to the hilt on one deep thrust, wringing a sharp gasp from her and a hot, shivery sigh that made his balls knot up tight with the need to spill.

He fucked her hard and fast, both of them desperate for release now.

When they came, it was together as one. Loud, unbridled.

Explosive.

Ethan shuddered as the pleasure broke over him and his cock spasmed hard inside her enveloping heat.

She felt like heaven, like coming home. Only to a home he'd never had until this woman had entered his life.

He should have known it would be like this with her.

It always had been.

Intense.

Consuming.

Something too goddamned close to perfect.

And now he realized how big a mistake he'd just made, thinking he could spend just one more night with Tori and it would be enough.

What a fucking fool he was.

Because as their joined bodies rocked together, their arms wrapped around each other as they both spiraled down from an impossible height, all Ethan wanted was the chance to do it all over again.

This one last night had only made him crave another one.

And then another one after that.

How am I going to find the will to walk away from her in the morning?

How far will I have to go to put Tori out of my mind?

Hell, he wasn't even sure the ends of the earth would be far enough to keep him from her this time.

12

Ethan had five condoms in his stash, and over the next several hours, they had burned through them all.

In between the multiple rounds of amazing sex and soul-shaking orgasms, they'd paused to nibble at their cold dinners and sip the warming champagne.

Afterward, they'd taken a long, hot soak together in the all-glass shower, but not even exhaustion was enough to cool their hunger. They'd kissed and stroked and teased under the spray, then fell into bed together in a state of boneless bliss.

The night hadn't played out in the order Ethan might have intended, but Tori couldn't have been happier.

Nor more satisfied, as she slept beside him in the big king-size bed, her naked body curled up close to his, caught in the warm circle of his strong arms.

She wasn't sure what woke her first—the erratic sound of his breathing, or the coil of tension that began to rake his entire body. His low, sharp moan made her eyes snap open in the darkened room.

He twitched fitfully, his eyelids and lips quirking in his sleep.

A nightmare.

And from the look and sound of its effect on a man as unshakable as Ethan, it had to be something awful.

He breathed rapidly, as if he was running a marathon.

And he was agitated, even terrified. A sheen of perspiration glistened on his furrowed forehead and in the shadowy scruff that darkened his cheeks and jaw.

Tori didn't know if she should wake him.

But watching him suffer through whatever horror was playing behind his closed lids was too much for her to bear.

Her voice was the softest whisper. "Ethan."

She hadn't even touched him before he sprang on her, eyes flying open, his large body trapping her under his hard weight as if she was the enemy. "Fuck!"

He muttered a swift apology, already rolling off her. He pivoted to the edge of the mattress, his long legs slung over the side.

"Jesus fucking Christ, Tori. You can't do that. I'm not…" He raked a hand through his bed-mussed hair. Swiveling his head to glance at her over his shoulder, he looked at her in pained regret. "I'm sorry, babe. I didn't hurt you, did I?"

"No. You startled me, is all." When he cursed again, more vicious this time, she crawled over to wrap her arms around him from behind. "It's okay. It was just a dream."

"It's not a dream," he murmured, a hard edge to his voice.

"A nightmare," she suggested, but the look he turned on her said it had been something more. Something much worse than that. "A premonition?"

He nodded. God, he looked absolutely sick with it. "I've been seeing it for the past three years, ever since the Phoenix program went dark. The same premonition, over and over and over. It's horrific and…incomplete somehow. I have to figure out what it means."

She listened, seeing the torment in him. "And this is all part of your work for the CIA—for the Phoenix program? They wanted you to see terrible things, then try to make sure they wouldn't happen? My God, Ethan. What that must do to you."

"It was important work. I've never been unable to handle it." He shrugged vaguely. "I could handle this too, if I only knew what it was I'm missing."

She tenderly stroked his muscled back, small caresses, unable to resist the need to touch him, to comfort him even in some small way if she could. "Tell me about the dream."

She didn't know if he was willing to let her in that close. But he hardly hesitated, pivoting around to capture her hand in his as he spoke.

"It's always the same. Brief glimpses of a bigger picture. I'm running full tilt through thick, yellow sand. I know I need to get somewhere fast—before it's too late—but no matter how hard I run, it's never enough. I'm getting nowhere. There's a building up ahead of me, but I can't get to it in time."

Tori stared at him, her own fear ratcheting. "In time for what, Ethan?"

"To stop what happens next." He glanced down at their joined fingers, frowning, his expression grim with his burden. "As soon as I see the SUVs, I know it's already too late. The clock is ticking. Time is running out too fast. I know the detonation is about to hit."

She couldn't speak now. Could only listen and wait as he prepared to tell her the worst of his premonition.

"The caravan is speeding across the sand, kicking up

a cloud of blinding dust," Ethan murmured. "I see the line of black vehicles with diplomatic plates—Christ, I have time enough to count all nine of them, but I can't turn them back. I can't make it stop. By the time the last SUV passes, the clock has run out. The explosion is…hellish. That's the only word for it."

Tori squeezed his hand. "Oh, Ethan."

"The fire washes over me," he said woodenly. "It burns my face, my hair. It melts my skin right off my bones. And all I can think of, as the flames engulf everything, is that I failed."

She felt sick for the misery his gift had caused him, at least with this horrific vision. An Armageddon-style nightmare that he'd been suffering through repeatedly for three years.

"Have you told anyone about this premonition?" she asked. "Maybe there's someone in the CIA who can help you."

"There's no one. No one left in the Company that I can trust." A sharp, weary sounding sigh gusted out of him. "The director of the Phoenix program, Henry Sheppard, gave explicit instructions on how to handle a potential betrayal of the program. 'Go to ground. Trust no one. Assume all is lost.' That was the message he sent me the day I disappeared. He would've sent the psychic distress call to all of the agents in the program that day."

Hope kindled to life. "If there are others in the program, Ethan, maybe we should try to find them. Maybe they will understand what the vision means."

"We," he said gently. "Tori, this isn't something you can be involved in. I won't allow it, especially not when there's a hired gun on my trail already. Shit, thanks to your involvement with me this far, you're already under more risk than I can accept. You're going home to Maine in the morning, before you're dragged any deeper into trouble that doesn't belong to you."

"And you?" she asked, too stung to pretend it didn't hurt to know her time with Ethan would be ending in just a few more hours. "What will you do? Where will you go?"

"I don't know. I'll keep moving." He shook his head. "Even if I thought it might be safe to trust any of the other Phoenix members, I wouldn't know where to find them. I've never seen any of them in person—not that I'm aware of, that is. We were referred to only by codenames. I was called Zephyr. And as far as I know, only a handful of our codenames were privy to anyone besides Sheppard."

"None of you met one another in your work for the program, not even briefly?"

"Aside from combat training exercises and other directives at The Farm, Phoenix operatives were kept apart," he explained. "It was done deliberately to avoid group-thinking our visions. The program required pure data from each of the agents in the field. We lived relatively normal lives once we were out of training, but it was our duty to stimulate our ability while we were on the outside by keeping up on current events, studying various sciences and arts, reading just about anything that caught our attention. We reported in regularly with any precognitive images or intel those exercises generated."

Another piece of the puzzle that was Ethan Jones clicked into place for her just now.

"That's why you were so well-read, and so informed on just about every subject under the sun. God, you must've thought I was an idiot that I never caught on to any of this."

"I never thought that." When she glanced away from him, he caught her chin and brought her gaze back. "Never. You were the only woman who ever challenged me, stood up to me. You always called me on my bullshit."

"Someone has to," she muttered, wishing he wasn't able to charm her so easily.

He didn't let go of her face, but his touch became a caress. "You're tougher and smarter than I can ever hope to be. Given the same training, you'd be one hell of a partner, I have no doubt. But this isn't your fight, Tori. It's not your problem."

"What do you plan to do, Ethan?"

A tendon ticked in his jaw. "I have to deal with the asshole who's been sent to kill me. That's objective number one. There's also a part of me that's itching for payback on all of this shit. Someone took down Phoenix and killed its founder. Henry Sheppard was a good man, one of the best. He didn't need to die. There are days when the need to take that price out in someone's blood keeps me going, even more so than the need to preserve my own neck or figure out what that nightmare vision means."

"He meant a lot to you, the head of the Phoenix program?"

"Henry Sheppard was a mentor to me from the time I was eighteen. I had no family—none that I cared to acknowledge, that is. He made me feel important when I thought I was worthless, a freak. He made me feel unique, valuable." Ethan chuckled. "Knowing Sheppard, he probably instilled that same sense of self-worth in every member of the program."

He let his hand fall away from her face, only to thread his fingers through hers again, as if he didn't want to be separated from her any longer than she wanted it either.

"I owe it to Sheppard to do what I can to ensure whoever started this war doesn't succeed. I'll do whatever it takes to see that through. That's my mission now. And you, Tori…keeping you safe is more important than all the rest of it."

He brought his other hand up and cupped it warmly around her nape. The kiss he gave her was slow and sweet and tender.

When he pulled back a moment later, there was an unmistakable heat kindling in his hazel eyes. "I just realized I have another critical mission objective. One that really can't wait."

She couldn't hold back her smile. "Oh, yeah? What's that?"

"I need to hear you scream my name at least three more times before morning."

"Three times?" she asked, laughing as he pressed her down onto the bed. "That's going to be a problem. We ran out of condoms hours ago, remember?"

He smirked. "Then I'll just have to get creative."

Slowly, he parted her naked legs, then sank his head down between her thighs.

13

Morning arrived much too early.

Ethan had kept Tori in bed with him for as long as possible, savoring the feel of her arms around him, their legs tangled together under the cool sheets. He groaned when the alarm went off at seven a.m., not at all ready to let reality intrude.

In less than three hours, Tori would be at the airport, boarding her flight back to Portland.

She seemed to dread it at least as much as he did. Her little moan vibrated through his chest where her cheek rested. "I don't want to wake up yet."

"Neither do I," he said, dropping a kiss on the top of her head. "But it's time."

The logical side of him knew that sending her home, away from him, was the best way to assure her safety.

The man hunting him was a professional, not a psychopath. He would have no cause to harm Tori, so long as she wasn't standing in the way of his true target.

Ethan couldn't think of any better place for her to avoid the assassin's crosshairs than all the way across the country.

But there was another side of him that could hardly bear the thought of letting Tori out of his reach. The part of him that didn't spend almost every waking moment watching for incoming enemy fire, or portents of a hellish disaster on the horizon, wanted nothing more than to keep her close.

As close as they'd been before Henry Sheppard issued the *Phoenix down* distress call.

Closer even than they had been before. Because now Tori knew him more completely than anyone ever had.

There were still things he hadn't told her, things he wasn't proud of. Things he'd left buried in his past, monsters he intended to keep hidden under the bed where they belonged.

But he'd been more real with her than any other person in his life. If he was being honest with himself, Tori Connors had found her way through his defensive walls and into his heart back in Maine.

If he thought he could bar her now, after their unexpected reunion and the incredible night they'd just shared, then he was a bigger fool than he should ever admit.

He caressed the slender length of her arm, and bent his head to inhale the sweet fragrance of her short blond hair. "It's time, babe. We have to get moving."

"I know." She pressed her lips to his chest, right above the cold knot that had taken up residence below his sternum. "Join me in the shower?"

One last time.

He was glad she didn't say it, but neither of them could ignore the weight of each minute that ticked rapidly past them.

They showered and got dressed in tender silence. Then, when reality could be avoided no longer, they went down to meet the taxi Ethan had arranged for with the hotel.

Tori's hand clung to his as they rode in the backseat of the yellow cab to the airport. The drive across town seemed to take mere minutes, even in the gathering rush hour. Of course, today of all days, there would be nothing but smooth traffic and no delays. A clear path to their personal end of the line.

Ethan's heart was banging behind his sternum as the taxi slowed to find a spot at the curb to unload. He didn't want to let Tori out of the vehicle. He didn't want to let her leave him. Not ever, if he had the choice.

"Here we are, folks." The cab driver's cheerful announcement made Ethan's regret tighten in his chest.

He paid the fare, but neither he nor Tori moved to get out. On a quiet cry, she flung her arms around him. Ethan closed his eyes and embraced her, savoring the feel of her against him for as long as he possibly could.

"Let's go, babe. We have to do this," he finally murmured, but still couldn't convince his arms to release her, even as the taxi driver came around to open the back door to the crowded curb outside the airline's departures terminal.

They climbed out together, but had hardly gotten to their feet on the concrete when Tori's cell phone gave a quiet chirp.

"Oh, shit." Tori said. "I told Hoshi I'd call her as soon as I could. That's probably her texting me, worried sick by now."

As the taxi rolled away, she fished the mobile out of her purse, then frowned. "It's not her. It's the airline."

Ethan scowled, adrenaline shooting into his veins. "What's it say?"

"My flight is overbooked. They've bumped me to standby." She glanced over at him. "It says I need to stop at the ticket counter as soon as possible to make alternate arrangements."

Something wasn't right. His realization was instant. So was his dread.

"No way." She handed him the phone to take a look at the message. He wanted to crush the damned thing in his fist. "This is a trap. No fucking way are you stepping foot inside this airport now."

Tori's face went white. "You think he's done this somehow—the man who's after you?"

Scanning the immediate area, Ethan gave a grim nod, but he feared it was even worse. Tori hadn't been taken off her flight by Ethan's assailant, but by whoever had sent the man.

Which meant now the assassin not only had Tori's visual description from the other day at the market, but her name and address too.

Jesus Christ. By now, they probably have everything on her.

"This phone is toast. We have to lose it. And we have to go."

The busy airport was clotted with people coming and going. Lines of cars idled near the curb, others weaving between buses and shuttles, everyone jockeying for positions.

As Ethan's gaze traveled his surroundings, he spotted the one thing he prayed he wouldn't find. The now-familiar rugged face and bald head of the assassin. He stood just inside the terminal near the windows, scanning the arriving throng.

"Shit." Ethan started calculating their options, few as they were. He grabbed Tori's hand. "Come on. We're getting the fuck out of here."

"Is it him? Oh, God. You see him somewhere, don't

you?" She looked so scared, it nearly killed him. "What will we do, Ethan? Where can we go?"

At that moment, he had no goddamned idea.

"Leave that to me. I'll get you out of here. I'll keep you safe."

And he would, to his last breath, if that's what it took.

14

Tori's heart lodged in her throat as Ethan pulled her along with him, stepping down off the curb to dart through the sea of vehicles clogging the pavement outside the terminal.

"Oh, God, Ethan. Do you think he saw us? Do you think he's coming after us?"

"Don't look for him," he ordered her, when Tori's dread compelled her to search every face in the crowd for the one hunting Ethan.

And now, apparently, hunting her as well.

"This way. We have to hurry, Tori."

With his backpack from the bus station locker slung over his good shoulder, Ethan's grasp was firm on her hand as he rushed toward a silver Impala standing vacant about four cars up the line. The driver's side door was carelessly left open. The sedan's former occupants, a young couple obviously in love, were in the midst of a long kiss goodbye in the white zone.

Ethan made a beeline for their car.

He swung Tori ahead of him as they approached the open door. He kept his voice low, urgent. "Get in. Do it quick."

She slid in. Hopped over to the passenger seat. Ethan was already behind the wheel as Tori clicked her seatbelt on.

Over on the curb, the passionate couple had suddenly realized there was something going on behind them.

Ethan shot Tori a less than repentant look, his mouth quirking. "They don't seem eager to part. We're probably doing them a favor."

He threw the car in gear and hit the gas.

He sped out of the terminal and through the city without consulting street signs or the vehicle's GPS, making a fast track for the interstate. He drove with full concentration on the task, his gaze distant, calculating, as the miles added up behind them.

They had been heading east on I-90 for almost an hour before he finally spoke. "You can't go back to Maine now, Tori. Not for a while. Maybe not ever."

"You think he'll try to kill me too?"

Ethan's mouth pressed flat. "I'm not about to chance it. The fact that they found your flight information—that they now know your name and probably everything else about you—means they also realize you're important to me. They'll know if they have you, they've got me too."

"They," Tori murmured. "You're talking about, what—the government? The CIA? Is that who you think sent this man to kill you?"

"I don't know. It could be either of those entities. Maybe even both."

God, she couldn't believe how calmly she was having this conversation. But the past couple of days had been a crash course in learning to believe the unbelievable.

Why not accept that she was now swept up in a potential government conspiracy with her covert agent, psychically gifted lover?

She might have laughed if the reality of it hadn't chilled her through to the bone.

Ethan kept his eyes on the road as they zipped along the forest-lined interstate. His hands were wrapped tight on the wheel, his squared jaw tense. "Someone wants to make sure the Phoenix program and everyone associated with it is eliminated. The question is, why?"

"What if it has something to do with the nightmare?" she murmured.

Ethan glanced at her, and his expression was utterly bleak. "Pray that it doesn't."

Tori sat back, a grave silence descending over both of them as the hours rolled on and the danger they'd left behind in Seattle faded farther and farther into the distance.

Heading south on a two-lane U.S. highway that had taken them into Oregon some hundred miles back, Ethan glanced at the dashboard and blew out a low curse. "Shit. We're going to need to stop for gas before long. And it's almost noon. You must be hungry."

She was starving, but she wouldn't have complained about an empty stomach when Ethan was doing his best to get them to safe ground. Wherever that might be.

"Where are we going, anyway?"

He gave a vague shrug. "Haven't decided. Unfortunately, we'll have to lose this car as soon as possible. We can't risk driving around in a stolen vehicle."

Tori nodded and glanced out the window as they approached a small town. There was a gas station up ahead less than a mile, and roadside signs that looked promising for something to eat.

"Ethan, look," she said, pointing to a double-wide trailer on the left side of the road as they rolled into town. In the front yard was a decade-old maroon minivan with a handwritten *For Sale* sign taped in the windshield.

Runs Good. $500 O.B.O.

She gave him a why-not shrug and a hopeful smile. "I doubt anyone will be looking for us in something like that."

He nodded. "Ugly as hell and cheap besides. It's perfect."

15

Ethan ditched the stolen car in the parking lot of a restaurant in Madras that specialized in pizza and Mexican food.

An hour later, a large pepperoni and mushroom decimated between them in the back of the minivan, he and Tori sat with the side door wide open in the car lot of a quiet state park.

Just beyond the tree-lined perimeter of the parking lot, a narrow stretch of the Deschutes River swept along rhythmically, early afternoon sun glittering off the surface.

Ethan glanced over at Tori, watching her sip soda from a styrofoam cup and plastic straw as she gazed out at their surroundings. As far as surreal moments went, this one ranked right up there. He and Tori trying to outrun a cold-blooded killer, yet sitting together as if they were on a frigging first date.

"Now, that was a great pizza," she said, giving her drink one last gurgling slurp.

Ethan chuckled. "Far cry from the standard I hoped to set last night, eh?"

She turned a smile on him that made his heart kick behind his sternum. "I think I like this even more. It's so beautiful here. How did you know about this park? We must be ten miles off the highway."

"More or less," he said with a shrug. "I spent some time in the area a while back."

She nodded and resumed enjoying the view. "I imagine you've spent some time in a lot of places. Did any of them ever feel like home to you?"

"Once," he said. Tori's face, lit up by the early afternoon sunlight, her short blond hair riffling in the light breeze, was more gorgeous than any scenery. "The closest I've ever gotten to feeling like I was home was the year I spent with you."

When she glanced over at him, a look of soft surprise in her blue gaze, Ethan let out a possessive-sounding growl and pulled her to him for a kiss.

He took his time, savoring the taste of her—spices on her tongue, sweet soda on her lips, and the warm, intoxicating flavor that was hers alone.

He'd never felt anything so right as the moments when he was holding this woman—his woman—in his arms.

She was smiling when he broke contact and rested his forehead against hers. "I feel like home to you?"

He grunted. "Even a rust bucket that smells vaguely of wet dog and kid vomit feels like home so long as you're in it with me."

She laughed, then wrinkled her nose. "Yeah, about that. Think we can trade this petri dish in for something else before we have to drive too much farther in it?"

"I think that's a definite affirmative. Should've asked for a sniff test before I plunked down my five hundred bucks."

Tori caressed his face with feather-light strokes of her fingers. "You know, speaking of home,

Ethan…you've never mentioned anything about where you grew up."

He pulled away before he could stop himself. A knee-jerk reaction that he hadn't been able to hide.

Not that Tori would have missed it anyway.

"Nothing to tell," he said, a dodge that sounded more wooden than casual. "I grew up in the Army. I don't really give my life before then too much thought."

A straight-up lie and she knew it. He saw her process his lame answer with a twinge of hurt in her tender blue eyes.

She gave a slow nod. "Okay. Well, maybe you'll tell me about it someday. When you're ready."

He should have let it go at that, but damn if he could ignore the sting in her gaze. He couldn't stonewall her, not after everything they'd been through.

Not when she meant more to him than any other person in his broken, fucked-up life.

As for his past, it was close enough that he could feel those bleak, early years breathing down the back of his neck.

Tori started to turn away from him. Ethan reached out to her. "My old man was a drinker. And when he drank, he was a mean son of a bitch." He blew out a humorless laugh. "The only thing my dad liked more than his whiskey was telling his kid what a fuckup he was. When he wasn't busy knocking me around, that is."

Tori had gone still, holding his eyes without pity or judgment. Ethan shrugged, forging on, too late to change his mind about spilling his life story in all its pathetic glory.

"The drinking got worse over time. Good thing about that was I knew I'd have some peace once the old man passed out."

"Ethan…" She settled her hand over his, swallowing hard as he explained.

"My mom tried to defend me from him. She'd distract Dad's temper with kindness or humor. Begging and pleading when nothing else worked on him. But that usually just pissed him off even more. I don't know why he hated me. Maybe he had no goddamned reason at all."

"He was an alcoholic. Addicts don't make good parents, even under the best conditions," Tori said gently. "Did you know about your ESP back then? Did they know?"

"Mom knew. He didn't, not for a long time. Not until later." And then his father really had begun to hate him. "My mother made me keep my gift a secret from him. She said it would only make things worse on me if we let on that I was different. God knows, he didn't need any other excuses to despise me."

He looked out at the river, recalling when his father's rage had escalated to its worst.

"I could've handled violence and insults. I was tough enough, even early on. But then one night he hit my mom. Sent her flying across the room. He'd found out she was cheating on him. Hell, who could blame her?" Ethan sighed sharply. "I was ten at the time. I was shocked that he'd struck her, scared shitless the way I never was when he hit me. I went at him for the first time, started hitting him. He knocked me out cold."

"Jesus," Tori whispered thinly. "Please tell me your mother called the police."

He shook his head. "The next morning, I woke up in the living room where he'd dropped me. Mom was acting like nothing was wrong—like she forgave him, if she even remembered what he'd done. That day in school, I had a premonition. I saw her packing up a suitcase and leaving us while the old man was delivering a truckload of vegetables to the farm stand in town."

"Oh, Ethan…"

"I got home and found Dad in a rage. There was a note on the counter. Mom said she'd forgotten to tell him about a meeting after hours at the library where she worked and would be home soon." He still recalled reading that note while his father was pacing around like a wild animal, a half-drained bottle of Jack in his hand. "I started gathering things to cook, but he barked at me that it wasn't my job. He said, 'Save it for your mother, boy, whenever the bitch finally comes home to look after her family.'"

Ethan chuckled, but it was a brittle sound. "I didn't want to out her, but I was hurt and angry. She left me behind that day too. I blurted out that she was never coming back. That she ran away because of him."

Tori's voice was hardly audible, filled with dread. "Oh, my God."

"He was pissed off, of course. And suspicious. 'How do you know that? Where'd she go? Did you help her leave me, you ungrateful little fuck?'"

The memories were vivid, but no longer sharp. He could tell Tori everything and not feel he'd been flayed to the bone.

"I told him that I saw her leave. I told him about the premonition, and that I'd had the ability for as long as I could remember. He beat the living shit out of me that night."

Tori squeezed his hand, silent now, her big blue eyes

welling.

"I wanted to run away, but I had nowhere to go. No one to turn to." He shrugged. "So, I made the best of my fucked-up home life. I avoided the old man as much as I could. Kept busy at school studying, or at the library, reading. I spent as much time as possible away from home. I guess it paid off in a small way. Dad left me alone pretty much after that, and somehow I ended up valedictorian of my graduating class. I finally left home for good the day I was supposed to speak at commencement."

"Supposed to?"

"He was in an ugly mood the night before my graduation, looking for a fight. I guess I finally had enough of his shit. I was seventeen, bigger than him by then. I told him what I thought of him. You can imagine how that went over."

Ethan blew out a wry exhalation and continued. "We fought, and he broke a bottle on my head. Split open my scalp, broke my nose. The next day, instead of showing up like that to the commencement, I skipped the ceremony and went to the Army recruiting office instead. Signed up on the spot. I bunked at a homeless shelter in town until I was able to ship out for Basic. Never spoke to my dad again. Never been back since."

"Ethan…" Tori wrapped her arms around him and just held him for a long moment. "What your father did to you and to your mom…it's inexcusable, unforgivable. But I can't fathom why your mother didn't take you with her."

"She did what she felt she had to," he murmured, feeling no ill will toward her, not in a long time. "I like to think she found some happiness with the man she'd fallen in love with. I never knew, because she died a couple of years after she left. Drunk driver. How's that for irony?"

Tori stared at him, tenderness in her expression. And something deeper. "You had no one to look out for you. No one on your side for so long, Ethan. No wonder you don't need anyone now."

He cupped her nape in his palm. "Not true. There is one person I'd rather not be without."

Drawing her into his arms, he kissed her slowly, holding none of himself back.

Hard to imagine when he'd started this journey three years ago—when he'd had to cut ties to everything he knew, everything that mattered to him the most. He'd never dreamed he'd have Tori back in his arms.

Back in his life.

He didn't know how he would be able to find a place for them to be together when his existence depended on how fast he could run and for how long. But a determination to make what he had right now with Tori a reality was burning strong inside him.

He needed time to think, to plan a course.

He needed to be somewhere no one would think to look for him.

Somewhere not even he was certain he should go.

Back to his past, so he could finally move forward.

But not just yet.

He wasn't ready to leave this temporary slice of tranquility with Tori. His demons would have to wait.

16

"I shouldn't have had all that soda," Tori said from the passenger seat of the minivan, her bladder feeling every rut and bump in the uneven pavement.

"We'll be stopping for the night in a few minutes. You be okay until then?"

She nodded, but crossed her legs just the same. Rather than get back on the highway, Ethan kept them on rambling back roads that followed the river.

Tori was well aware of the tension that had settled over him since they'd left the state park a short while ago, but as he contemplated their course in sober silence, she couldn't help being captivated by the rugged scenery that slid past the window.

Breathtaking, rust-colored rock formations jutted up behind wide, rolling farms and green pastures. Livestock paddocks and pole barns let out onto acres of well-tended land, most of it hemmed in by low white fences that seemed to go on for miles on the winding valley road. Against the far horizon, hazy, snow-covered peaks of jagged mountains loomed, making even the highest ridges in the Northeast look like meager hills.

After a few miles, the picturesque homesteads, farms, and clusters of rural neighborhoods gave way to less prosperous-looking patches of land. Few homes or trailers sat on the stretch of twisting asphalt ahead of them now. The land was flat and dusty, most of it gone to seed or littered with rock and boulders. Here and there a rundown farmhouse or neglected camper squatted at the end of an unpaved driveway.

It was near one such place that Tori noticed they had begun to slow down.

Up ahead on the left, a rusted metal mailbox with the name "Wm. Davis" painted onto it sat atop an S-curved length of plumbing pipe. At the end of the long, dirt path leading back from the road was a ramshackle, sun-bleached gray two-story farmhouse with a sagging, faded red barn behind it.

She glanced at Ethan as he brought the van to a crawl as they approached. A strange shiver worked its way up her nape as she took in the sad, sorry condition of the house and land.

It was a lonely place. A home that had been long in ruin, devoid of joy.

And suddenly she knew where they were without needing to ask him. "You spent some time in the area," she murmured quietly, his words back at the river. "This is the house where you grew up."

He stared at the old house, the van now paused in the empty road. "Yeah. This is it."

"The mailbox doesn't say Jones on it," Tori pointed out, looking at him in question.

"I dropped the family name after I got into the Phoenix program. Henry Sheppard helped me start fresh, bury my past. I've been Ethan Jones ever since." He turned into the narrow driveway.

Tori could see that he wasn't happy to be there. His fingers were coiled around the wheel, his jaw clamped tight.

"What are we doing here? Are you sure you want to do this?"

"Staying anywhere else right now is too much risk. We could be spotted at a motel, and I'm not going to make you sleep in this van tonight."

"But here, Ethan?"

"I'll keep you safe." A solemn reassurance, spoken like a vow.

He kept driving, the silence in the vehicle punctuated by the pop and crunch of gravel as they rolled slowly toward the old house.

She didn't understand until now how deep Ethan's dread must be that the killer on their tail, or the ones who hired him, might find them.

If he thought seeking shelter at his father's house was less terrifying than facing his other enemies, then Tori could only hope they survived the night so they could run far and fast again tomorrow.

She sat ramrod straight as the van crawled up the driveway to the side of the house. Inside, a curtain swung back into place in a dingy bay window, as if someone had just peeked out. Before the van had slowed to a stop, the side screen door opened.

An old man stepped out onto the covered wooden porch. Tall and thin, hunched at the shoulders, he poked his thinning, gray-haired head around one of the rails and scowled at his uninvited visitors.

He wore a white, short-sleeved undershirt and dark green work pants. Sagging, faded black tattoos rode his forearms. His glower was piercing, terrifying and forbidding.

He peered at the van's windshield for a long

moment, then the glare faltered. Just a fraction, and only for a moment before he called it back and scowled even more furiously.

Ethan put the van in park, but left the engine running as he opened his door and got out.

Tori didn't feel quite as brave as him, yet she couldn't let him face his father on his own. She climbed out too, and stood beside the vehicle as Ethan walked around the front.

"If you come here for the readin' of the will, you're too early." His father's voice was scratchy, not nearly as deep or smooth as Ethan's. "I ain't dead yet, boy."

Tori stared, unsure what to do or say in the face of this cold reunion. Ethan seemed thoroughly unfazed. He stood his ground as the old man hobbled down from the stoop and made his way onto the dirt drive.

Fog-gray eyes stared out of a skull covered in tissue-thin, sallow skin. His cheeks were sunken, lips dry and cracked.

He wasn't healthy, but there was still an air of couched aggression in the man. God only knew what he'd been like with a few more pounds on him and thirty fewer years of age.

The old man's shadow-ringed gaze slid to Tori for no more than a second before he turned his displeasure back on his son. "You gonna tell me what you're doing here? You didn't come for my funeral and you sure as shit ain't here on a social call."

"We need a place to crash. Just for the night." Ethan didn't phrase it as a question, and there was no fear or hesitation in his voice or the steely stare he fixed on his father. He reached into the pocket of his cargo shorts. "If you need money—"

"I don't want your goddamn money, boy."

The sharp retort made a rattle crawl up the old man's throat. He wheezed and coughed, then spat at the dusty ground once he'd composed himself again.

He pursed his pale lips, looking from the van to Tori, then Ethan. "Just for one night?"

Ethan gave a curt nod. "We'll be gone by sunrise."

His father studied him for a long while, then his head bobbed absently in consideration. "Okay, then. If that's what you need, boy. Come on inside."

Ethan cleared his throat. "I'd like to park the van in the barn."

The wiry gray eyebrows rose a fraction. He grunted, then motioned for Ethan to follow him as he started heading for the weather-beaten red outbuilding.

Ethan didn't follow right away. He walked over and brushed his fingers through the hair over her brow. "There's a bathroom just inside the house. Second door on the left."

"Oh, no, that's okay. I'd rather wait for you—"

He gave a faint shake of his head. "I need to get a few things straight with him. And I need to do it alone."

"Okay," she agreed.

He kissed her, tender and sweet.

Then he pivoted to go confront the monster of his youth.

17

Ethan pulled the van inside the open barn, amazed to see the place had hardly changed since he'd last been there. It was time-worn and brittle though, suffering from an obvious, prolonged dereliction and neglect.

Rather like his father.

Ethan glanced at the old man who waited inside the barn with him. He looked worse than unhealthy.

The strong, rangy, combative drunk who used to simmer with explosive rages had become a stooped, jaundiced shadow of the terror he once had been.

And Ethan had been shocked not to detect the sickly sweet, ever-present whiff of whiskey on his father the instant he got close to him.

"You been on the road for long?" the old man asked as Ethan got out and shut the driver's side door.

"Not long."

His father grunted. "Where'd you say you were headed again?"

"I didn't."

Another grunt, this time with an edge of annoyance to it. "Gotta tell you, boy, figured I'd be dead and dust before I ever saw you around here again."

Ethan swung an indifferent look toward him. "Yeah, that makes two of us."

"You in trouble of some sort?"

Jesus, was that a flicker of genuine concern in those cataract-clotted eyes, or was he imagining things?

Ethan wasn't about to trust that idea at face value.

His father considered him for a long moment. "Yeah, you must be mixed up in something bad. I'm thinking you gotta be in some kinda dire straits, to come running back home to me."

"This isn't home," Ethan said sharply. "You don't even know the meaning."

"Yet here you are."

Ethan wheeled on him. To his shock, the old man shrank back, cowering from him. "Don't think for a second I'd be here unless I had no other place to go. If it was just me, I'd sleep on the street before I asked you for a fucking thing."

But he had to think about Tori, about her comfort and safety. He wouldn't risk them sleeping unsecured in the van. And with a hired killer behind him somewhere, they couldn't chance staying at a motel or other public place where they might be seen by the assassin or anyone else.

They had to lie low, and hope the danger either passed them by, or gave Ethan the chance to eliminate it permanently.

Right now, he needed to keep his head down and come up with a plan. A roadmap for where they should go, where they might be safe for a while.

He glanced at his father, who had gone quiet, recoiled from Ethan's fury. "I don't want to argue with you. I don't even want to be standing here talking with you right now. I'm just passing through. Like I said, we'll be gone in the morning. Then you can carry on with your life and I'll carry on with mine."

"Carry on, you say." His thin mouth pressed flatter and he clucked his tongue. "Did you know I stopped drinking?" When Ethan didn't respond, his father went on. "Naw, you couldn't know that. You've been away for too long. Well, I did. Two and half years now, not a single drop."

Ethan blew out a sharp sigh. "Better late than never."

"Late is right." The old man chuckled, and the wet, scraping sound of it echoed in the quiet barn. "Too fucking late for me. I'm not well, as you might've guessed. Cirrhosis. Terminal, so they tell me. I've had one foot in the grave for the past eight months."

"That's too bad." Ethan knew it sounded cold, unfeeling. But there wasn't much emotion in him when he looked at the man who had terrorized him so often and driven his mother away.

"You hold a grudge, just like she always did," his father remarked tonelessly. "Well, I suppose it's no use apologizing now. What's done is done."

Ethan scoffed. The old man was true to form, he'd give him that. He might be dying. He might even be wrestling with some personal regrets. But damn if he was going to accept any blame for his past sins.

And truly, Ethan had no need to hear it from him either. "Don't worry. I'm not looking for sorry from you. I'm long past that."

His father stared at him. "Where you been all this time, anyway?"

Ethan shrugged. "Around. Here and there."

"Been gone what, almost twenty years?"

"Seventeen," Ethan replied. "Didn't expect you to

be keeping track."

"I heard you joined the military," his father pressed. "That true?"

Jesus. Ethan started to bristle at all of the questions. "What do you care?"

Those filmy gray eyes that used to instill so much dread in him when he was a kid now narrowed with a spark of animosity in them.

This was the man Ethan recalled. Not the bent, apparently sober, dead man walking who'd assumed he could prod for answers and poke around for sympathy just because he'd gone a couple of years without a drink and a couple of decades without punching his kid.

The old man crossed his withered, tattooed arms over his tattered undershirt. "I hope for your sake you did join the service. God knows, you needed the discipline. Needed someone to put you in your place."

"I thought that was your job," Ethan muttered.

"Your mother made you soft. She made you arrogant, all those books she put under your nose, letting you sit in front of that computer for hours. You were so smart, always acting like you were better than me, better than the life I provided for you." He scowled at Ethan. "You and your mother, you never appreciated what I did."

Ethan met the accusing gaze leveled on him now with one of his own. "Guess you showed us both real good, huh, Dad?"

He expected his father to bellow back in fury, or lash out with flying fists. But he did neither.

He got quiet, contemplative. He stared at Ethan, studying the unswaying glare he'd never seen directed at him before in his life.

He looked down at his scuffed work boots, then glanced vaguely back toward the house where Tori had gone a few minutes ago. "You gonna tell me about the girl?"

"She's with me," Ethan said firmly. "She's mine. That's all you need to know."

"Yours," the old man mused. A slow smile played at the edges of his mouth. "Well, I'll be goddamned. Did you go off and fall in love, boy?"

He tensed with a spike of fierce protectiveness. "I'm not a boy anymore, and you need to know that woman means everything to me. Anyone touches her, I will kill him. Anyone."

His father shook his head. "What do you think, I'm gonna hurt either one of you? Look at me, son. I'm not the same person I was back then. I'm sober. I'm also old. And I'm dying."

"I hope you're not looking for sympathy from me."

"No, son...I'm not." He paused for a long moment, his hard eyes going distant. The lines of his face seemed to deepen with what looked astonishingly like regret. It was there and gone, dismissed by the rattled clearing of his throat. "If you have anything to bring inside, go on and gather it up. We can close up the barn when you're ready."

His father didn't wait for a reply, just shuffled outside and left Ethan standing there behind him. Tori passed him on the way out of the house. He gave her a nod, but kept walking, his gait hitching, humbled by age and disease.

"Fuck." Ethan raked a hand over his scalp. He didn't want to feel even a twinge of forgiveness for the son of a bitch. He wanted to hate him.

He still did, in fact. Part of him probably always would.

But as he watched Tori approach, he couldn't deny the sense of gratitude that overcame him. William Davis might be the sorriest excuse for a father, but for all his faults, he was still willing to shelter Ethan and Tori from the even bigger terror that was still breathing down their necks.

A terror that Ethan felt certain would not relent until one of them was dead.

18

Hours later, after a quiet, awkwardly hospitable dinner with Ethan's father, Tori found herself in the attic bedroom that was to be their lodging for the night.

She'd gone up alone. Ethan had decided to take a shower after he and Tori cleared the table and washed the dishes.

She had only planned to change out of her shorts into the pair of yoga pants she'd stuffed into her purse when she left Hoshi's place, but once she was inside the cramped little room, she couldn't help lingering over the artifacts of Ethan's childhood.

Opposite the wall with the sole window in the room sat a narrow twin bed with a bookcase headboard, crammed with paperbacks, all sporting aged, barely legible spines.

A wheeled chair and battered particle board desk stood across the small space, its veneer faded and filmed with dust in some areas, scarred and peeling away in others.

Wall-mounted pine shelves served as displays for a collection of model aircraft, rockets, and sports cars.

There was something heartbreaking about the normalcy of Ethan's room. How it bore no signs of the trauma he'd suffered in this house, under his father's alcohol-fueled fury and his mother's eventual abandonment.

Then again, maybe it did.

She drifted over to the bed and sat down, looking at Ethan's boyhood library. There were easily close to a hundred books on the shelf. So many, they were packed in like sardines, some standing up and others filed on their sides. A veritable hoard, collected by a boy with a sharp, intellectual mind and a hidden gift that made him all the more extraordinary.

But he was also a child living in a private hell.

Each book on Ethan's shelf, every last one, was a story about magical lands and faraway adventures. Each crumbling spine and bleached out title spoke of escape.

She glanced at the models he had clearly built with his own hands. High-speed jets. Spaceships. Fast cars.

His yearning to get away from his upbringing couldn't have been more obvious to anyone inclined to take a closer look.

Tori's mouth went dry with heartbreak as she absorbed the reality of Ethan's past. She pulled one of the old paperbacks off the headboard bookcase and carefully opened it, the knot in her throat burning even more as her eyes lit on the scrawled handwriting penciled onto the title page.

Property of Ethan Michael Davis.

She touched the juvenile letters, feeling a connection to him now that could never be broken. He had trusted her with this part of himself, of his past.

He had, at last, shown her his whole truth.

And she had never loved him more.

Tori glanced up at the sudden, soft creak of the attic bedroom door.

Ethan's hazel eyes found her on the bed and he smiled as he stepped in and closed the door behind him. "I should warn you, those books are rare literary treasures. There's a steep fine if you're late returning any of them."

She grinned despite the weight of her emotions. "Well, that could pose a problem, since I don't have a lot of cash on me right now. Maybe we can take it out in trade?"

Barefoot, dressed only in the jeans he had in his backpack, he strode over to sit beside her on the bed.

"What are you reading?" He took the paperback out of her hands and chuckled lightly. "I must've read this one a dozen times. All of them, more than likely."

As he reached around her to put the book back on the shelf, Tori let her gaze soak him, from his handsome, now clean-shaven face, to his broad shoulders and the stitched, healing stab wound from yesterday. Her heart was so full of love when she looked at him, it felt on the verge of bursting inside her breast.

She pulled him into her arms and kissed him, slowly, deeply. He encircled her in his embrace too, returning her kiss with the same tender fervor.

"What's this for?" he murmured against her mouth.

"For trusting me," she whispered. "With this. With your life. With who you really are."

He said nothing, just looked into her eyes with an intensity that stole her breath. When his mouth met hers again, it was achingly sweet.

Raw and honest.

And much too brief for her liking.

"Where's your dad now?" she asked, still holding Ethan close.

"He was just going to bed downstairs when I came up." Ethan exhaled a sigh. "Is it wrong that seeing him now, I feel more pity for the son of a bitch than hate?"

She stroked his smooth cheek, the hard plane and firm jaw. "No. You lived it, Ethan. You feel what you feel."

"I pity him for all the things his addiction and his rage cost him. My mom loved him once. I did too. He destroyed all of that."

Ethan brought his hand up to her face now, his strong fingers ghosting over her skin, making her tremble. His gaze searched hers, as tender as his touch. "For so long, I worried that I had destroyed anything you might've felt for me. I thought you'd hate me too."

"No," she said. "It wasn't hate. It was hurt. And that's a much different thing."

He cursed quietly. "I didn't want to leave you, Tori. It about killed me to walk away that day."

"You had to do what you did, how you did it. I understand that now."

He shook his head. "It's not over yet. I could be on the run for a long time. Maybe the rest of my life. I don't want to wreck your life because of the way I have to live mine now."

"I'm right where I want to be—with you. I waited three years for you, Ethan. I would've waited longer." She brushed her fingers into his damp hair. "Besides, I've always wanted to see other parts of the country. Or the world, if that's where we end up."

He laughed ruefully. "Preferably not with a target on your back."

"What kind of life would you expect me to have somewhere else without you, knowing that you had a target on your back? I need to be with you, Ethan. I don't care where that is, or under what circumstances it will have to be—"

"You didn't choose this kind of life," he argued, frowning. "It's not fair for me to ask you to sacrifice your job, your home, your friends—your entire way of living—just to risk your neck with me."

"You haven't asked," she pointed out.

"And I won't." He drew back now, withdrawing from the conversation and from her. "I don't want you to regret it, Tori. I don't want you to regret me."

Anger spiked through the softer feelings she'd been having in Ethan's arms. "Regret you? Regret what we have right now?" She shook her head. "The biggest regret I could ever have is not being with you. If you don't realize by now that I am in love with you, then maybe you're not as brilliant as I thought."

He stared for a long moment, his expression unreadable. "In love with me?"

"Head over heels, Professor Jones." He was still staring, but now a tendon had begun to tick rapidly in his cheek. "I think I've been totally, irrevocably in love with you since St. Patrick's Day four years ago."

Ethan said nothing, but then he grabbed her on a fierce growl and drew her into a fevered, heart-stopping kiss. Yet for all his fire and passion, his hands were tender, reverent on her face and in her short hair.

When he finally released her, Tori laughed breathlessly. "This is traditionally the part where you say you love me too."

He shook his head. "No. That's not a strong enough word for what I feel about you. When you said I'd been alone all my life, you were right. I made sure I never had to rely on anyone. I never let myself trust anyone. Letting myself love someone?" He exhaled a sharp gust of breath. "I didn't even know what that meant. Not until you, and the year we had together."

"Ethan…" she whispered, hardly able to form words for the joy that had taken up residence in her breast.

"You mean everything to me, Tori. You are the only love I've ever known. The only one I've ever needed." His long fingers were still caressing her cheek, his thumb stroking her jawline and throat. "I used to lie awake in this room, wishing, waiting for my first chance to get away. This house has always been nothing but bad memories. Not now. Tomorrow, I'm going to leave here with another memory. This memory—right here and now."

Tori bent toward him on a soft cry and kissed him.

"Damn, woman," he uttered against her lips. "This is torture, having you here on my bed, kissing me like that, telling me you love me…looking so beautiful and sexy, I can hardly keep from tearing your clothes off."

"Who's stopping you?"

He drew back and held her in a hooded, dark gaze. Tori didn't wait for him to object or have any sudden attacks of honor.

With deft movements, she took off her tank top and shimmied out of her shorts. She sat before him on her knees in just her bra and panties.

Ethan swore, but it sounded like a prayer. "Tori Connors, you are the most beautiful thing I've ever seen. I can't control myself around you for a fucking second."

He reached out to her, caressed her breasts over the satin of her bra. She sighed at his touch, wanted more of it. Wanted to feel it all over her.

Ethan rasped a low curse. "My thirteen-year-old self would explode on the spot to see you now, like this, in a bedroom that has never known any action, other than the nights it was just me and my hand and a head full of horny teenage fantasies."

Tori grinned. "Then brace yourself, because this bedroom's cherry is about to get popped."

19

She stripped him naked in mere seconds. His jeans and boxers hit the floor, then Tori went straight for his jutting cock.

"I don't have protection," he murmured, the words thick, difficult to spit out.

She sent a heated glance up at him. "I don't care. Not tonight."

"Thank God." Ethan let his head fall back on his shoulders, sucking in a sharp breath as she licked him slowly from root to tip.

Her lips were soft and wet, her tongue scorching as she closed her mouth around the crown of his cock and slid down his length. Her enthusiastic moans as she swallowed him up vibrated through him straight to his balls, turning his already aching need into something fierce and primal.

She was his woman.

The only person he needed, and the only one he would ever want.

He loved her.

Holy fuck, he loved her with all of his being.

And damn, did he love what she could do to his body.

She took him deep, twisted her devilish little tongue

along the sensitive underside of his shaft and up around the plum at its top.

He was on fire from her attention. He fought the roaring build of his climax, wanting to feel this pleasure for a while longer. Forever, if Tori was willing.

He would never have enough of her, and if he ever doubted it in any moment they'd been together, tonight, after everything they'd come through and had yet to face, Ethan knew he would never let her out of his life.

All his noble talk about moving on without her, keeping her safe by keeping her away from him, had been obliterated when she'd confessed her love for him so openly tonight.

He would protect her with his life.

With his death, if it came down to that.

The only thing that mattered was this woman—*his woman.*

She owned him, a fact that was all the more clear to him as she suckled him and kissed him, picking up a tempo that was too pleasurable for him to endure much longer.

On a growl, he pulled her off him before he lost all control. "Now it's my turn."

He tossed her beneath him on the bed and rolled onto her, kissing her with tongue and teeth, his need firing even wilder.

With clumsy, impatient fingers, he unfastened the dainty clasp on her bra and freed her breasts. Her nipples were hard and flushed as deep a shade as her lips. He suckled the tight little buds, spurred on by Tori's breathless, throaty cries.

He didn't want to leave the delicious feast of her breasts and mouth, but there was a sweeter temptation that awaited. Ethan moved down the length of her body, kissing a trail over her sternum and delicate rib cage, then on to the creamy plane of her abdomen.

As he descended lower, he hooked his fingers in the hem of her panties and drew them down her slender legs. His palms were too warm, skidding up the velvety skin of her thighs.

He spread her open to his gaze, his senses full of the pretty wetness of her sex, the sugared cream scent of her arousal. She watched him admire her nakedness, her eyelids heavy over the dark blue pools of her eyes.

Eyes that looked at him with such trust and affection, such carnal need, he nearly spilled himself just sitting there.

"So beautiful," he murmured hoarsely.

Then he bent his head and indulged in a deep, unhurried taste of her.

He brought her to a swift, thrashing orgasm, showing her no mercy until she had to bury her screams in the thin pillow on the bed.

He needed release too. She'd worked him into a state of pleasured anguish with her mouth, and now her climax had him beyond all sanity.

He needed her now.

All of her.

Forever.

"I have to be inside you." Ethan rose between her parted thighs, crawled back up on the narrow bed.

Tonight, all their filters were stripped away, gone. Including this last one.

He rocked against her slick folds, nothing but skin on skin. Her juices coated him in warm honey as he thrust inside.

"Oh, God," she gasped, reaching for him, pulling him down atop her as their bodies joined and began to move in perfect tempo.

He wanted to take it slow, but he was too far gone before they'd even started. With Tori writhing beneath him with the start of another climax, Ethan drove harder, deeper, faster. She broke around him, her tiny muscles rippling against his shaft as he chased his own release.

Finally, he could take no more.

His orgasm rolled up on him. On a low roar he withdrew, nestling his cock between their bodies as he spilled in a stream of slick heat.

"Ah, Christ," he gasped, burying his forehead above her shoulder on the mattress. "This bedroom's cherry is more than popped. It's been fucking obliterated."

Tori laughed softly and wrapped her arms around him as they caught their breath for the next round.

20

They made love several times during the night, then again as they woke that early morning before sunrise.

While Ethan had gone down to find them some coffee and toast, Tori had showered in a state of blissful exhaustion, her body aching deliciously in all the right places after enjoying his apparently endless stamina.

His desire for her had seemed equally infinite, his love even deeper, and she could only imagine how intense and passionate their future together would be.

She couldn't wait for that future to begin.

He was alone in the kitchen when she went in, dressed and ready to hit the road. Standing bare-chested at the sink in his low-slung jeans, his sandy brown hair sleep-rumpled, Ethan palmed a mug of steaming coffee as he stared out the window at the gathering light outside.

Tori recalled another morning like this one, when she'd found Ethan standing in her kitchen back on that late-February morning in Maine.

She had loved him then too, but now she saw a different man before her.

And although it hardly seemed possible to her, she loved this newer, truer man even more.

He glanced over as she walked into the room, and

his warm smile melted her. Tori went to him, wrapping her arms around his waist from behind. She rested her cheek on his muscled back. "Where's your father?"

"Just waking up, I think. Heard him in his shower about the same time you were getting out of the other one." Ethan caressed her clasped arms with his free hand. "You want coffee? I can make you some toast to go with it."

She kissed the center of his strong spine. "Sure. When do you want to leave?"

"As soon as I'm showered."

He broke out of her loose hold and gestured to the table where her purse and bag sat beside his black backpack. "I brought everything down from the bedroom. My burner phone is in the pack. If you want to call Hoshi do it now, on the burner. Keep the details to a minimum and don't say where we are. I know we can trust her, but the less she knows for certain the safer she'll be."

Tori nodded as he poured her a cup of coffee.

"We'll trash the phone before we leave," he said, handing her the cup and then sticking a slice of bread in the toaster on the counter. "Better to start fresh with a new one at our next stop. Hopefully we can trade the van for another vehicle at the same time."

After the incredible night they'd spent together, it was easy to forget that the morning would put them back on the run, trying to stay ahead of Ethan's enemies. Her enemies now too, because wherever he was—whatever he might face as a former member of the Phoenix program—Tori intended to be with him every step of the way.

He smoothed her hair off her forehead and placed a

tender kiss on her brow. "I'm going to clean up now. Have your toast, call your friend. Then we need to get out of here."

"Okay."

He caught her face in his hands and brushed his lips over hers. He groaned as the affectionate meeting of their mouths sizzled with renewed desire. She felt that very obvious, very enticing desire swell firmly against her abdomen as he kissed her.

When he broke away, his breath was ragged and heavy. "I'm gonna have to take a cold shower now. Make that glacial. Otherwise, I'm not going to make it more than a few miles today without pulling the van over to attack you."

She laughed as he kissed her again, then gave a little yelp as he palmed her ass in both hands and gave her backside a possessive squeeze over her clothes. As he strode out of the kitchen to head for the bathroom, Tori let herself admire the fine form of her man.

She would let him drive in peace today, but as soon as they stopped to rest, she intended to indulge in every delectable inch of him.

With that thought buoying her, she retrieved her slice of toast and nibbled at it as she sipped her black coffee at the small kitchen table.

She was about to pick up the phone to call Hoshi when she heard shuffling footsteps behind her. Ethan's father walked into the kitchen, giving her a short nod of greeting.

"Good morning." Tori offered him a brief smile over the rim of her cup. "There's fresh coffee in the pot."

He grunted noncommittally, but made his way over

to the machine and poured himself some. "Imagine you two will be heading out soon."

"In a few minutes," Tori replied. "Ethan's just taking a shower before we go."

Another grunt, this one quieter, thoughtful. He took a drink of his coffee, pensive for a long moment.

"I won't ask where you're heading, because I know he won't want me to know. Not my business anymore what he does, or where he is. I know that." There was no animosity in his words, only a frank understanding that he wasn't part of Ethan's life and probably never would be again.

Tori heard a softer note in the sickly old man's voice too. And when he turned his head to look at her, she saw sorrow in his cloudy eyes.

She saw a father's deep, unspoken regret.

She saw the man Ethan said he couldn't hate, the man who had driven away or destroyed every precious thing he once had.

But she also saw a stubborn, irascible man who might have felt all those things, yet would never put them into words. Not with her.

Most certainly not with the son he'd wronged so terribly, for so long.

Tori felt sorry for Ethan's father all the more because he would never know the good, honorable man his son had become in spite of the way he'd been raised.

"Well, I gotta get on with my day," he murmured. He took another swallow of his coffee, then dumped the rest down the drain. "Not gonna hang around and wait on goodbyes, and I don't wanna be in the way as Ethan and you head on out. I have work waitin' on me out back, so I'm gonna get on to it now."

He wiped his hands on a dish towel and glanced over at Tori for a long moment. "You look out for the boy, all right? Let him know I wish him Godspeed, to the both of you, wherever that road is gonna take you."

"I will," Tori said. "And…thank you, Mr. Davis."

He gave an abrupt nod. Then he turned away and strode out the back door.

As his heavy boots clopped down the stairs of the porch and faded into silence, Tori picked up Ethan's backpack and drifted outside to call her friend.

21

Ethan stood under the sputtering metal showerhead in the small guest bath's tub.

As the lukewarm water poured over him, he considered the road that lay ahead—both the physical route he'd need to resolve, and the journey he was about to embark on with Tori at his side.

She was his, and that fact made everything else seem insignificant.

Even the assassin they'd left behind in Seattle.

Christ, he hoped they'd left the hired killer behind.

Unfortunately, Ethan knew too well the way these men operated. They were relentless machines, driven by the need to finish their lethal tasks—perhaps even more so than by any reward promised to them upon completion.

There would be no rest for Tori and him unless the killer was stopped permanently. And regardless of the chase, Ethan knew he would have no lasting peace until he had answers about his nightmarish vision and what it was that he was supposed to prevent.

And for that, he knew he would need help.

No matter the risk in placing his trust in anyone besides Tori, Ethan had to find the other members of the Phoenix program.

The only question was, where to begin?

Mentally weighing the options, he squirted a dollop of shampoo into his palm, then soaped and rinsed his hair. He closed his eyes and let the water sluice down his face and shoulders, suds sliding down his abdomen and limbs.

When the first flash of premonition hit him, he staggered under the spray.

Holy fuck.

The vision hit him again—sharper now, a clear image of the property outside.

He saw the old gray farmhouse and the dirt drive. Saw the faded red barn where he'd hidden the minivan last night. The door stood wide open. Then his father emerged, the nose of a pistol held tight against his head.

Ah, Christ.

No.

They didn't have to hope to outrun the assassin from Seattle today.

He'd already found them.

"Tori!" Ethan roared as he scrambled out of the tub and yanked on his jeans. Barefoot, his hair still dripping, he raced out to the kitchen where she'd been a few minutes ago.

She was gone.

So was his backpack. The bag that held his own gun and the one he'd taken from his assailant back in the city.

He had no weapons. No immediate means to face off against the threat he knew was about to play out.

And then he realized he didn't even have the benefit of time.

Out on the porch off the back door, Tori let out a terrified-sounding whimper.

The premonition he'd seen in the shower was taking place right this very second.

Woodenly, he walked to the screen door and pushed it open. Tori's cry just about killed him, it was so thready and fearful.

"Ethan, don't," she whispered from the other end of the porch. "Don't come out here."

As if he would leave her out there to face this danger alone? It was him the assassin came for, not Tori. And not his father either.

But as Ethan stepped out, he saw his premonition manifest in reality.

His father was being walked out of the open barn door, the hit man holding a pistol in his left hand, the nose of the weapon jammed up hard against the old man's temple. There was a clear warning in the assassin's narrowed, unfeeling eyes. He would use whatever means necessary to get Ethan in his sights.

He would kill anyone who tried to thwart him.

"Keep your hands where I can see them, Mr. Jones." The assassin smiled ruthlessly. "Or do you prefer I call you Mr. Davis?"

Ethan's blood chilled. Somehow this son of a bitch had been given access to classified information on Ethan's background. Information that had been buried years ago and not resurrected since.

Which meant Ethan's dread that his kill order had been issued from within the Company or somewhere else in D.C. wasn't far off the mark.

No, more like dead-on.

Ethan lifted his hands, even as he assessed the situation before him. In his peripheral vision, he spotted his black backpack lying unzipped at Tori's feet on the porch. His burner phone was on the wooden floor nearby, no doubt dropped on the killer's command.

Both much too far for him to reach.

He could dive for the pack and hope he might wrestle out one of the weapons, but by the time he did, his father would have a bullet in his skull. Hell, by that time, Tori might too.

No fucking way can I risk that.

"Step forward," the assassin ordered him. "Step forward now, or the old man eats a bullet meant for you."

"Don't do it, boy!" his father shouted. "We both know I ain't worth it."

Maybe he wasn't, but Ethan would be damned before he let anyone be used as a pawn to get to him.

And he needed the time, however fleeting, to run his odds. To calculate his chances of somehow reaching his backpack.

He edged a bit farther onto the porch. "Let my father loose first. Then it's you and me."

The hit man grinned, white teeth gleaming like a jackal's. "Did I say anything about bartering? I only see one of us with a gun. That means the only one making demands is me."

Ethan felt a growl rumble in the back of his throat. He'd never be able to reach his own weapons. Not without someone losing their head.

As if the killer knew Ethan was stalling for time, he gave the old man a shove, walked him farther out onto the dirt driveway.

Closer to where Tori stood at the other end of the porch.

"Step forward, Mr. Jones," the killer said tonelessly.

"Let me do my work here. I'm sure you would prefer a clean shot as much as I do."

Ethan saw his father's anguish written all over his gaunt, weary face.

He couldn't see Tori's expression, but he knew it would be twisted in worry for him, ashen with fear.

But Ethan saw no other choice.

His hands held up, he walked all the way out onto the porch.

22

Panic stabbed Tori as Ethan crossed the width of the porch on the assassin's command.

"Oh, my God. No!" Heart lurching, terror spiking, she turned to run for him—to physically stop him from doing it. "Ethan, no!"

He held her back with a halting hand, his bare feet paused at the top step. The look he gave her was both courageous and resigned.

He really was going to do this. Ethan was left little choice but to obey, or see his father shot in front of him for his son's inaction. And Ethan was not the kind of man to let that happen, no matter the complicated tangle of feelings he had for the man who raised him.

But there was something else shadowing his hazel eyes. Something dark and rueful. A secret knowledge that pained him, conflicted him. Tori didn't know how to read him now. She simply had to trust.

Even if her heart was breaking in the process.

"Son, don't do this. Not for me," his father pleaded now. "Goddamn it, boy!"

Ethan began to descend the short steps, down to the unpaved drive.

And then, everything happened in an instant. Yet it played out in Tori's mind, frame by agonizing frame.

Ethan on the first step, the second.

Tori looked to the man with the gun, saw the cold intent on his face. The chilling triumph.

The pistol at Ethan's father's temple started to relax. Started to move away from his head.

But then the ominous black barrel of the weapon pivoted forward.

The assassin set his aim on Ethan.

Tori screamed.

At the same instant, she saw a look of defiance cross his father's weathered, weary face. His eyes were fixed on his son, unflinching. Tori saw a grave and fearless understanding in William Davis's gaze.

She saw love.

Rusty, late-arrived, yet selfless parental love.

And she saw sacrifice.

On a bellow, Ethan's father reared with all he had, his arms going up and back. The assassin's gun jerked wildly in his hand, but he held fast to the weapon.

The old man wheeled on him, slamming head and shoulders into the hit man's torso.

They went down in a struggle, dust kicking into a yellow cloud around them.

Ethan was back on the porch before Tori realized he was moving. He grabbed the backpack. Pulled out one of the pistols.

Out on the driveway, a shot rang out.

The assassin got to his feet, pistol aimed down at Ethan's father. He didn't get the chance to shoot again.

Ethan stalked forward, blasting rounds into the killer in rapid fire, even after the body had dropped in a lifeless heap on the ground.

"Ethan!" Tori ran down and wrapped herself around

him, tears streaming down her cheeks as her fear receded and a flood of relief swamped her.

Ethan was safe. He was unharmed.

But his father...

Together they walked over to where the old man lay. He was bleeding profusely, one obviously mortal shot to his gut. He had moments left. A few short minutes at most.

"Dad," Ethan said thickly as he stuck the spent pistol in the back of his jeans, then hunkered down beside his father. He tried to say something else, but his words seemed to dry up in his throat.

"Was heading this direction anyway," his father rasped. "Might as well put both feet in the damn grave and get it over with."

Ethan shook his head. "If I'd known...I wouldn't have come here."

"Don't you dare, son." The old man wheezed, blood sputtering out of his mouth as he panted and struggled to speak. "Don't you...go apologizin' to me. I'm the one owed you that...never gave it. So you take it now. You take it now...and you...you and your girl...go on now."

A harsh, broken curse leaked out of Ethan as his father's eyes closed and he exhaled his last breath.

He stood up in silence and took Tori's hand in his. Started leading her away from the carnage, back to the barn where their vehicle waited.

"I saw it," Ethan murmured. "While I was in the shower, I saw the whole thing. Right to this moment."

Tori looked at him in astonishment. In sorrow. "You mean, you saw your father..."

He nodded. "I saw what he did, before it happened. I thought I could change it. Maybe I could've stopped him."

"No, Ethan." She stroked his face tenderly. "You couldn't have. He did what he intended to do—probably from the moment the gunman put the pistol to his head. He did this for you. I don't think you could've changed any of this, Ethan. Sometimes there's no changing fate."

He nodded soberly. "This isn't over, you know. There will be more like him, coming after us. We won't be safe. Not for a long time. Maybe never, Tori."

"But we'll be together," she whispered, wrapping him in her arms.

"Yeah, we'll be together."

"Then none of the rest of it matters."

"No, it doesn't. Not as long as I have you." He cupped her head in his strong hands and drew her to him for a sweet, tender kiss. "Let's get out of here."

23

Ethan leaned against the van at a highway rest area about an hour east of his father's house.

He'd just phoned 9-1-1 from his burner phone. In a short while, police would be arriving at the old Davis farm on an anonymous report of gunshots heard on the property. There would be no weapons found; Ethan had both the gun used to kill his father and the assassin's second firearm zipped up in his pack in the van. He figured he and Tori might need the extra firepower at some point.

Especially considering where they were headed.

She got out of the van and came around to join him as he brought the burner phone away from his ear and disconnected the call. "All set to go?"

"All set." He dropped the phone and crushed it under his heel.

Tori crouched down along with him to pick up the broken shards and toss them in the trash bin on the curb. "How far is it to D.C. from here?"

Ethan considered the route he'd planned when they'd parked a few minutes ago. "About forty hours, just about due east."

After facing death up close and personal that morning, they had decided together that trying to outrun

Ethan's enemies was no longer an acceptable option. They needed to confront the danger in order to take it down.

And to do that, Ethan realized he would need help.

He would need to find the Phoenix program's other operatives. He would need allies, people he could trust.

He only hoped he'd find both soon.

As for where to begin searching, it seemed to him that some of those answers might be waiting in the place where the program began.

He couldn't kid himself that there wouldn't be obstacles in the way, some of them sure to be lethal. But he had the best reason in the world to keep on moving, to keep on fighting. To make sure the nightmare vision that haunted him never came to pass.

He had only to look at Tori to see that he had all the reason he could ever need to win this war he hadn't started.

She embraced him, pressing her cheek against his chest where his heart beat hard and determined, full of love for her.

The road ahead was uncertain, but they had each other.

And nothing could stop them now.

~ * ~

ABOUT THE AUTHOR

LARA ADRIAN is a *New York Times* and #1 international best-selling author, with nearly 4 million books in print and digital worldwide and translations licensed to more than 20 countries. Her books regularly appear in the top spots of all the major bestseller lists including the *New York Times*, USA Today, Publishers Weekly, Amazon.com, Barnes & Noble, etc. Reviewers have called Lara's books "addictively readable" (Chicago Tribune), "extraordinary" (Fresh Fiction), and "one of the consistently best paranormal series out there" (Romance Novel News).

Writing as **TINA ST. JOHN**, her historical romances have won numerous awards including the National Readers Choice; Romantic Times Magazine Reviewer's Choice; Booksellers Best; and many others. She was twice named a Finalist in Romance Writers of America's RITA Awards, for Best Historical Romance (White Lion's Lady) and Best Paranormal Romance (Heart of the Hunter). More recently, the German translation of Heart of the Hunter debuted on Der Spiegel bestseller list.

With an ancestry stretching back to the Mayflower and the court of King Henry VIII, the author lives with her husband in New England.

Visit the author's website and sign up for new release announcements at **www.LaraAdrian.com**.

Find Lara on Facebook at
www.facebook.com/LaraAdrianBooks

RUN

Tina Folsom

1

Scott Thompson wiped his hands on the oil-drenched rag on the workbench and glanced back at the Ducati Diavel he was working on. He'd had one just like it a few years earlier, but circumstances had dictated that he switch to a Multistrada Touring bike, a model which was much more conducive to being on the run. Locked in its side cases he kept the essentials that made it possible for him to disappear at a moment's notice: money, a firearm, fake IDs, a change of clothes, an untraceable phone, keys, and other electronics. He was ready to leave should it become necessary again. Like it had, three years earlier.

He pushed the thoughts into the back of his mind, not wanting to be reminded of the past. He hadn't been back to the house he'd grown up in outside Washington, D.C. It was too dangerous to claim what belonged to him now. Instead, he worked at a motorcycle repair shop in Cicero, just outside Chicago, and kept a low profile.

"Are you Scott?"

The tentative female voice made him swivel on his heel and look to the open garage door. The woman who stood there wasn't the typical motorcycle chick who frequented a shop like Al's. He bet she'd never even sat on a bike, let alone ridden one.

"What can I do for you, ma'am?"

She gave him a seductive smile while her eyes wandered over him. He was glad it wasn't an overly hot day and he hadn't rolled down his blue overalls to his waist like he often did to allow the light breeze to cool his body. Because the way this woman ogled him already now in his fully clothed state made him feel more than just a little annoyed. As if he were a piece of meat. He'd never liked that sort of woman—the rich femme fatale who thought she could throw money around to lure a stud into her bed. He preferred more down-to-earth women. Women who had a little bit of innocence left in them. Well, not *too* much innocence. Just enough for a guy to pretend he was the one in charge.

"I was told you could help me select a motorcycle for my husband. It's a birthday present," she purred.

Scott jerked his thumb toward the attached shop which belonged to the same owner as the repair shop— Al, a good-natured second-generation Polish immigrant with a beer belly and a balding head. "All the salesmen are next door. I'm sure they'll be happy to help you find the right bike."

He turned back to the Ducati and picked up a wrench from the workbench before crouching down again. His ears picked up the sound of her footsteps as she came closer instead of leaving the garage to enter the shop. Involuntarily, he tensed.

"My friend mentioned that you're such an ace at what you do."

Ace? Shit! Nobody had called him by his codename in three years. This wasn't good news.

At her words, his training kicked in. It was something so ingrained in him that even now he couldn't switch it off. He reared up and whirled around, coming face-to-face with the woman. In the next instant, he had her pinned against the workbench, trapping her arms so she couldn't reach for a weapon.

"Who sent you?" Scott growled, almost snarling at her.

When he glared at her, she looked at him with the frightened eyes of a doe caught in the headlights, her chest heaving.

Her lips trembled, attesting to her fear. "What are you doing?"

"Who?" he insisted, not loosening his hold on her arms.

"Jenny."

Scott's forehead furrowed as he tried to place the name. "Jenny who?"

"Markovitz. From the hair salon," she elaborated, trying to shrink back from him.

The name rang a bell. It took two more seconds for his brain to make the connection. A few months ago, he'd had a one-night stand with a hairdresser named Jenny. It dawned on him then. The woman he was currently pressing against the workbench wasn't here to kill him. She was here to fuck him.

"You've got the wrong Scott," he claimed and released her.

She glared at him, adjusting her clothes and huffing indignantly. "Yeah, I can see that now. Jerk! Attacking me like that! That's no way to treat a customer! I'll complain to your boss about you! He'll fire you!"

Scott narrowed his eyes. "While you're at it, make sure you don't forget to tell him you came here to proposition me."

"How dare you?" she gritted through clenched teeth, her ample chest lifting. "I had no intention of—"

"Didn't you?" he interrupted, stepping closer. "Lady, let me tell you one thing. I'm a man, and I know when a woman is coming on to me. I don't sleep with women like you. So if you want to get laid, why don't you seduce your husband for once, and leave men like me alone? Because the next time you come up to a stranger, you might run into somebody who's less gentle than I am." And she had no idea just how close she'd come to death by uttering the wrong word.

Her lips parted. Scott could see how she was searching for a comeback, but no words came out of her mouth.

"Something wrong?" Al's gravelly voice suddenly came from the door to the showroom.

Scott turned his head. "I believe this lady is looking for a bike for her husband, but couldn't find the right entrance." He glanced back at her. "Isn't that right?"

Without a word, she turned away and approached Al.

"Well, let me show you what we have in stock, then, Mrs. uh…?"

"Elroy," she answered and walked through the door that Al held open for her.

Al tossed him a quizzical look, and Scott answered with a shrug before turning back to the Ducati. He knew he'd overreacted, but maybe it would teach Mrs. Elroy something. Namely that propositioning strangers for sex was never a good thing.

At the same time he recalled his interactions with the hairdresser. He had a rule not to divulge much about himself to any woman he slept with, but one night Jenny had shown up at the local bar he frequented, where several people knew his first name and where he worked. It was the only reason she knew how to get a hold of him. Scott made a mental note never again to screw another woman who knew where she could find him, though he was a little surprised that women would trade one-night stands with their girlfriends.

But then, what did he know about women? He'd never had an honest relationship with a woman. Flings, one-night stands, yes, and plenty thereof, like any healthy thirty-six-year-old man. But no real relationship where the woman knew who or what he was. It had been a necessity to hide his true identity, now more so than ever before. If certain people found out who he was, he would already be dead. And he planned on staying alive.

Scott picked up the wrench he'd dropped on the workbench when he'd grabbed Mrs. Elroy and turned back to the Ducati, when his vision suddenly blurred. His hand instantly released the wrench and gripped the bench for support.

"Shit," he cursed and closed his eyes, knowing instinctively what was happening to him.

Instead of darkness greeting him, a scene played out before his eyes. A scene taking place somewhere else.

The man sat in the driver's seat of the school bus. Behind him, the voices of excited kids talked over each other. There were giggles and laughter, then the voice of a woman, but the kids were making too much noise for Scott to hear what she was saying. Nor did he get a visual on her or the kids. She was probably the teacher, though it was odd that she would be in the bus with the kids. Maybe a field trip.

His vision focused back on the bus driver. He wore a short-sleeve striped shirt and khaki pants, but Scott didn't see his face, only the back of his head. His brown hair was in need of cutting, and his scalp was showing through the bald spot on the top of his head. He'd made an attempt at a comb-over, but his hair wasn't long enough.

The man grumbled to himself, looking to the right and the left as he approached a railroad crossing. He glanced at his wristwatch. Three minutes before two o'clock. It was afternoon, Scott noted, and by the way the sun shone into the bus and the clothes the driver was wearing it appeared to be summer. The driver's hand reached for the radio. He turned up the volume, maybe to drown out the kids' voices.

At the railroad crossing he slowed, glancing to the left once more. He rolled onto the rails, then brought the bus to a stop.

Scott held his breath.

The bus driver switched off the engine and pulled the keys from the ignition. His hand went to the mechanism to open the door, but instead of opening it, he seemed to wiggle it slightly. Scott focused on it and saw that it had been cut through and was hanging on by only a sliver. It would break off the next time somebody touched it.

The driver didn't lose any time. He pushed the window to his left open and wedged himself through it with such grace that it looked like he'd practiced it beforehand. Once outside, he slid the window shut and pulled something from his pocket.

Scott peered through the window and watched him jam a lock into some hooks outside the window—hooks that shouldn't be there in the first place—rigging it so it couldn't be opened.

Where the driver disappeared to, Scott couldn't tell, because at that moment a movement caught his attention. The gates of the railroad crossing were lowering.

Shit!

Scott glanced down the railroad tracks, first to the left, then to the right, when he saw a movement in the distance. From the right, a train was approaching.

The occupants of the bus were oblivious to their fate. The train wouldn't be able to stop in time. It would hit them full-on. Horrified, he let his eyes wander, trying to find any indication as to where and when this event playing out before his eyes would take place.

He focused, knowing he had only a few seconds more until the vision would disappear. It always did as soon as the disaster occurred.

On the opposite side of the railroad crossing a car was parked, and another one on the other side of the street. Both with Illinois license plates, a good indication that this railroad crossing was in Illinois. He was searching for street signs, anything that would help him identify the location, when he saw a phone number on a billboard. A realtor was advertising his services with a 312 prefix, the area code for Chicago. Good, realtors only advertised locally, so the railroad crossing had to be in the Chicago area. But Chicago was big and there were many train lines leading into town, and even more railroad crossings.

The song on the radio stopped and the DJ came on instead. "And that was Stevie Nicks from Fleetwood Mac. How's that for nostalgia?"

Another voice joined him, this one also coming from the radio. "And can you guess who's going to be singing the anthem at tomorrow's baseball game, the White Sox against Kansas City right here in—"

The train hitting the bus cut off the radio.

Scott's knees buckled and he fell forward, feeling the impact physically. His eyes shot open and he saw the ground coming toward him. In the last second he braced himself with his hands and slowed his fall before he hit the hard concrete floor of the garage.

His breathing was ragged when he pushed himself up to sit. He shoved a trembling hand through his dark hair, feeling cold sweat on his nape.

The kids from his premonition would die unless he intervened. He knew it for certain. He'd seen too many of his visions become reality to doubt their authenticity. And he had enough information to find out where and when this collision would take place: the time on the wristwatch told him the time of day; the mention of the baseball game told him which date; and with the help of photos from Google Maps, where the sun was coming from and from which direction the train had hit the bus, he could find the correct railroad crossing in the Chicago area.

But he also knew one other thing for certain: if he interfered in this looming tragedy, he could expose himself and lead his enemies right into his arms. If they found him, they would kill him.

His heart beat into his throat. Could he let all these kids die to protect his own life? Could he live with the guilt of knowing he'd done nothing to save these young lives?

2

"Crap!" Phoebe Chadwick cursed under her breath and put the receiver back on the cradle.

Her colleague Kathleen, who occupied the desk across from hers, looked up and cast her a quizzical look. "Something wrong?"

Phoebe was already rising from her chair. She motioned to the glass-enclosed office at the other end of the large open-plan area which housed more than two dozen cubicles. "He wants to see me in his office. Now."

"Uh oh."

"Yep."

With trepidation, she made her way to the office on whose door the words *Bruno Novak, Editor* were stenciled. During the last few weeks, several of her colleagues who'd entered Novak's office had cleared out their desks shortly afterward. Her heart beat into her throat.

She needed this job to support herself. She didn't have a family or a husband who could help her. She was on her own. Her parents were divorced and had their own financial problems, and she'd broken up with her last boyfriend over six months earlier because he was only mooching off her instead of paying his own way.

Though she hoped she was wrong, Phoebe knew the

paper was in a dire situation. Budget cuts had to be made, and since personnel costs were the largest line item, staff had to be let go.

She felt everybody's eyes on her as she stopped in front of the door. Her palms were sweaty when she knocked and entered after a grunt from inside. She shut the door behind her quickly, not wanting her colleagues to overhear the conversation.

"Bruno, you wanted to see me?" she asked as casually as possible, willing her voice to sound calm when she was anything but.

Novak didn't lift his head, but grunted once more and motioned her to sit in the old chair in front of his desk.

She swallowed away the bile that was rising and followed his unspoken command.

"You probably heard," he started, finally lifting his head from the stack of papers in front of him.

Her heart sank into her stomach. "Yes."

"Well, I'll make this short, then. You haven't been with us for very long."

"It's been over a year," she protested quickly, but he stopped her by lifting his hand.

"I've been here for over thirty years. Trust me, one year isn't very long. I had to put you on the list. There are three people on that list, and one more will have to go."

Phoebe shot up from her chair. "I need this job, Bruno. Please."

"I'm not the one making the decisions here. The editor-in-chief will pick who's going to be axed and who stays."

Her heart plummeted into her knees, making them

wobbly.

"Who else is on the list?"

"You know I can't tell you that." Novak sighed. "But let's just say the other two never spilled any coffee on his expensive Italian shoes."

Phoebe cringed. She'd only once met the editor-in-chief in person, and the exchange had not only been awkward, but also embarrassing. She knew already now who would get the axe.

"Eriksson doesn't like me."

"Then you'll have to make him like you."

Phoebe felt her face scrunch up in disgust. "You must be kidding. I'm not going to—"

"Christ, Phoebe!" Novak rolled his eyes. "What the hell do you think I was talking about?"

"Uh, well, I thought you…" she mumbled, feeling heat rise into her cheeks.

"What I'm suggesting is that you'll have to prove to him that you're an excellent journalist and that he can't afford to lose you."

"I can do that!" she said with more confidence than she possessed. She would do anything to convince her editor-in-chief that she was the best reporter this paper ever had. The newspaper business was in her blood. Her father had been a journalist and her mother an editor. Both had switched to different careers after the divorce. Her father was now back in Nashville, where Phoebe had grown up, and was working as a PR and media consultant for the police department, while her mother lived in Los Angeles and had married a struggling writer, whom she supported by working as a secretary. But none of that was of any consequence. "I'll get you a good story. Something you can be proud of."

Novak nodded slowly. "And you'd better make it quick. I have to hand this list to him in one week. And once he's got the list, you know what'll happen. He's gonna take one look at it and make his decision. So find something good."

"One week? That's insane! How am I gonna find a great story in such a short time?" It was practically impossible. Any exposé, whether it concerned a politician or a business, would take time to research.

"Then you've gotta buy yourself some time."

"But how? How am I gonna do that? You said yourself that he'll pick me once he sees the list."

"Then do something that makes him hesitate." Novak motioned to the door. "Now get out of here and get to work." He dropped his head back to his papers.

Phoebe left his office and exhaled. At least she had another chance, though she didn't know how realistic it was to come up with a killer story in one week. As for making Eriksson hesitate, as Novak had called it, she had no idea how she would manage that. She never saw the editor-in-chief. He worked two floors above her and the few times she'd seen him in the distance, he'd always been surrounded by other people. There was no way she'd ever catch him on his own. And even if she did, how would she change his opinion of her? She had nothing with which to impress him.

Phoebe ignored the clandestine stares of her colleagues and slumped down in her seat. "I'm so screwed."

"Did he fire you?" Kathleen whispered back, leaning over her desk, her eyes darting to the side.

Phoebe dropped her head into her hands. "He might as well have."

"What do you mean?"

She lifted her face to look at Kathleen. "He gave me a week to come up with a killer story to impress Eriksson so he won't fire me."

"A week? What a prick!" The soft pinging of Kathleen's computer indicated an email had landed in her inbox. She glanced at the screen. "Speaking of the prick, here's another one of his mass emails." She huffed. "Urgent! Yeah, right!"

Phoebe sighed and signed onto her computer. She might as well start scouring the internet for anything that could be turned into a story. When her screen came up, her email inbox pinged too, and she looked at the list of new emails. Eriksson's was the latest.

Subject: Substitute needed—urgent

The email was marked with a priority flag, as if that was anything new. All of Eriksson's emails were marked priority.

Phoebe's eyes flew over the message.

Need somebody to ride on an outing of my son's class today. School bus leaves in two hours.

Kathleen groaned. "Like I wanna be stuck with a bunch of eleven-year-olds asking questions about my job."

"What?"

"Are you the only one who hasn't heard about this?" Kathleen asked. "Eriksson has been telling everybody and his dog that he's doing this school outreach program, getting kids interested in journalism by taking them on research trips." She made air quotes around her last two words. "And now he's chickening out and dumping it on one of the staff. I sure ain't volunteering."

Phoebe reached for the phone and dialed a four-digit

extension. She'd just found the perfect thing to buy herself some time.

"Mr. Eriksson's office," the secretary answered.

Kathleen whispered, "What are you doing?"

But Phoebe waved her off. "It's Phoebe Chadwick. I'm calling about the school outing with Mr. Eriksson's son."

"Hallelujah," the woman on the other end of the line responded, overly dramatic.

There was a click. Then a male bellow. "Yes?"

Phoebe swallowed. There was no way out now.

3

Phoebe forced a smile and patiently tried to answer the same question again though one of the other kids had asked the very same thing only ten minutes earlier.

The old school bus jostled along the city streets on the way to a warehouse on the outskirts of Chicago the newspaper used as its archives, and where it stored old printing presses which the publisher of the paper kept for sentimental reasons.

Phoebe sat near the rear of the bus, surrounded by at least two dozen eleven-year-old boys and girls who were all talking over each other. Several were fighting over the small notepads with the emblem of the newspaper she'd handed out earlier. Clearly, she hadn't brought enough for everybody. Above all the noise, the bus driver was listening to the radio, which alternately played music and news.

Several kids were standing on the seats, trying to look over kids who were blocking their view of Phoebe, thus obscuring Phoebe's view out the window. She sighed. What had she been thinking, volunteering for this? Dealing with a bunch of kids who talked a mile a minute was more exhausting than chasing down a politician unwilling to answer her probing questions.

You can get through this, she coached herself. *Eriksson*

will owe you one. It will make him hesitate when it comes to firing you. And she hoped it would buy her enough time to find a juicy story with which to save her job. It was all for a good cause.

"No, if a story is important enough, then we'll stop the printing press and reset the front page. It's been done many times before. And it's a lot easier these days. It's all done by computer," she now answered the question the girl with the red hair and freckles had asked.

"I have a computer," a boy in a blue T-shirt piped up. "It's brand new."

Another boy used his elbow to get past him. "And I have an iPad. I got it for my birthday."

"Me too," a girl in the crowd replied.

"Yeah, but mine is newer," the second boy replied.

"Hold it, kids," Phoebe said, trying to get the bragging under control. "It doesn't matter whose tablet is newer."

"Does too!" somebody protested.

More voices chimed in and all the kids were suddenly talking all at once, trying to establish who had the newest iPad or computer. Within seconds Phoebe felt as if her head wanted to explode from the din of their combined voices. She was definitely not meant to be a teacher. Already now, her patience was wearing thin.

"Miss Chadwick, Miss Chadwick!"

Phoebe turned her head to the girl who was calling out to her, but couldn't see her.

"Miss Chadwick!" the same girl insisted, her voice tinged with not impatience, but anxiety.

"What's wrong?" Phoebe shot up from her seat, worried now that the girl might have hurt herself. She saw her standing toward the front of the bus, pointing out the window.

"Miss Chadwick, why did we stop in the middle of a railroad crossing?"

Phoebe spun her head to the side and stared out through the windows. The girl was right; the bus stood in the middle of the railroad crossing.

"Driver!" she called out, turning her head to the front while shoving her way through the kids.

When she saw the empty driver's seat, she froze.

"What the—" She stopped herself from using profanity in front of the children.

"Why's the driver gone?" a boy asked behind her.

Phoebe took several steps forward while she tried to be as level-headed as possible. "Maybe the motor stopped and he's checking something under the hood."

She reached the driver's seat, her eyes instinctively scanning the area. There was no key in the ignition. She looked outside, first to the front, then the left and right, but the driver was nowhere to be seen.

"Maybe the driver is in the back," another boy claimed.

Phoebe twisted her head and saw several of the kids crowding toward the rear of the bus and peering out the window.

"He's not there," a girl said.

"Shit!" Phoebe cursed.

Why had the bus driver left? And right in the middle of a railroad crossing, of all places? Without the keys to the bus she couldn't move it off the rails. Her heart beat faster, but she tried to keep a cool head. She was the only adult here. The teacher who was supposed to be accompanying them had had a flat tire on the way to the school, and Phoebe had therefore arranged with her to reroute the bus, so they could pick her up on the way. However, in the meantime, Phoebe was responsible for these kids. If she showed that she was panicking, then the kids would surely panic too.

"Get all your belongings, your bags and things, and we'll get off the bus until we can find out where the driver is. And no pushing and shoving, okay?"

She might as well have saved her breath with her last instruction, because the kids suddenly all tried to be the first to reach the front of the bus, all talking over each other.

Phoebe leaned over the dashboard and scanned it. There were several switches. She tried the first and looked to her right, but the door didn't open. Then the second. Nothing.

"Open the door, Miss Chadwick!" a girl started to whine.

"I'm trying," she answered tersely and touched the next switch. When she flipped it, it broke off. Her heart stopped as she looked at her fingers holding the black switch.

"You broke it!" the girl cried out. "Miss Chadwick broke the switch!"

Phoebe felt the smooth area where the switch had broken off the console, while several kids started to scream. "He cut it through," she murmured to herself. "The bastard sabotaged the bus."

Dread filled her stomach. This was no accident. This was deliberate. The bus driver was trying to get the kids killed.

"Somebody call 9-1-1 and tell them where we are." She rushed to the door and looked up. There had to be a manual release somewhere above the door. Her eyes searched every inch, but the spot where the manual release for the door was normally located was covered with a piece of metal that had been screwed over it. "Fuck!"

In the background she heard several kids crying, while others were already talking on their cell phones. But Phoebe knew she couldn't rely on the police to get here soon enough. At any moment, a train could approach.

Her eyes flew back to the back of the bus where the emergency exit was located. "Let me through to the emergency exit!"

She paved her way through the kids and reached for the lever to open the back exit. She pulled in the direction indicated on the door, but nothing moved.

"Why is it not opening?" a girl whined.

Phoebe yanked at it again, but the thing didn't move. Shit!

She turned back to the kids. "It's jammed. The windows! Push the windows out! Lift the latches and push on the bottom until the window opens." She had no idea whether the windows would simply fall out or be locking at a ninety degree angle. In either case, the kids would be able to get out, though they'd have to jump.

"What latch, Miss Chadwick?" a boy asked.

She rushed in his direction. "The red latch on the bottom of—" Her eyes fell on the window the boy was pointing to.

"There's no latch," the boy said, his eyes now filling with tears. Phoebe focused her eyes on the red contraption at the bottom edge of the window, but the latch that was supposed to be there had been sawed off.

"There's no latch on this one either!" a girl screamed from the back of the bus.

The kids rushed to the windows and Phoebe watched helplessly as they hit their fists against the glass. Before she could stop them in their futile attempts to break the windows, a sound from outside made her snap her head around.

The crossing gates were lowering and the warning lights started to flash.

Her mouth went dry, while the horrified screams of the children filled her ears.

4

Scott let a vile curse roll over his lips.

It had taken him longer than expected to find the correct railroad crossing on Google Maps. Figuring out that the train would collide with the school bus today at about two p.m.—the same day he'd had the premonition—had been easy. It had only taken him a minute to check the schedule of the White Sox to realize they'd be playing Kansas City the next day and that Stevie Nicks from Fleetwood Mac was supposed to sing *God Bless America* at the seventh-inning stretch.

Kicking his Ducati into a higher gear, Scott raced down the street. He knew this part of the Chicago suburbs well. Well enough to avoid any known speed traps, where the police lay in wait. He couldn't afford to get held up by a cop. Every second counted. All he'd had time for, once he'd figured out the location of the impending accident, was to shove the largest wrench he could find in the garage into his leather jacket and jump on his bike. An axe or a steel cutter would have been better tools, but he'd had no time to look for them. He could only hope that what he'd brought would be strong enough.

Scott slowed at the next intersection, cursing at the red light. When it switched to green, he was already in the middle of it, turning left, leaning almost forty-five degrees to the side with his bike, before the oncoming traffic had moved even an inch. Honking sounds chased him, but he ignored them and gained speed again.

"Three more blocks," he ground out as he drove past a bank. He caught a glimpse of the display on the outside, which announced the temperature as well as the time: two p.m. The driver would have already left the bus and locked the kids and their teacher inside.

Another intersection, but this time he didn't have to slow down. The side streets had stop signs.

"Two more blocks." It was almost like a chant, a prayer he sent to the powers that be, the powers that had given him this gift of foresight. A gift he'd at first cursed because it had made him different. But one he'd learned to appreciate with the help of his adoptive father, the man with whom he had so much in common, including this gift.

Scott's entire body was tense, the muscles in his neck rigid, his jaw clenched. The thought that he might be too late made him turn the handle even harder, sending more gas into the engine to make the Ducati go even faster. If the police caught him now, it wouldn't matter. In a few seconds he'd be at the railroad crossing, and once they saw what was happening, they wouldn't stop him.

"Come on," he ground out and saw the yellow vehicle in the distance now as he cleared a slight hump in the road.

The street was almost deserted. No other cars waited at this side of the railroad crossing, the gates of which had already lowered. The bus blocked his view of the street on the other side of the crossing, making it impossible to see if there was anybody else on whose help he could count.

Just before the gates, Scott skidded to a halt, jumped off the bike, killed the engine and with the same movement, pulled the kickstand up. He didn't bother taking his helmet off. There was no time for it.

Running between the middle of the gates, he charged toward the bus, pulling the wrench from the inside of his leather jacket and gripping it tightly with his gloved hand. When he reached the passenger door of the bus, he saw several kids kicking against the glass from the inside. Screams accompanied their fruitless efforts. Safety glass didn't break that easily.

"Get away from the door!" he screamed, but realized they didn't hear him.

He lifted his visor and tried again. "Away from the door!" He slapped his hand against the door and lifted the arm holding the wrench.

The kids finally looked at him and seemed to understand.

"Step back! Cover your eyes!"

The moment the kids had backed away from the door, he lowered his visor again and hit the glass panel with his wrench. The glass of the left panel shattered. Then he did the same with the right panel, until it too shattered. He gripped the frame and pulled it toward him to open at least one side of the door. He jerked it open with sheer force and willpower. He tried to do the same with the right side, but it was stuck and didn't move an inch. The opening he'd created was narrow, but it would have to do. The kids would be able to squeeze through.

"Now all out!" he commanded, throwing a glance over his shoulder. In the distance there was a movement: the train.

"Quickly!" he screamed and reached for the first child, lifting the girl down. "Run to the side of the gates! Run!"

One child after the next he helped out of the train, while he continued to urge them to hurry. "Quickly! Faster! Get to the other side! Run, damn it!"

The kids were crying and screaming. He couldn't avoid them cutting themselves on the glass shards as they tried to brace themselves while exiting the bus, but a few cuts and bruises were better than the alternative getting closer with each passing second.

In the distance he heard sirens approaching. Somebody had called 9-1-1. But they wouldn't be here in time to help with the evacuation. Despite his helmet, he heard the radio from the bus. Stevie Nicks was still singing, but he was familiar with the song, and knew it was coming to an end. And once the radio announcers were speaking, Scott knew he only had a few more seconds until the train would smash into the bus.

"How many more?" he yelled.

"Three!" came the panicked voice of an adult. The teacher.

"Quickly!" Scott dragged the next child out of the train and shoved the girl in the direction of the gate. The next boy almost fell out of the bus, stumbling over his own feet. He righted him, making sure he had found his feet again, before reaching for the last one.

"Run!" he commanded, his voice hoarse now, his heart beating like the locomotive that was fast approaching.

Scott recognized the song reaching its last chords. "Shit!"

A young woman appeared on the top step, hurrying

down. She turned sideways to squeeze through the narrow opening, and he reached for her and pulled, but met with resistance. His gaze flew to her face. Her eyes went wide in horror as she tried to pull free of the bus, but failed.

"Fuck!" he cursed behind his helmet and reached past her where her top had caught in a jagged edge left by the broken glass.

Suddenly the music stopped, and the announcer now spoke. "And that was Stevie Nicks from Fleetwood Mac. How's that for nostalgia?"

He knew he had only seconds now.

Her eyes darted past him, and he didn't need to look over his shoulder to know how close the train was.

"Run!" she urged him. "Save yourself!"

"No!" Scott yelled and tore at her top. Finally, it ripped free of the glass and the teacher almost fell into his arms. He whirled around, the next words of the radio announcer in his ears.

"And can you guess who's going to be singing *God Bless America…*"

With the woman in his arms, Scott jumped to the side, landing beside the tracks. He rolled over her, shielding her, when a moment later, the train hit the school bus behind them. His helmet and heavy leather jacket—though it was open in the front—protected him from the flying debris while he covered the woman beneath him as best he could.

"Don't move," he urged her, though he had no idea if she heard him through his helmet.

But he knew she was alive. He felt her breathing against his chest, her hands holding on to his shirt in a death grip.

The screeching of the train braking was the next sound he heard. Only when there were no more sounds coming from the train, indicating that it had stopped, did Scott lift his head.

He took a breath, his first conscious one since reaching the bus, and felt his heart thunder. The teacher in his arms had her eyes squeezed shut.

"Are you all right?" Scott asked, but she didn't reply. He jerked his helmet off and tried again. "Are you okay?"

Finally she opened her eyes. The first thing he noticed was that they were a vibrant blue. The second thing he realized was that for the first time he looked into a woman's eyes and felt he could trust her with everything.

Shocked by the strange feeling, Scott pulled back and lifted himself off her, sitting back on his knees, flinching slightly as he did so. He'd hit the asphalt hard, taking the full brunt of the fall before he'd rolled on top of her. His ribs were bruised, but he knew nothing was broken.

"You saved my life." She squeezed his hand and pulled herself up to sit. She turned her head toward the gate.

Scott followed her gaze and saw the kids standing there, dazed, in shock, but only a little worse for wear. Several cars had stopped in the meantime, and drivers and passengers were running toward the children.

"You saved all those kids."

Her words made him look back at her. She was prettier than he'd noticed at first. Her shoulder-length dark brown hair had gentle waves, and her skin was bronzed, her lips full and red and a tantalizing complement to her blue eyes. If any of his teachers had looked like that when he'd been a kid, he was sure he would have liked school a lot more.

"Are you sure you're unhurt?" he asked now.

She nodded, pressing her lips together, her eyes now growing moist with unshed tears. "I don't know how to thank you."

"I was just there at the right place at the right time," Scott answered and wanted to get up, but she suddenly slung her arms around his neck and hugged him to her so tightly he couldn't resist putting his arms around her and hugging her back.

So much innocence and honesty lay in her embrace that he found himself caressing her hair and rubbing her back to comfort her. And oddly enough, the gesture comforted *him*. For the first time since he'd lost his father and mentor—and at the same time his purpose—he felt needed.

"I've got you," he murmured into her hair.

5

Around her body, Phoebe felt the comforting arms of the stranger who'd rescued her. She could finally breathe again. The anxiety and mortal fear that had gripped her only moments earlier was seeping from her. For certain, she'd thought her final hour had arrived. The train had been so close, and when her clothes had caught somewhere she'd seen her life flash before her eyes. At that moment she'd realized she hadn't really lived yet. Nor had she loved.

"I've got you," the stranger now murmured once more. His deep, melodic voice soothed her and made her tense muscles relax while her body suddenly stirred with awareness. She was pressing herself against a strange man who was practically straddling her. The intimacy of this position didn't escape her.

Nor him, apparently, because he now peeled himself from her embrace and started to rise, lending her a hand to get up. "Are you all right?"

She stole glances at his face. His hair was dark, almost black, and a little longer than most guys wore their hair these days, but it appeared well-groomed, just like its owner. His green eyes were framed by long dark lashes and strong eyebrows. He was clean-shaven, and his lips were full and oddly tempting.

"Miss?"

She tore her gaze from his mouth, embarrassed that he'd caught her staring at him. "I'm fine. I'm all right," she answered quickly. Her gaze drifted past him to where the children were gathered beyond the crossing gates. "The kids." She had to make sure all of them were unhurt.

Her feet already carried her toward them, while her eyes scanned the area. An ambulance screeched to a halt and two paramedics jumped out, running toward the scene. A block away she saw lights flashing, accompanied by police sirens. The police car reached the railroad crossing at the same time Phoebe reached the kids.

"Miss Chadwick, Miss Chadwick," some of them wailed.

"Is everybody okay?" She tried to look at all the kids individually, but they kept moving around in the huddle, anxiety rolling off them. "Is anybody hurt?"

She heard several kids crying.

"Just a few scrapes," the voice of her rescuer assured her from behind. "Your pupils all got out safely."

Phoebe turned her head halfway, but before she could thank him for his reassurance the paramedics had reached the group of kids and suddenly everybody was talking over each other.

The female paramedic caught her eye. "Ma'am, did everybody get out?" She motioned to the remnants of the school bus, which were strewn about the railroad crossing. Pieces of it were caught underneath the train's wheels. The train had long stopped. The locomotive now stood several hundred yards past the crossing.

"Everybody got out."

"Are you hurt?"

Automatically, Phoebe shook her head, but when she lifted her arm to point at the kids, she felt a stinging pain in her back, where her shirt had caught on a glass shard. "I'm fine. Check the kids first."

"You're bleeding."

The words came from her rescuer and sounded like an admonishment.

"It's nothing. Just a scratch." She turned back to him just in time to catch him shaking his head, a soft smirk curving his lips.

"You're an interesting woman."

Phoebe tilted her head, not really understanding what he meant by that.

"Still, you should have it looked at."

"Later." She extended her hand. "I'm Phoebe Chadwick."

He nodded and shook her hand without taking his glove off. "Scott."

Her reporter instinct kicked in instantly when he didn't offer a last name, and another question already sat on the tip of her tongue, but she didn't get a chance to voice it.

"Are you the teacher?" an authoritative voice called out to her, making her whirl around. A policeman was approaching her. "What happened here?"

She nodded at the police officer. "I'm Phoebe Chadwick. I'm from the Daily Messenger. I was—"

"A reporter. How do you guys get here faster than we do?" The police officer was clearly annoyed.

"I was on the bus! I was chaperoning the kids," she defended herself instinctively.

"You were on the bus? Where's the teacher? What

happened?"

Her heart beat into her throat as she conveyed in as few words as possible what had happened once she'd realized the bus driver had abandoned them on the railroad crossing. "And then this man here came and smashed the door in." She turned to Scott, but he wasn't standing behind her anymore. Her eyes searched for him.

~ ~ ~

A reporter! Shit! That was just his darn luck. Scott suppressed a curse and pushed his way through the crowd of kids and adults who had now started arriving—curious bystanders, neighbors, business owners, motorists, as well as more paramedics. A second ambulance had arrived already and another police car was approaching from somewhere, though Scott couldn't yet see the car, only hear its siren. In a few minutes, the first parents would get here, concerned about their kids' welfare. Considering the cell phones the ten- or eleven-year-old children wielded, it wasn't hard to guess they'd already alerted their parents.

And in a few minutes the news vans would be flocking to this accident site with their cameras and microphones, interviewing everybody and anything that moved.

Scott knew he had to get out of here fast. He'd already stayed too long. The moment he'd rescued the woman who he'd believed to be the teacher—but who by her own admission was a reporter by the name of Phoebe Chadwick—he should have hightailed it out of here. He'd done what he considered to be his duty. He'd saved the children from certain death. Now he had to save himself from exposure.

Intrigued by Phoebe, he'd stuck around for a few minutes longer than he should have. From a teacher, he would have expected the kind of selflessness she'd displayed. She'd made sure all the kids had gotten out of the bus before her. From a reporter, her actions surprised him. She hadn't even allowed the paramedic to treat her injury, more concerned about the children than her own wellbeing. Even from a female teacher he would have expected she'd at least have flinched at her injury and asked the paramedics to check it out.

Scott shook his head and stepped past a crying girl. Phoebe wasn't his problem. So he did what he always did in situations like these. He kept his head down and avoided eye contact. A few more seconds and he'd be gone. He quickly retrieved his helmet where he'd dropped it after he'd jumped out of the way of the moving train with Phoebe in his arms.

From the periphery he noticed a news van park on the other side of the street and two people jump out. The woman was holding a microphone in her hand; the man carried a large camera on his right shoulder. They ran across the street, approaching the accident site.

"What happened here?" the female reporter called out. "Is anybody hurt? Anyone got killed?"

Scott scoffed. Yeah, that would have made quite a story, wouldn't it? *Dozens of school kids murdered by bus driver.* Because that was what it would have been had Scott not interfered: murder. With only a shrug, Scott walked past the reporters. It was best never to engage with people like that. They would soon find somebody else who would answer their curious questions.

The kids seemed more than happy to reply to the reporters, as he could hear now from their excited voices. Scott continued walking, almost running into a girl who was sobbing uncontrollably. He hesitated for a moment and couldn't resist running his hand over her hair in a gesture of comfort.

"It's all right, little girl. Everything's all right. Your parents are gonna be here in a moment. They'll take care of you."

She sniffed and looked up at him. Recognition lit up her face. "You saved me." Unexpectedly she slung her arms around him, burying her face in his stomach.

He took her arms and gently pried them off him. It was time to leave before other kids got the same idea and tried to thank him.

"He's a hero," he suddenly heard a boy call out in Scott's direction.

Scott snapped his head toward him.

The boy pointed at him, while he addressed the two reporters. "He saved us all."

Shit!

The two reporters were staring at him. They were already moving in his direction. "Sir! Sir! A word."

But Scott spun around and charged toward his motorcycle, slipping the helmet over his head. He jumped onto the Ducati, kicked the stand back and engaged the engine. The reporters had no chance in light of his speedy escape.

He was racing down the main street and turning at the next corner before they could voice another question. It was unlikely the camera had even been turned on yet. And if they had really gotten a glimpse of him, it would have been with his helmet on. As for the license plate on his motorcycle, it was registered to a mailboxes place which couldn't be traced to him, and as soon as he got home he would switch the plate out for another one. They wouldn't be able to find him.

The only regret he had was that the moment of peace he'd felt with Phoebe in his arms had been just an illusion.

6

"Novak is furious!" Kathleen greeted her as Phoebe made her way through the group of excited colleagues who had stormed toward her as she'd entered the newsroom. The news of the bus accident—if it could be called an accident—was everywhere.

"What's he got to be furious about? I was in a fucking train collision!" And still a little shaken by it.

"Yeah, over four hours ago!" Novak yelled behind her. "We're going to press in two hours and we've got nothing!"

Phoebe spun around, facing her pissed-off editor.

"Why didn't you call in with the story? You were on that damn bus! Firsthand account! Shit!"

Phoebe braced her hands at her hips. "Because the police dragged me down to the station to make a statement. And the paramedics insisted on treating me." She pointed to her back, where beneath her fresh shirt she now sported a bandage over a superficial cut. "And by the way, I almost died today, so don't mind if I take a few minutes to breathe, okay?"

Her heart raced now, and she noticed her colleagues surrounding them had gone quiet, listening to the heated exchange with her editor.

Novak clenched his teeth. "My office, now!" He

turned on his heel and marched into his office.

The moment Phoebe entered behind him he glared back at the other employees, making them scurry away, before slamming the door shut.

Once they were alone, Phoebe took a breath and opened her mouth, intent on defending herself, but Novak cut her off with one swipe of his hand.

"Not another word out of your mouth, young lady! First you listen to me." He sucked in a breath. "For starters, you nearly gave me a heart attack when I heard about the bus having been hit by a train. When you didn't call in right away, I had to call a contact at a news station to find out if anybody knew anything. Only when Eriksson heard from his son did we know you were all right. So don't ever do that again!"

Surprised that he'd actually been concerned about her, she was speechless for a moment. But she wouldn't be a reporter if words failed her for long. "We were all very lucky. The police are already looking for the bus driver. They've promised to give me first dibs on any information on him since I was on the bus." Maybe she'd even get an exclusive once they'd caught the guy. "This might be just the story I need for Eriksson."

Novak frowned. "Eriksson isn't interested in the story about the driver." He walked around to his computer and motioned her to follow him. Pointing to the screen, he added, "He wants to know who this is."

The computer screen showed a picture of Scott walking through the crowd of kids.

"Scott." She looked up at Novak. "He rescued us. He smashed the door in and pulled us out."

Her boss nodded. "Scott? Do you have his full name?"

Phoebe shook her head. "He left right after the police and the ambulances got there." She pointed to the screen. "How did you get this picture?"

"Eriksson's son took it with his cell phone and told his father this is the guy responsible for saving his life. Eriksson wants this to be the lead story—the hero, the mysterious rescuer. Find him! Do whatever you have to do to get his story."

Phoebe cast Novak a doubtful look. "It didn't look like he wanted to be the hero, or he would have stuck around. If he wanted the fame, he had his chance when Debbie Finch from WYAT News arrived. She practically ran after him to get a statement from him."

"And did she?"

"No. He jumped on his motorcycle and sped away." He'd practically fled the scene, now that Phoebe thought of it. "Maybe he's shy." Well, not even she believed that. He'd seemed self-confident in the little interaction they'd had. Strong, self-assured, decisive.

"Shy?" Novak scoffed. "That's not it." He tapped at the screen, pointing at Scott's face. "Get the story! Find him and I can guarantee you that Eriksson won't fire you. You've bought yourself some time now. Use it well. Prove to me and to Eriksson that you're the kind of journalist I always thought you were."

Her eyes drifted back to the photo on the screen. "Can I get a copy of that?"

"I'll email it to you."

"Did the other kids take any pictures too? Maybe of his motorcycle?"

"I'll have Eriksson's son talk to his classmates. Knowing those kids, everybody got something. They've probably already texted each other their pictures. I'll forward you what I can get."

"Thanks." She turned to the door.

"And Phoebe?"

She stopped.

"I'm glad you're all right."

She smiled to herself and opened the door. Novak wasn't as much of a hard-ass as he made others believe. When it came down to it, he cared about the people who worked for him. And he was a journalist with integrity and an eye for a good story. Focusing on the hero of this disaster was the positive spin the parents of these kids needed, rather than highlighting the likely mentally sick individual who'd driven the bus onto the railway crossing and rigged it.

She would introduce the citizens of Chicago to Scott, the hero who'd saved twenty-seven lives today and wasn't expecting any public recognition for it. And maybe once she found him and got his story, she would be able to thank him in a more personal way than she'd had occasion to this afternoon.

Full of determination, she marched toward her cubicle when somebody turned up the volume on the TV that hung at one wall of the newsroom.

Debbie Finch of WYAT News was at the accident scene, talking into a microphone. Behind her the train had moved, but forensic investigators were still sifting through the debris of the bus.

"...earlier this afternoon. From the children we interviewed, we heard reports of a man dressed in motorcycle clothing, who saved all twenty-six children and the one adult riding in the bus. Unfortunately, the person left the scene of the accident before he could be identified." She touched her earpiece and listened intently for a few seconds, before speaking again. "I'm being informed as we speak that about two years ago a similar disaster involving a mentally ill taxi driver who'd locked his passenger in the back of his cab was prevented when a motorcyclist rescued the passenger before the cab was hit by an oil truck."

Phoebe froze and sucked in a breath. Was the reporter suggesting the two incidents were connected?

"The station is encouraging anybody who was near the accident site today to send in any photos they might have taken with their cell phones so we can assist the police in finding the hero of today's disaster. Please email the photos to…"

Phoebe didn't listen any further. To assist the police? Right! She knew Debbie well enough to guess she wasn't interested in assisting the police. She wanted the scoop on Scott. Clearly Debbie's editor had the same idea as Novak, namely that Scott was the story, not the deranged bus driver.

"Fuck!" she cursed. With Debbie encouraging everybody to send pictures from the accident to her, she might find Scott before Phoebe did. "Pedal to the metal," she encouraged herself. "You can do this, Phoebe." Arriving at her desk, she leaned over to Kathleen. "I need your help. Do you still have contact with that guy at the DMV?"

"The one who st-st-st-stutters?" She chuckled and blushed.

"Yes."

Kathleen bent closer. "Saw him last night. And guess what—he doesn't stutter when he's getting down to it. If you know what I mean."

Phoebe couldn't help but laugh. "You're terrible!"

But thanks to Kathleen's active love life, Phoebe would have a leg up on her competition, because she'd memorized the license plate of Scott's motorcycle before he'd sped away.

7

Scott opened the refrigerator and took another beer from the bottom shelf, popped the cap off with his thumb and took a long gulp. It was sweltering hot in his apartment, and his landlord still hadn't fixed the air conditioning. But that wasn't the only reason he was feeling uncomfortable.

For the hundredth time since returning from the accident site, he went through his actions again step-by-step. Had he made any mistakes along the way? His biggest mistake had of course been to follow his premonition in the first place to prevent the disaster from happening. But apart from that action, had there been anything that he could have done differently? Every time he went through the event, he came to the conclusion that he couldn't have done anything differently in light of the circumstances.

After returning home, he'd changed the plates on his Ducati and disposed of the old ones. Tomorrow he would repaint the motorcycle at the shop to make it harder to identify, should anybody be looking for a black Multistrada Touring bike. And should there be any fallout from his actions today, he was fully prepared to leave the area.

He sighed and pulled his shirt off, standing in front

of the open refrigerator door in only his shorts, his bare feet planted firmly on the cool tile floor.

He'd never truly had a choice about what actions to take today. Just like he'd never had a choice when he'd first started to have premonitions. He'd been an orphan and had lived in an orphanage for most of his young life.

~ ~ ~

Richmond, Virginia
25 years earlier

Thirteen-year-old Gary used both his hands to slam Scott's face into the dirty puddle. This wasn't the first time the two-year-older bully was having his fun with Scott, using his superior physical strength against him.

Scott jerked his elbow back and jammed it into Gary's chest, managing to lift his head enough to gasp for air. The voices belonging to the children watching their fight became louder, their excitement rising as the prime bully of the orphanage once again showed off his physical superiority over one of the younger boys. Withdrawn and quiet, Scott was Gary's favorite target for such demonstrations.

Again, Gary pressed Scott's face into the puddle, making Scott swallow dirty water. Panic rose, kicking his heartbeat up, his pulse racing now, his chest heaving for a breath he couldn't take. He saw it then—a scene playing out in front of his eyes, though his eyes were closed to protect them from the dirty water. Nevertheless he watched something happening as if it were reality.

A moment later, the voice of a teacher sliced through

his head and somebody pulled him up. Scott coughed, expelling the water from his lungs. But his rage was at a boiling point now. He whirled around and glared at Gary.

"You'll break both your legs when you fall down those stairs and then I'll be the one taunting you!" Scott yelled at the bully, teeth clenched.

"Enough!" the teacher demanded. "Both of you! You'll get detention. Now! Move it."

~ ~ ~

A week later Gary fell down the main stairs of the orphanage and broke both his legs. Despite his protests that he had nothing to do with the accident, Scott was commanded to appear in the office of the orphanage's director, Mr. Peabody. Trembling with fury about the injustice of being accused of something he hadn't done, Scott clenched his fists by his sides and defiantly glared at the older man.

"What have you got to say in your defense, Thompson?"

"I didn't do it! I wasn't even in the house! I was out back on the playground."

Peabody slapped his fist onto the desk. "Stop lying, Thompson! I know it was you! Several people heard you say last week that you were going to push him down the stairs so he'd break his legs. Next time when you plan something nefarious like that don't be so stupid as to announce it to everybody," the director thundered.

Scott didn't know what nefarious meant, but it was probably nothing good. But he did know what stupid meant. And he wouldn't be called stupid by anybody. "I didn't say I was going to push him! I saw him fall!"

Peabody leaned over the desk. "You just said you were on the playground. You can't see the stairs from there. So you were in the house, just like I suspected!"

"I wasn't in the house. I saw it. Before," Scott corrected, crossing his arms over his chest.

"If you keep lying, your punishment is going to be even more severe!" Peabody claimed. "Do you know what could have happened? You could have killed him. He's lucky he only broke his legs. He could have broken his neck. So tell me the truth. Admit what you did!"

Scott expelled an angry breath, tears welling up in his eyes. But he pushed them back, swallowed them, because boys didn't cry. "I didn't do it! I didn't push him. I saw him fall. I saw it last week. In my head. I saw it in my head. Like all the other things too."

Peabody froze and pulled back a little. "What? What are you seeing?"

Scott sniffed. "All the other things. Things that haven't happened yet. And then they happen." He dropped his head. He'd never told anybody, because he didn't want to be different. It was hard enough in the orphanage, hard enough to stand up to boys like Gary. It wouldn't help him one iota if they found out he was different, that he was a freak.

"Tell me what you see," Peabody now demanded, though his voice wasn't as harsh as before.

Scott looked up and met his gaze. But he'd already said too much. It was better to take the punishment than be labeled a freak of nature. He pressed his lips together and shook his head.

~ ~ ~

His next summons to the director's office came three days later. This time the director wasn't alone. A man sat in the chair in front of the desk and rose when Scott entered after a hesitant knock at the door. When the stranger turned his head, Scott pulled in a breath. He recognized the man.

"Thompson, this is Mr. Sheppard. He's come to talk to you," Peabody said.

Mr. Sheppard smiled, a kind, gentle gesture. "So this is the boy." He extended his hand. "I've heard a lot about you, Scott. I'm Henry."

Scott shook his hand and let go of it again quickly, eyeing Peabody, who had remained seated behind his desk.

"You're not a mute, Thompson. Greet your visitor."

Scott ran his eyes over the stranger. He looked younger than Peabody, who Scott knew had recently celebrated his fiftieth birthday. But older than his English teacher, Mr. Langenfeld, who was a little over thirty. Mr. Sheppard's hair was dark brown, as were his eyes. He wore a business suit, but no tie. This man reeked of authority though he didn't inspire the kind of fear Peabody conjured up in Scott.

"Thompson," Peabody repeated, but Mr. Sheppard stopped him by lifting his hand.

"Give the boy a minute."

A feeling of gratitude swept through Scott. Everything would be all right soon. "I saw you in a house surrounded by a brown fence and a wooden swing in the back, covered in snow."

"When was I there?" the stranger asked softly.

"Next winter."

185

"Why do you think it'll be next winter?"

"Because I was staring out the window from my bedroom on the second floor while you were shoveling snow. On that path, the one that leads to the back gate, down to where the little creek is. It was frozen. You promised to take me ice skating there."

Mr. Sheppard smiled broadly and exchanged a triumphant look with Peabody before addressing Scott again. "Well, then you'd better pack your things so we can leave before we miss the snow."

"Are you sure?" Peabody interjected.

Mr. Sheppard turned back to the director. "He's got the gift. You didn't tell him I was coming, did you?"

Peabody shook his head. "Not a word. Just like you requested."

"Then he couldn't have known about me or my house. Or the creek behind it." He turned back to Scott. "Scott, tell me when you saw me."

"A long time ago. Every fall I was hoping you'd come. And every time the snow melted, I knew I had to wait another year."

"I've waited for you too. It just took me a long time to find you." He reached his hand out to Scott, who clasped it instantly.

He was finally getting a real home. A home with a man who understood him, because he was just like Scott. A man who saw the things Scott saw and wouldn't consider him a freak. Finally somebody would understand him, and he wouldn't have to hide anymore. A future was waiting for him.

But years later that dream had shattered and Scott had lost everything.

Henry Sheppard, the man who'd become his father,

was gone.

Scott's future was uncertain.

He was on the run and would remain so until he took his last breath.

8

Phoebe took a deep breath. She'd come this far, she couldn't back down now. It had been hard enough to track Scott down. Though Kathleen's DMV contact had gotten her the address to where Scott's motorcycle was registered, that lead had culminated in a dead end, or rather a UPS Store, not a residential address. Luckily she'd remembered something about Scott's outfit when he'd rescued her. He'd worn overalls under his leather jacket and when the jacket had fallen open she'd glimpsed an emblem on the breast pocket. *Al's*, it had said. She'd searched for all businesses that went by Al's and had been surprised at how many repair shops were named Al's something or other. But after two hours she'd found a motorcycle repair shop in Cicero that employed a man named Scott.

It had taken her far less time to find the owner of the shop at his home and charm him into telling her where she could find Scott. Any more charm and Al would have handed her the keys to his shop and asked her to help herself to anything she wanted. Sometimes she really hated how she had to lie to people to do her job.

Nervously, Phoebe glanced back down the stairs again, where Scott's motorcycle was parked behind a dumpster as if he didn't want it to be seen from the street. That in itself didn't surprise her, since many residents in the area didn't exactly want to advertise that there was something valuable to steal. But when she'd looked at the license plate, she'd had to do a double-take. The numbers she'd memorized were different from the ones on the plate, though this was definitely the bike he'd ridden.

Was she now standing at the front door of a criminal's apartment, about to knock? Was it safe? If he'd changed his license plate, not only did this mean he had something to hide, but he also had the means to do so. After all, who kept a spare license plate on hand?

Her heart thundered in her chest. Was she asking for trouble, coming to Scott's home when he so clearly didn't want to be found? Would she be putting herself in danger?

You need this story, she told herself. *Don't be such a chicken. Maybe he's just avoiding child support.*

Right. He'd probably gotten some woman pregnant, who was now trying to get him for child support. After all, who wouldn't sleep with a hunk like him and throw caution to the wind?

Her heart fluttered at the thought. And this time it wasn't fear that made her pulse race. She still remembered the moment he'd pulled her from the bus, when she'd stared death in the face. The seconds after it, when she'd been cradled beneath his protective body, she'd felt safe. And when she'd pressed herself to him, hugging him tightly, other sensations had raced through her body, sensations that had nothing to do with being safe. That in a moment like that she could feel desire and arousal awaken her body had seemed impossible, but after having cheated death, she'd felt more alive than ever before.

No matter what Scott was hiding or who he was hiding from, she knew he wouldn't hurt her. He'd risked his own life to save hers and those of the children in her care.

Gathering all her courage, Phoebe knocked at the apartment door. She heard somebody move inside, then a low curse. Her gaze drifted to the peephole in the door. She didn't need to have x-ray vision to see that Scott had spotted her.

"Scott, I know you're there."

A few more seconds passed, then the door was finally opened. Scott appeared in the frame, opening it only wide enough for himself, so she wouldn't be able to squeeze past him to slip inside.

"The reporter," he said by way of greeting. "How did you find me?"

For a moment, Phoebe was speechless, not because of his question, but because her eyes were busy ogling him. Scott wasn't wearing a shirt. His chest was bare, hairless, and sculpted. He didn't look like a bodybuilder, but like a very fit man who was no stranger to a gym. His biceps were defined, his pectorals strong, and his stomach sported a six-pack. In the center of it, a thin line of dark hair grew thicker and disappeared into his shorts. She tried to moisten her dry throat by swallowing.

"You done looking?"

Embarrassment sweeping through her, she lifted her eyes to his face. "Uh…"

"Then maybe now you can answer my question. How did you find me?"

"Your license plate."

Scott raised an eyebrow. "As we both know, that

wouldn't have led you to this address."

"Which made things a little harder, but I got lucky."

"Lucky?" He narrowed his eyes. "The jury is still out on that."

Phoebe shifted uncomfortably. "Listen, I just wanted to talk to you about—"

"How did you find me?"

Clearly, he wouldn't talk to her until she'd answered his question. Phoebe sighed. "Fine. If you insist. I saw an emblem on your overalls under your jacket. I figured you work in a repair shop of some sort, so I looked for all businesses called Al's, and found out where you worked. I spoke to Al and asked him where I could find you."

His jaw tightened. "I'm gonna have to have a serious word with Al."

Phoebe reached her hand out and touched his forearm. "Please don't be angry at him. I buttered him up so he'd give me your address."

"No doubt." He pointedly looked at her hand that still lay on his arm. "That approach isn't going to work on me."

She pulled her hand back. "Please, I just want to talk to you about what happened this afternoon."

"I don't talk to reporters." He took a step back and made an attempt to close the door.

"Please, Scott. Let me come in. We can talk. Off the record."

He let out a bitter laugh. "Nothing is ever off the record with a reporter."

"I'm sorry if you had a bad experience with reporters, but I'm not like that. You risked your life for me today, even when I told you to save yourself. My readers want to know why you did it. Everybody wants to read about a hero."

"A hero? I'm no hero," Scott scoffed. "It doesn't matter why I did it. Now leave."

"No!" She slammed her hand against the door, opening it wider again. "I won't leave until we've talked. There's so much that needs explaining. How you got there in time. How you knew what to do." And why he'd had a wrench with him. After all, what mechanic carried a wrench with him just on the off chance he'd need it to smash in a glass door?

"You don't get it, do you? There's nothing to talk about."

"Please, let me come in."

He suddenly took a step toward her, his face only inches from hers. "I'm not interested in talking. There are only two things I want right now—a beer and sex. And I already have the beer. So, unless you want to provide the sex, I'd suggest you leave now."

Her breath caught in her chest. Had he just propositioned her? Her heart started to thunder. Her pulse raced and blood rushed through her body, spreading heat into every cell of her being.

"Leave," he ordered.

Phoebe found herself shaking her head, her hand pushing against the door, opening it wider. She walked past him and entered the apartment before looking over her shoulder, where Scott still stood in the door, frozen and staring at her in disbelief.

"You don't expect me to have sex with you out in the hallway, do you?" she asked. "Are you gonna close the door or were you planning on having your neighbors watch us?" If he could bluff, so could she.

Scott let the door fall shut behind him then flipped the deadbolt. With two steps he stood opposite her. "You have no idea what you're getting into."

Was he warning her? She had no time to contemplate his words, because in the next instant he pulled her to him, one hand encircling her waist, the other cupping her nape. His mouth descended on hers. Hot and firm, his lips pressed against hers, immobilizing her.

Phoebe realized then that Scott wasn't bluffing. He really was planning on taking her to bed. And there was one other thing she realized simultaneously: she wanted to go to bed with him.

~ ~ ~

Scott felt Phoebe's lips yield to him, her body molding to his and her arms coming around his back to pull him closer to her. Her soft palms caressed his naked back, and a shiver raced through him. He slanted his mouth and swiped his tongue over the seam of her lips. Phoebe parted them instantly, inviting him to explore her delicious mouth. Greedily, he swept inside, his tongue stroking against hers, his lips sliding against hers. There was nothing tentative about this kiss, no hesitation, no holding back. Phoebe was kissing him with a passion and wildness he'd rarely seen in a woman.

Fuck! This wasn't what he'd expected to happen. He'd been certain that Phoebe would flee, shocked by his outrageous proposition. After all, they were strangers, and all she wanted was a story for her newspaper. She'd said so herself. And she was asking all the right questions, questions he had no intention of answering.

But if all she wanted was a story, why was she now allowing him to kiss her? Would she stop him when he got down to business, when he was at a point where he couldn't stop anymore and had to have her? Would she then insist on him telling her his story before she would go to bed with him?

No, he couldn't allow her to use him like that.

Scott ripped his lips from hers. "You'd better go now, before we both do something we'll regret."

With lust-filled eyes she stared at him, her lips plump and red, her mouth slightly parted. "I won't regret it."

Scott shook his head. "If you think by sleeping with me I'm gonna give you anything for your story, you're wrong." He pulled away from her, but she gripped his upper arms.

"This is not about the story."

He tilted his head toward the door. "It was, a moment ago."

"I know. But sometimes things change."

"Not even you believe that." And as much as Scott wanted to believe it, he wasn't naïve enough to believe anything a reporter said. Even if that reporter was the hottest woman he'd ever touched.

"All I know is that today I would have died had it not been for you. Believe what you want. Whether I do this for the story, or because I want to thank you for saving my life, or just because I want to feel a man's body, what does it matter to you?"

Scott clenched his jaw and jerked her to him, her pelvis slamming against his groin. "It matters. Everything matters." He cupped the back of her head and brought her face to his. "So tell me the truth now. Why would you want to sleep with me? I could be a serial rapist for all you know."

Phoebe trembled, and her lids lowered by a fraction as if she couldn't look at him. Her cheeks flushed and a rose blush spread over her entire face. She looked almost innocent now.

"I want to feel a man's body." She took a deep breath. "No." She shook her head. "No, not just any man's. I want to feel *your* body." When she lifted her lids to look straight at him, the desire in her eyes was unmistakable.

"Uh, damn it, Phoebe!" Scott cursed. Had she said anything else, he would have tossed her out on her ass. But her confession that she wanted him made him weak. Too weak to resist her. And despite the knowledge that he was getting into something he couldn't control, he couldn't stop his next words.

"I won't stop until I'm done. You understand that? Once I kiss you again, you're not going to leave my bed until we're both thoroughly satisfied. Last chance to leave. I won't stop you if you leave now."

"Scott?"

"Hmm?"

"Where's your bedroom?"

He twisted his lips into a half smile. "You keep saying stuff like that, it's gonna get you into trouble one day."

"But not tonight."

"No, not tonight." Scott brushed his lips against hers. "Tonight all you get is pleasure."

9

Scott laid Phoebe on his bed and slipped the sandals off her feet before he joined her. He wasn't going to rush this, despite the fact that his cock had already pumped full of blood and was rock hard just from kissing her.

Her dark hair fanned out on the pillow, rendering her face more innocent than she was. After all, no reporter could be innocent, but for the next hour he would forget about what she was and concentrate on only the woman in her, not the reporter who was looking for answers.

"You're beautiful," he murmured, and captured her lips before she could say anything in response.

Bracing himself halfway over her, he kissed her passionately, while he pulled her shirt from her slacks and opened the buttons to get to the prize below. With every button he slipped from its hole, he exposed more of her creamy flesh to his touch. With it, his body heated even more and he was grateful he only wore shorts and nothing else.

Phoebe responded to his kiss as if she'd not kissed a man in a long time, with a hunger that he welcomed and a skill he appreciated even more. He wasn't kissing an inexperienced woman but one who knew what she wanted and how to get it. Making love to her would be a special treat.

Finally he'd opened all the buttons of her shirt and peeled the fabric back. She wore a thin bra which didn't impede him from feeling the lush fruit beneath, almost as if she were already naked. He slid his hand over one breast and gave it a tentative squeeze. Her flesh was firm and soft at the same time. Perfect. Just how he liked it. Beneath his fingers, her nipple hardened, and a moan issued from her lips.

How he loved a responsive woman.

Scott released her lips amid a disappointed mewl coming from Phoebe, and dropped his head to her breast. He pushed the bra aside enough so her nipple popped free. A moment later, he licked over the rosy bud and took his first taste. Underneath his mouth, Phoebe trembled and released another moan.

"Yes," she murmured in encouragement.

He hummed his approval against her nipple and sucked it into his mouth while he squeezed her flesh in his palm. He loved the heavy feel as her breast filled his hand, almost spilling over. Despite her slim waist, Phoebe had curves. Her breasts were full and lush, and her hips were cushioned just enough to welcome a man when he thrust into her body. But he was getting ahead of himself. Before he plunged into her, he wanted to thoroughly explore her body and pleasure her until she was begging him to take her.

He'd always loved that, driving a woman so far that she was mad with lust and need and could only think of one thing: to have him inside her. And with Phoebe he wanted it even more. No, not just wanted. He needed her to beg him to take her. And he needed her to scream his name when she came. So he'd know she was truly alive. Because now that she was in his bed, he felt a shudder travel through his body at the thought that she could have died in that collision today. A few seconds later, and it would have been too late for her. A few seconds later, and he would have had to abandon her and save his own skin.

That thought made him lick her breast harder. When he felt her hand slip to his nape and caress him there, he groaned from the intense pleasure of her touch. He knew once she touched more intimate parts of his body, he would erupt in flames. Maybe he'd gone without sex for too long. Or maybe he sensed everything so intensely tonight because of what had happened earlier in the day. Because of the danger they'd been in.

Wanting more of her, Scott let go of her breast for a moment and freed her of her shirt and bra, tossing the garments to the floor. Her ample flesh spilled into his waiting hands. He shifted on the bed. Phoebe understood and spread her legs so he could move into the space and bury his face in her breasts, alternately licking one and then the other peak.

He loved her softness and the openness with which she greeted each of his caresses, whether he was tender or demanding, passionate or gentle with her. No matter what he did, her sounds of pleasure bounced against the walls of his bare bedroom, while her hips ground against him in an unmistakable fashion.

Keeping his lips wrapped around her nipple, Scott slid one hand down her torso until he reached the top of her light linen pants. Phoebe's breath hitched, and he slowed his descent. Her pelvis arched into his palm, and he moved lower until his hand cupped her sex. Warmth emanated through the fabric.

"Yes." She hissed out the word in a desperate plea

for more.

He lifted his head for a short moment. "Patience, baby."

Then he was kissing her breasts again, sucking her hard nipples, while his hand moved to the button of her slacks and opened them. The zipper followed. He felt her chest rise and fall with a sigh of relief.

"You want me?" he murmured, his hand resting on her stomach now, his fingers brushing up against her panties.

"Yes, please, Scott, touch me."

He pushed his fingertips beneath her panties, then slowly moved south, through the nest of coarse hair. Lower still. Phoebe lifted her pelvis, silently asking for more. Gently he complied and bathed his fingers in her wet heat, caressing the aroused flesh with unhurried movements.

Scott lifted his head from her breast and looked up at her, then shifted to bring his lips to hers. "Like that?"

"Perfect."

He felt a smile curve his lips. If Phoebe thought this simple touch was perfect, she hadn't experienced anything yet that he could give her. He brought his lips over hers and kissed her, while farther below he extended one finger and carefully drove into her. In response, she bucked against him.

God, she was tight! Her interior muscles gripped his finger as if she didn't want him to leave again. But Scott had other plans. He pulled his finger from her and moved north to her center of pleasure. When he found the engorged piece of flesh and stroked over it, Phoebe moaned into his mouth. He captured the intoxicating sound and felt it reverberate in his chest.

Rhythmically her pelvis ground against his hand. She rubbed herself against him, spurring him on, her chest now heaving, her breaths coming in erratic pants. But he could do better than that. He could get her even hotter, even wilder.

Severing the kiss, he slid down her body, released her sex and gripped her pants. As he slid them off her legs, she helped him by lifting her backside off the bed. Her panties followed. Finally she lay naked before him. A veritable feast for the eyes.

Scott took hold of her thighs and spread them wider, before he dropped his head to her sex.

A surprised gasp was her answer as she reared up. "Scott!"

"Shhh," he murmured. "Just enjoy it." Because he didn't go down on every woman he had sex with. In fact, he rarely did. It was too intimate, something reserved for a person with whom he had a deeper connection, and not the one-night stands he had from time to time.

But it was different with Phoebe. He wanted to taste her to experience the intimacy of sensing her shudder under his mouth. He craved that closeness. If just for this one night, he wanted to feel a connection to somebody. To Phoebe.

When he swiped his tongue over her moist folds and tasted the dew that had seeped from her, his entire body coiled with excitement. Behind his shorts, his cock pressed against the mattress, and he thrust his hips as if he were thrusting into Phoebe. Already now he could feel pre-come ooze from the tip. How long he could hold back now before the need to take her would overwhelm him, he didn't know for certain. But it wouldn't be long.

Desperate to pleasure the woman in his arms, Scott licked her sex, teasing her center of pleasure with firm strokes of his tongue and gentle caresses with his fingers. Phoebe twisted beneath him, rubbing herself ever more rapidly against his tongue and fingers.

"Oh, yes, more, yes!"

Her words were like a chant, and he welcomed each and every one of them. Her hands dug into his shoulders as if holding on for dear life.

"Please, please!" she begged. "Scott! Please!"

He knew what she wanted, what she needed. Not letting go of her clit, he drove two fingers into her and felt her buck against him. Simultaneously, he sucked the engorged bundle of nerves into his mouth and pressed his lips together.

Phoebe erupted. He could feel the waves charging through her body physically as the vibrations reached his fingers and lips.

Fuck! He'd underestimated how intense this feeling would be. Just by feeling Phoebe climax, he was dancing on the verge of his own orgasm.

He lifted his head and removed his fingers reluctantly, but he had to hurry now. If he didn't get inside her in the next few seconds, he wouldn't make it.

Frantically, Scott freed himself of his shorts, glad he was going commando, and reached over to his bedside table. He pulled a condom from the drawer, opened it and slipped it over.

When he looked back at Phoebe, her eyes were on him.

"You want me?"

She reached for him, pulling him closer. "Yes."

When she tried to touch his cock, he gripped her

wrist, preventing her action. "If you touch me now, I'm gonna come."

"We can't have that," she murmured seductively and lay back on the bed.

Scott moved over her, settled in the vee of her legs and braced himself on his elbows and knees. With a look into her eyes, he drove into her, seating himself to the hilt. "Fuck!"

Despite the condom that normally robbed his cock of some of its sensitivity, the feeling of being inside Phoebe was intense. And he wasn't even moving yet. He was simply lodged deep inside her, taking steadying breaths in the hope of warding off his imminent orgasm.

"You feel good," Phoebe said, sliding her hands onto his ass and crossing her ankles behind his thighs.

"Yeah?" He dropped his head to her face and pulled her lower lip into his mouth, swiping his tongue over it. "Are you ready for more?"

"Mmm."

"I take that as a yes."

He pulled his hips back and withdrew almost completely from her silken sheath before slicing back into her. Like a tight glove, she enveloped him, and he began to thrust steadily. Though he wanted to keep his tempo slow, he couldn't. His body was dictating his actions now, and he had no control any longer. Driven by the need to find release, his body took on a mind of its own. His hips worked frantically, his pelvis slamming against hers in rapid succession, his cock sliding in and out of her without pause. His movements grew wilder and faster with each passing minute.

His torso was covered in sweat, and every time their bodies came together the sound echoed from the walls, underscoring their combined moans and sighs. Heavy breathing mingled with it. With every thrust, Phoebe arched into him.

"Yes, come with me," he encouraged her, wanting to feel her body spasm when he climaxed, knowing it would only add to his own pleasure.

"Harder! More!" she demanded.

Scott welcomed her demand. Instinctively he'd held back, not wanting to hurt her, but now that she spurred him on to take her more ferociously, he let himself go. He braced himself on his knees, gripped her hips with both hands and tilted her pelvis upward, immobilizing her. Then he plunged into her, harder this time. Faster too. Phoebe gasped, her chest heaving, but she didn't stop him, didn't voice a protest. Instead, her eyes locked with his, approval and desire shining back at him.

"Yes! Scott! Yes!"

He felt his balls burn and knew there was no going back now. Gritting his teeth and clenching his jaw, he drove into her, while he used his hands to pull her pelvis to him in the same movement, doubling the impact.

Phoebe moaned, then a shudder ran through her body. Before it reached him, Scott felt his semen shoot through his cock and explode from the tip. "Fuck!"

His cock kept thrusting back and forth, his hands still holding Phoebe's hips immobile so she couldn't escape. Though it didn't look like she had any intention of escaping. On the contrary, she reached for his face, pulled it to her and kissed him. His movements slowed, and after what felt like an eternity, he stilled.

"That was...wow."

Scott pressed his forehead against hers. "Yes, wow is the right word." He rolled off her and rid himself of the condom then pulled her back into his arms. He took a few breaths and leisurely stroked her back before sliding his hand down to her behind and resting it there.

"I hadn't expected this," he admitted.

Phoebe lifted her head from his chest. She looked thoroughly loved, and he had to admit, he liked the look on her.

"Expected what?"

"That you'd accept my challenge."

"Was that what it was? A challenge?" She chuckled softly. "I had the impression you wanted to shock me with your proposition."

"And? Did I succeed?"

"I wouldn't be here if you had."

Scott raised an eyebrow. "Fearless, huh?"

"You don't strike me as somebody I should fear."

"You have no idea." If only she knew what he'd been, who he'd worked for, the things he'd done, and the things he was capable of. But she would never find out. Because despite the incredible sex they'd had, he wasn't going to tell her anything about himself. She was still a reporter.

"What's with that frown on your face?"

He shook his head. "No questions, remember?"

Phoebe rolled her eyes and started to rise.

"Where are you going?"

"Where do you think I'm going? I'm leaving."

"Why?"

"Because you can't even tell me why you're frowning just after we had sex." She swung her legs out of bed. "As if you regret it already."

Scott sighed and reached for her. "That frown had nothing to do with you."

Phoebe rose. Scott jumped up and wrapped his arms around her from behind, pulling her against his body. He knew he should let her leave now, but he couldn't. He didn't want her to think badly of him.

"I don't regret what just happened between us. I loved every second of it. You're an amazing woman, Phoebe. It's just, well, it's complicated. And I can't talk about it."

"Complicated? What man hasn't said that after having sex with a woman? Let me make this easy on you. I'll leave, and you won't have to come up with any excuses later why you want me gone."

She was right about so many things. He would make up an excuse eventually so she would leave. And he should take the out she was presenting him with just now. But for whatever inexplicable reason, he couldn't.

"Phoebe, please spend the night with me. Stay here."

She turned her head, looking at him in disbelief. "You want me to stay here? What happened to *it's complicated*?"

Scott brushed his knuckles over her cheek. "Forget about that. It doesn't matter tonight. Sleep here, with me, in my bed. I love having you in my arms."

She tilted her head back in a clear invitation, her lips parted, her lids lowered halfway.

"Thank you," he murmured. "I'll make it up to you."

"How?"

"Give me a few minutes to recover, and I'll show you."

And a few minutes was all it would take before he was ready to make love to her again.

10

Scott raced toward the building, but his feet didn't want to comply. The faster he ran, the farther away he seemed to find himself. As if he were running in reverse. He reached out his arms, wanting to grasp what was in front of him, but his fingers touched nothing. His lungs burned from exhaustion but he couldn't stop, knew he had to continue, because the fate of so many people depended on him.

But he wouldn't make it. He knew it instinctively. When he saw the six Marines carry the coffin from the cargo hold of the plane, he knew he would be too late. The American flag draped over the coffin fluttered in the breeze as the six walked stoically toward their doom.

Scott tried to scream, to warn them to take cover, to find shelter, though he knew even if they did, they couldn't save themselves.

The explosion knocked him off his feet. The shockwave that followed slammed him against a wall. Then there were only flames and fire so hot it was coming from hell itself.

Scott felt his skin melt. The pain rendered him immobile. He couldn't even scream, because the fire was burning away his face, until only one thought remained: the Phoenix had failed in their ultimate mission.

Phoenix down.

At the command, Scott shot up to sit. He was in his bedroom. The fiery inferno was gone and he was alive. He rubbed his hand over his face, instinctively checking that he was all right.

It was the same nightmare he'd had many times before, though he knew it wasn't a true nightmare. It was a premonition, even though this particular one seemed to only hit him when he was asleep, while most of his other visions came over him when he was awake.

But just like the other nights he'd had this premonition, he hadn't glimpsed enough information to allow him to figure out where and when this disaster would take place. There was no indication as to the location, though the six Marines in his vision seemed to suggest the inferno would take place on U.S. soil.

Scott had no idea what was causing the explosion or how large it was, but from the shockwave he always felt hitting his body, he had to assume it was of massive proportions. Not just one building blowing up, or even one city block, but something on an even larger scale.

There was however one thing that he knew wasn't part of the premonition: the command, which always signaled the end of the vision. *Phoenix down.*

He'd received it three years ago. It had come from his father and mentor, Henry Sheppard. And Scott had known immediately what it meant: the program had been compromised. The protocol for such an event had been drilled into him ever since Sheppard had started the Phoenix program.

"You hear that command, you leave everything behind, son, you hear me?" Sheppard had urged him. "Assume you're on your own. They'll hunt you down for what you are, for what you're capable of. But you have to live. Do you understand that?"

Scott had nodded reluctantly. "And you? Won't they hunt you too? You have the same skills as I do."

Sheppard had squeezed his hand. "When you get that command, my life will already be forfeit. Don't look for me. Assume I'm dead, because most likely I will be."

Scott shook off the painful memories when he heard a sound next to him. He wasn't alone, and only now he remembered that Phoebe was still in his bed. Sleeping soundly.

Quietly, not wanting to wake her, he pulled back the thin blanket and swung his legs out of bed. He reached for his shorts and put them on, then walked into the living room, easing the door to the bedroom shut soundlessly behind him.

Still shaken from the premonition, he walked to the refrigerator and poured himself a glass of water. He gulped it down and felt the refreshing liquid cool his body from the inside.

He knew he couldn't sleep any longer. His mind was racing again, reliving every moment of his vision in the hope that he remembered something that would help him decipher the secret hiding in his premonition. So he could prevent the disaster. Because that had been the reason his father had started the top secret program within the CIA. To foresee and prevent disastrous events. Until somebody had decided that having agents who could see the future was a liability and a danger in itself. Until that somebody had killed Sheppard and thus made the members of the Phoenix program go underground.

Scott had no idea how many had made it out, how

many were alive. The program had operated in such secrecy that not even Scott knew which of the agents he'd met during his training at The Farm had been selected for the Phoenix program, or which were going to enter regular CIA field work. However, he'd always sensed there were others like him and his father, others with the same skill.

"It's better if you don't know who the others are. It's safer for all of you," Sheppard had said when Scott had pressed him for more information. However, Scott had been given a list of their codenames—Fox, Ranger, Zephyr, and the like—to help with identifying his fellow Phoenix in a time of crisis, though he couldn't put any names or faces to the codenames. After memorizing the list, Scott had destroyed it and heeded his father's warning. "Never reveal your codename unless you find yourself in a life or death situation."

In the living room, Scott reached for the remote and switched on the TV, setting the volume to low in order not to wake Phoebe. It was barely past five o'clock, and neither of them had gotten much sleep. Scott had found Phoebe more than just a little tempting and made love to her a third time, waking her shortly past two o'clock after she'd fallen asleep for a while. Luckily she hadn't been upset at all about Scott robbing her of her sleep, and had been more than welcoming when he'd thrust into her as he'd spooned her. In fact, she seemed to enjoy herself even more that third time, confessing that she loved to be woken like that.

Scott smiled to himself. He'd have to remember that fact for the future. He suddenly stopped himself, shaking his head. Such thoughts were futile. He couldn't carry on with Phoebe. A relationship was out of the question. He was still on the run, still hiding from his enemies, and there was no place in his life for a woman. It wouldn't be fair to her. Besides, for all he knew, her motive for being with him was to get her story. He had no reason to believe she even liked him, though he had to admit that sexually they were a hundred percent compatible.

Scott glanced at the TV, the announcer's last words having drawn his attention. The photo of a middle-aged white man was displayed in the top left corner of the screen, while the announcer spoke.

"Following a tip from a relative, Martin Lee Warren, the bus driver who abandoned a school bus on a railroad crossing in Brookfield, Cook County, yesterday afternoon, was apprehended by Chicago police in the early hours of the morning. He did not resist arrest, but police sources told us he was spouting anti-American propaganda. Sources close to the investigation confirm that Mr. Warren has a history of mental illness."

Scott scoffed. "Sicko!" These days mental illness seemed to be a blanket excuse for committing any crime in the book.

He was about to switch the channel when the picture of the bus driver was exchanged for another picture, this one not a posed photo like the one of the driver, but one taken on the fly.

He suppressed a curse. Though the picture was only showing about three quarters of Scott's face, he was definitely recognizable.

"One man has emerged as the hero of this tragedy, which could have resulted in as many as twenty-seven deaths, twenty-six of which were schoolchildren aged eleven," the announcer continued. "One of the rescued children shot this photo of the rescuer who seemed to come out of nowhere. According to Debbie Finch from WYAT News, the first news team on the scene, this man left the scene of the accident before the police could question him. While he is not suspected of any involvement in the crime, he's a person of interest who may be able to shed light on the events of yesterday. Anybody with information about this man—"

Scott switched off the TV. He'd heard enough. Though he'd been right that the news team hadn't caught him on their camera, one of the kids had and had promptly sent the picture to the press.

This changed everything. Once his enemies—the people who'd killed his father and destroyed the Phoenix program—saw this picture, they would find him. Hell, Phoebe had found him, and she had far fewer resources at her disposal than the people who were after him. It would take them only a few hours to track him down. And kill him.

He had to leave now if he wanted to live.

~ ~ ~

He pressed the pause button, freezing the picture on the TV screen. The man whose face was currently staring at him from the screen was the hero who'd saved the twenty-six kids and the teacher.

There was something he didn't like about the scenario. How often did it happen that a hero emerged at the eleventh hour to save the day? He grunted to himself and wiped his face with a towel, then tossed it back over the handrail of the treadmill and stopped the machine.

He could sense that the man whose face was frozen

on the TV had had prior knowledge about the impending disaster. From the reports he'd seen earlier, the interview with the children this man had saved, he'd had the impression that the man who'd arrived on a motorcycle had acted very deliberately, knowing exactly what to do.

And now that he saw the picture, he knew with certainty that his hunch was correct. The man looked familiar, and he realized now where he'd seen him before.

He stepped off the treadmill and marched up the stairs to his home office. His computer was already on. He logged in, navigated to the file he kept on his desktop for easy access and opened it. He didn't have to scroll long until he found what he was looking for.

The man in the picture was a little younger, but it was clearly the same one as on the TV. Beneath it, his information was displayed.

Name: Scott Thompson

Codename: Ace

Notes: First to enter the Phoenix program. Adoptive son of Henry Sheppard, director and founder of the Phoenix program.

Special skills: Premonitions/ESP

Status: Program terminated

Current location: Unknown

Not anymore. He grinned and saw his own face reflected in the monitor.

"Gotcha."

11

Music drifted to her ears. Phoebe stirred, her entire body aching pleasantly from the activities of the previous night. Scott had been more than she'd expected. She felt a little pang of guilt emerge, because she'd planned on using her female wiles to get him to tell her his story. But the moment he'd kissed her she'd forgotten all about the story and why she'd looked for him. Suddenly nothing had mattered other than the pleasure they could give each other. In the end she hadn't slept with him to get his story, but because she felt drawn to him like a moth to the light.

She'd never met a man with such magnetic sex appeal, and despite the fact that she knew nothing about him other than that he was possibly hiding from something or someone, she had thrown caution to the wind and let herself go in his arms. The reward had been well worth it—many times well worth it.

She sighed contentedly and rolled over, her hand already reaching for him. With a start she sat up. Scott wasn't in bed anymore.

She listened for any sounds in the apartment, but heard nothing except the radio on the bedside table. Curious, she got out of bed and snatched a T-shirt that lay on a chair. It was long enough to cover her to mid-thigh, and it smelled of Scott.

Barefoot, she walked into the living room. "Scott?"

But there was no response. Only silence. He wasn't in the living room, nor in the attached open plan kitchen. The door to the bathroom was open, and it was empty too.

Had he gone to buy breakfast and bring it back? She walked into the kitchen and opened the refrigerator. There was milk and a container of ground coffee. Other than that it was empty. The cupboards didn't yield much more either: some crackers and jam. Nothing fresh to speak of. She'd seen more food in a vacation rental than in Scott's kitchen. Almost as if he didn't really live here.

Phoebe marched back into the living room and glanced around. She hadn't really had a chance to take a look the night before, but now she noticed it immediately: the place was barely decorated. There were no personal effects, no pictures on the walls, no books on the built-in bookshelves. Just a stack of newspapers and flyers from the local supermarket.

The furniture was secondhand and didn't match: a sofa, two armchairs, a coffee table. She noticed a white piece of paper on the table. When she approached, she realized that somebody had written a few lines on it.

I'm sorry. You wouldn't understand. Please don't look for me.
It wasn't signed.

She didn't have to be a detective to figure out who'd written the note and that it was meant for her. Scott had just ditched her, fled his own apartment and dumped her.

"Bastard!" she cursed.

You wouldn't understand. Yeah, right! A typical male excuse. How dare he treat her like that? Why had he even asked her to stay the night, then? Just so he could screw her twice more, until he'd had his fill? Damn it, he'd even woken her in the middle of the night, his cock already thrusting into her, and she hadn't protested. No, she'd found it exciting. What an easy lay she'd been! Stupid!

She ran back into the bedroom and peered out the window. The motorcycle was gone. Figured. A more thorough search of his apartment revealed that he'd left nothing worth coming back for. She couldn't even find a single piece of mail with his name on it. Instead she found a shredder and a bag with shredded paper. Since she hadn't heard him use the shredder during the night, she had to assume he made it a habit to shred every piece of mail as soon as he'd read it. Who did that? Such action appeared downright paranoid. And it made her more than just curious. It made her suspicious. What did Scott have to hide? Not even a guy trying to avoid making child support payments did that. No, Scott had to be involved in something more nefarious. And she would find out what it was.

The reporter in her couldn't just walk away. But it was the spurned lover in her who made the final decision: she needed to know why he'd left after the amazing night they'd spent in each other's arms.

Phoebe grabbed her phone and dialed a number. The call was answered on the second ring.

"Hey, doll! What's up?" chirped the cheerful voice of Andrew, her go-to guy for electronics.

"Oh thank God you're up already."

"Already? Doll, I haven't been to bed yet. So, what's cooking?"

"Remember that tracker chip you gave me a few months ago when I was trying to get the scoop on that politician?"

"Sure, what's wrong with it?"

"Nothing, I hope. Does it still work?"

"What do you mean?"

"I mean, I put it on somebody's motorbike yesterday. And I need to find out where that bike is heading."

"Sure, it's gonna work. Let me just log in." There was a short pause. "Okay, got it, but it's still moving, heading southwest on Highway 6."

"Can you somehow keep me up to date on where it's going?"

"Yeah, but that'll take me about fifteen minutes. I'm gonna have to set up a live update for you. Do you want me to send it to your cell?"

"Can you do that?"

"I can do anything, doll," he said confidently.

"You're the best! Fifteen minutes?"

"Give or take. I'll send you a link to an app you'll need to install, and as soon as I'm done programming it, it'll ping and you'll get live updates every thirty seconds. It's almost as good as a live feed."

"Thanks, Andrew! I owe you one."

"By my count, that's more than one so far. But who's keeping track?"

Phoebe chuckled. "You are, I'm sure. Talk soon." She disconnected the call and charged into the bathroom. She would have just enough time to shower and get dressed before she could head out and follow Scott.

She wouldn't be a journalist if she didn't try to get to the bottom of this. Something stank to high heaven, and she would find out what it was. And not just because she needed a good story to keep Eriksson from firing her. Now it was personal. Nobody ditched Phoebe Chadwick as unceremoniously as Scott had done and got away unscathed.

A little voice in her head piped up. *You wouldn't be doing this if he were ugly and bad in bed. Admit it—you've got the hots for him and want more.*

"Ridiculous!"

12

Scott had driven over five hours with barely any breaks, having filled his tank once at a small gas station which didn't appear to have any security cameras mounted. Just to be sure, he'd stopped his motorcycle at an angle from which the gas station attendant couldn't read his license plate. He'd paid cash. He never paid by credit card. In fact, he'd ditched all his cards from his former life, and when there was need for a credit card, he purchased a pre-paid card in a supermarket and paid cash. Cash was king to a man on the run.

He'd stayed off the freeways, preferring the smaller highways and country roads with less traffic and less chance of running into the highway patrol. Though he'd changed the license plate of his motorcycle the moment he'd returned from the train collision, he hadn't yet had a chance to repaint the bike. He should have known better and spent the night at Al's shop, letting himself in with his spare key, rather than screw Phoebe as if he could afford the luxury of such a distraction. Now he was paying for having indulged in the pleasure of spending the night in Phoebe's arms.

He couldn't change it now. And a part of him didn't want to change anything about the previous night. He recalled the words of one of his instructors at The Farm, where he'd spent countless months training for the CIA.

"Acknowledge your mistakes and move on. Dwelling on them will only lead to more mistakes," he'd said more than just once. "Instead, examine what you did and see if there's any advantage you can glean from it."

Scott involuntarily smiled. The advantage of having spent the night with Phoebe was that he felt content for the first time in three years. Sated, satisfied, whole. While he knew this feeling would vanish soon, he appreciated the energy he'd garnered from it. As if he'd filled his tank just like he'd filled the tank of his Ducati.

He knew he would never see Phoebe again, but he also knew it was for the best. He couldn't drag her into this. Danger followed him everywhere he went, and while he was trained for this, Phoebe wasn't.

Maybe in another life they could have had more than just one night, but he only had this life to live and he wasn't going to do anything to endanger her or himself. He'd promised his father to continue what he'd started. Maybe not under the protection of the American government, but there had to be other ways to fulfill his destiny and use his gift to protect those who needed him.

Feeling tiredness creep into his bones, he started scanning the neighborhoods he drove through. He had to find shelter for the rest of the day. He needed to sleep, eat, and shower, and would continue his journey south around midnight, when the streets were deserted.

Scott slowed his motorcycle, staying only slightly below the speed limit. Any slower and he would have attracted attention. Going too slow piqued people's interest just as much as going too fast. His surveillance instructor had taught him that.

"Always be ordinary," he'd advised. "Ordinary means invisible. That's what you want to be—a ghost who people walk past without seeing. Don't do anything that makes them remember you."

Well, he'd epically failed at that with Phoebe, that much was certain. As Scott thought of her, he hoped that his note had pissed her off enough that she'd left his apartment posthaste and was gone by the time his enemies had found out his address. Not that he thought she could tell them anything that would lead his enemies to him, but he didn't want her involved in something that could put her in danger. Because once they found out she was a reporter, there was no telling what they'd do. That's why he'd written the note the way he had.

You wouldn't understand was a red flag for any woman. Waved at a woman, she would turn into a fury and stomp out, slamming the door behind her—*after* she trashed his place. Considering there wasn't much to trash, Scott estimated that it had taken her less than twenty minutes to leave his apartment after he'd made sure she was awake by setting the radio alarm on his bedside table for half an hour after he'd left.

Outside a convenience store he stopped and pulled a free real estate circular from a display on the side of the street. Every small town had a rag like it. Some were thicker, some thinner, but they all contained the same: homes for sale and rent.

Scott tucked the paper into his leather jacket and continued on. A mile outside town, he pulled off the road and parked behind a copse of trees. He got off the bike and stretched. He was used to spending long hours riding a motorcycle, and the Multistrada was a comfortable bike for long rides, but he felt stiff nonetheless. Soon he'd be able to lie down and rest for a few hours.

Scott pulled the paper from his jacket and started scanning it. He quickly found what he was looking for.

Foreclosures, it said halfway down one page.

The ads read mostly the same: *Three bedroom, two bath house in good neighborhood, large yard.* All good, but he was looking for something in particular.

Vacant, he finally read. Perfect. Plus the real estate agents were even advertising where the houses were located. Some even noted the house number and the street. That was all he needed. Several ads fit his criteria. Then he found one other crucial piece of information.

Showings on Wednesday and Saturday only, one ad read.

He was in luck. Today was Tuesday. Nobody would be showing up at this particular house until the next day. By then, he'd be gone.

He punched the address into his GPS device and headed for it. It wasn't far. When he saw the house, he drove past it. He needed to check out the neighborhood to see if there was anything he had to be aware of. To his relief, the house wasn't in a subdivision where you could practically hear your neighbors flush the toilet. The house stood on a large lot, mature trees in the front and back, overgrown grass and bushes in the front.

Scott turned right when he saw a path leading to a street behind the house. He took it and looked around. There was no fence at the back of the house, enabling him to approach it without anybody from the street seeing him. The shed in the backyard was in disrepair as was the entire house by the looks of it, but it would do nicely to hide his bike. He killed the engine and jumped off.

His eyes and ears were vigilant while he pushed his motorcycle out of sight and took what he needed from the side cases. Then he closed the shed door and walked to the back entrance of the house. It was a ranch style, one-level home with a pitched roof.

Scott spied through the window next to the door. Like he'd suspected, this was the kitchen. And like in so many houses, the back doors were easy work for any intruder. With one of his trusted tools the lock sprang open within thirty seconds.

He stepped inside and listened. No sounds.

On the kitchen counter, the real estate agent had left flyers about the property and his business cards. He glanced at them. Correction: *her* business cards. The agent's plastic smile beamed at him from her cards.

Scott tested the light switch. It worked. The electricity hadn't been disconnected. He walked to the sink and turned on the faucet. Clean water flowed from it. Good. It was all he needed.

As he inspected the property, he was pleased to see that several pieces of furniture had been left by the previous owners, including a single bed in one of the rooms. At least that meant he wouldn't have to sleep on the floor. He opened all the cupboards, and in one of them he found a few mismatched pillowcases and sheets. They would be sufficient to serve as makeshift towels to dry off after his shower, which he would take right after he'd eaten something.

He placed his emergency sack of food on the kitchen counter and unpacked what he'd brought.

13

Scott woke with a start. It was pitch black around him, and for a split second he didn't know where he was. But then it all came back. He was sleeping on a bed in a foreclosed home on the outskirts of St. Louis, Missouri.

And despite all his efforts, they'd found him.

They were good, Scott had to admit. But they wouldn't succeed. He wasn't going down that easily.

The intruder was too loud. While he certainly made an effort to be quiet, he'd made the mistake of keeping his shoes on. Had Scott been tasked with sneaking up on a target, he would have taken his shoes off and approached silently. His target wouldn't even have woken and realized what was coming. Whereas this would-be assassin was behaving like an elephant in a china shop.

Scott rose silently. He was fully dressed except for his boots and leather jacket, which lay on the floor beside the bed. His Glock was locked in one of the cases on his Ducati, but his knife was right where he wanted it, in his hand. In a place like this, he preferred to defend himself with a knife, instead of shooting a gun which might alert nosy neighbors to his whereabouts. A knife was silent and just as deadly if you knew how to use it.

Scott had left the door to the hallway open, which

now benefited him. The intruder wouldn't hear him coming. On bare feet, he snuck into the hallway, his eyes already adjusted to the darkness around him. He breathed silently, taking shallow breaths, avoiding anything that could alert the intruder to the fact that Scott was already onto him.

The sounds came from the back. Somebody was coming out of the kitchen and entering the hallway. Scott darted into the next room, the largest of the bedrooms, and pressed himself against the wall next to the open door.

The footsteps got louder. A few more seconds and the intruder would be even with the door. Scott counted in his head, holding his breath all the while.

Another sound, and Scott pounced, emerging from his hiding space and jumping onto the intruder, slamming him against the wall, knife drawn and ready to plunge into him.

A high-pitched gasp broke the silence.

Simultaneously Scott noticed something else: the body he'd slammed against the wall was lighter and smaller than he'd expected. And softer too. They'd sent a female assassin after him?

"Fuck!" he cursed, though it wouldn't matter. He'd kill a woman just as easily as a man.

"Scott?"

His hand holding the knife arrested in mid-thrust. It nearly dropped from his grip, so shaken was he by the voice he heard. "Phoebe?"

A relieved breath came from her, echoing his own. But his relief wasn't long-lasting.

"What the fuck are you doing here?" He pulled her into the kitchen, where moonlight shone through the large windows and allowed him to see her properly without switching on a light.

"I was following you. And why the hell were you attacking me?" She glared at him and ripped her arm from his grip.

Scott clenched his jaw. "Because you don't break into a house and sneak up on somebody in the middle of the night."

"It doesn't look like this is your house. There's a for sale sign out front. So don't lecture me on breaking and entering!" Phoebe braced her hands on her hips in a show of defiance.

Right now, Scott felt like paddling her ass. He'd nearly killed her, and as a result his hands were still shaking. "That's beside the point! How the fuck did you even find me?"

"I have my ways."

He made a step toward her, growling. To her credit, she didn't flinch. "How?" If he'd inadvertently left a trail, he had to know about it. Now. Before his enemies followed it and got to him.

"I'll tell you if you tell me why you left."

"I don't play that game."

Phoebe narrowed her eyes. "Well, like it or not, now you do. And I have a whole bunch of questions I'd like answered."

"Not a chance. I told you before that I won't answer any of your questions, no matter how good the sex was." And the sex had been amazing.

"Yeah, and while we're on that subject—how dare you leave me that insulting note? *You wouldn't understand? Jerk!*"

She glared at him, and despite the dim light in the

kitchen, Scott could tell she was hurt. He shoved a hand through his hair, combing it back. There was a reason why he never got involved with anybody. It only led to complications. "Shit, Phoebe! Why couldn't you just trash my place and let out your anger on me that way? Why did you have to come looking for me?"

A perplexed look spread over her face. "You purposely pissed me off? Why?"

"It doesn't matter now."

"It does to me," she ground out.

"I wanted you gone from my place, okay?" Gone, so his enemies couldn't hurt her.

"Of all the rotten guys I've been out with, you really take the cake!" Her lips trembled now.

"I'm sorry, Phoebe, but I never made any promises to you."

"No, you didn't. My mistake, expecting the hero who saved twenty-seven lives not to behave like an asshole!"

"Damn it, Phoebe!" He gripped her upper arms and dragged her body against his. "I'm not an asshole. I was trying to protect you."

She scoffed. "Protect me?"

"From the people who're after me. I had to make sure you left my place before they got there."

Phoebe shook her head. "You're just making that up to pacify me. I'm not that naïve."

Scott let out a bitter laugh. "If I wanted to pacify you I'd employ another tactic."

"Oh, yeah, what kind of tactic?" she spat.

"This one."

He cupped the back of her neck and sank his lips onto hers. After a stunned split second, she struggled, hammering her fists into his chest, but her lips parted upon his urging tongue and he swept inside, tasting her. Instantly his entire body was aflame again, just like the night before when they'd made love. He encircled her waist and yanked her to him, grinding his groin against her.

Shit, he knew this was wrong. Wrong for so many reasons. Phoebe was angry at him, and rightly so. He'd left without a word, and now he was using their mutual attraction to placate her, even though he knew there could never be anything between them.

Just as he wanted to sever the kiss, her hands curled into his shirt and she clung to him. She angled her head and her tongue stroked against his. For a few seconds he enjoyed the contact and responded to the caress, while his hand slid down to her backside to press her against his hardening cock.

Then he ripped his mouth from hers, breathing hard. "Damn it, Phoebe, we shouldn't be doing this. You shouldn't even be here."

Her lips parted and moist, she lifted her eyes to look at him. The vulnerability he'd seen in them before was there again.

"You shouldn't be anywhere near me. It's too dangerous. I don't want you to get hurt." Scott brushed his thumb over her cheek and down to her lips, tracing them. "You have to go back and forget you ever met me."

"I can't do that," Phoebe murmured, avoiding his gaze.

He took her chin between his thumb and forefinger. "You have to. Please. But first, you need to tell me how you found me. Both our lives may depend on it."

She gave him a doubtful look.

Scott brought his lips to hers and brushed over them in a feather-light caress. "Please, Phoebe. I need to know. If *you* found me, it means I didn't cover my tracks. And that means my enemies will find me too. Do you really want them to kill me?"

A jolt went through her lithe body, her eyes widening at the same moment. "Kill you?"

He nodded solemnly. "If last night meant anything at all to you, then please tell me how you were able to find me here." And by the way Phoebe had kissed him back only moments earlier, he guessed that it had meant something to her. No woman traveled three hundred miles to chase down a guy she didn't give a rat's ass about.

"I put a GPS tracker on your motorcycle before I knocked at your door yesterday."

"Shit!"

She shrugged apologetically. "Sorry, but I figured if you left before I could get my questions answered I would have a way of finding you again. It was hard enough the first time."

Scott released her, all business now. "Are you using a cell phone to get the data from the tracker?"

She nodded.

"Fuck! They're probably already on my tail."

"Don't worry, I'm the only one who has access to the info. My computer guy set up the site just for me."

Scott shook his head. "Anything sent over an unsecured line can be picked up. We have to get rid of the tracker and your cell phone now. Give it to me."

"No!" she protested.

"Phoebe, you don't understand who you're dealing with here. The people who are after me don't play games. By now they'll have identified who you are. Once they saw my picture on the news, they will have figured out who I've been in contact with. They will already be searching for you in the hopes you'll lead them to me."

"Who are they?"

"I don't know."

"But—"

"We don't have time for explanations. Give me your cell phone."

Phoebe finally dug into her handbag which was slung diagonally across her torso and handed him the phone.

"Where did you put the tracker?"

"Back wheel, underneath the covering."

He nodded and turned toward the door leading into the backyard.

"What are you planning to do?"

"Cover my tracks."

"And then?"

"Then you and I will have a talk."

14

It hadn't taken long for Scott to take the GPS tracker off his motorbike, race to the next gas station and plant it on a truck. He'd struck up a quick conversation with the driver, asking him where he was heading, and decided the truck would provide a good enough diversion should anybody have caught on to the signal it was emitting. Instead of smashing Phoebe's cell phone, he slipped it underneath the driver's seat of a car whose driver had just entered the 24-hour convenience store attached to the gas station after filling up his tank.

Scott jumped back on his bike and headed back to the house, where he'd instructed Phoebe to wait for him, something she'd done reluctantly, probably suspecting that he would ditch her again. It was his plan, though this time he was going to actually say goodbye instead of disappearing without a word.

But sometimes not even he could plan for everything. Fate had a way of intervening.

The moment Scott pulled into the backyard once more and switched off the engine, his vision blurred.

"Shit, not now!" he cursed, but there was nothing he could do.

He'd never been capable of stopping a premonition from coming over him. His father had told him not to try. "It's impossible, Scott. Just accept it. It's part of who you are. There's no fighting it."

He managed to get off the bike before the full brunt of the vision hit him and forced him to his knees.

He didn't know whose hands wrapped around the graceful neck and squeezed. But he knew the woman: Phoebe. Her face turned red as she struggled for air, and her fingernails clawed at the large hands choking the life out of her.

"Scott! Scott!"

But her lips didn't move, couldn't have produced the words that now drifted to his ears. He fought to push the vision back, but the pictures kept coming, the horror of it chilling him to the bone.

~ ~ ~

Shocked, Phoebe rushed to Scott. She'd heard the motorcycle return and had watched him from the kitchen window. She'd seen him stumble and fall to his knees. Was he hurt? Had whoever was after him gotten to him while he'd tried to cover his tracks, as he'd put it?

"Scott!"

She grabbed him by the shoulders and though he looked at her, he didn't seem to see her. His eyes didn't focus, didn't appear to recognize her.

Frantically she scanned his body, but she saw no blood and no obvious injuries. "What's wrong, Scott? Please talk to me."

His body jerked, making a few uncoordinated movements. Was he having a seizure? Oh God, she had no medical training whatsoever, had no idea what to do. She was helpless in a situation like this. All she could do was hold on to his shoulders and make sure he didn't fall and hit his head on something.

"Phoebe." All of a sudden Scott stared right into her eyes. "Phoebe."

Then he pulled her to him so violently she nearly toppled over. He hugged her close to him, burying his face in the crook of her neck.

"What happened?" Phoebe asked, relieved that he seemed to be better.

Slowly he released her. "Nothing. It's fine."

But his voice called him a liar. He wasn't fine. She could see that. "Are you sick?"

"I'm fine." He rose to his feet, pulling her up with him. "It's nothing."

"But you were having a seizure," she protested. "Do you need medicine?"

"No. Don't concern yourself with it. You can't catch it."

Her concerns hadn't even gone in that direction. "You didn't look fine."

"Trust me, I am." He cupped her cheek and pressed a kiss on her lips. "Now let's go. We've gotta get out of here."

"We?" Had Scott really said we? "You're not sending me back to Chicago?" She'd been sure he'd intended to do just that when he'd told her they would talk once he got back from ditching the GPS tracker.

Scott shook his head. "I don't think you'll be safe there right now. They probably know who you are, and they may use you to get to me."

"But I don't know anything."

"Doesn't matter. They'll try to hurt you in the hope that I'll come back to help you."

"But why would you do that?"

Tenderly he caressed her cheek. "Because I'm the reason you're in danger in the first place." Their eyes met. "And because I like you."

His confession was unexpected but no less welcome. But she couldn't let it influence her now. He was a smooth talker, and his kisses had a way of softening her up. That much she knew. But everything else about him still lay in the dark. What if he was a hardened criminal and she was becoming his accomplice by going with him? She didn't want to turn into Bonnie from Bonnie and Clyde.

She swallowed hard. "Are you a wanted man?"

"By the police, you mean?"

Phoebe nodded.

Scott smiled. "I wouldn't be worried if the police were after me. But I'm afraid the people who want to kill me are more powerful than that. And more resourceful."

"The mafia?"

"You watch too much bad TV. Let's get going." He grabbed her hand to pull her toward the house.

"Can't you please tell me what I'm dealing with here?"

He stopped and turned back to her. "How old are you, Phoebe?"

"What's that got to do with anything?"

"How old?"

"Twenty-nine, if you must know."

"Do you want to turn thirty?"

Her breath hitched in her throat. "What kind of question is that?"

He looked at her intently. "If you want to live, Phoebe, you need to come with me. Otherwise I can't guarantee your safety. I promise that as long as you do as I say, you'll be safe."

The sincerity of his words hit her. Scott wasn't joking, nor was he bragging. He was merely stating a fact. And to her surprise, she believed every single word he was saying. For the first time in her life her reporter brain, which wanted an explanation for everything, stilled and accepted a statement without asking for proof.

Either Scott was telling the truth, or he was the best liar the world had ever seen and she was about to make the biggest mistake of her life. One that could cost her her life if she was wrong about him.

"Do you trust me?"

Phoebe met his eyes. "Yes."

Scott squeezed her hand reassuringly, and she followed him into the house to collect her things.

15

Scott had driven her car into a small lake, and Phoebe had watched it sink. At that moment the finality of her decisions had hit her like a freight train. But she couldn't turn back now. She had no cell phone, no car, and an unknown perpetrator on her heels. If she didn't go with Scott now, there was no telling what would happen to her.

Once this whole thing had unraveled, maybe she would be able to publish the story about her adventure and thus save her job. If she came back with something juicy like a chase around the country, Eriksson and Novak would maybe even forgive her for having disappeared without a word. For now, she would take things as they came and hope for the best.

"Ready?"

Phoebe met Scott's inquiring gaze and hopped onto the motorcycle behind him. He handed her the helmet and she put it on. On the way to the lake, he'd stopped at a biker bar and stolen a second helmet off another motorcycle, and he now slipped the stolen helmet over his head.

"Hold on tight," he commanded. "Move with me when I go into curves, all right?"

"Okay."

She slung her arms around his waist. He put his hand over one arm and squeezed. Then he turned the ignition key and pressed the starter button before lifting the kickstand and driving off into the night.

She'd never been on a motorcycle, but she had to admit she liked the feeling of freedom it inspired in her. Though Scott drove fast, he took every curve with skill and confidence and soon she found herself clinging to him not with the death grip she'd employed at the start of the trip, but with a more relaxed hold. He seemed to notice it too, because on occasion he would remove one hand from the handlebar and briefly squeeze her hand as if wanting to thank her for adhering to his instructions.

During the long drive she also became more aware of Scott's body. Her legs were pressed against his outer thighs, and she could feel his muscles flex underneath his pants. She wasn't sure how long they'd ridden, but on the horizon the sun was about to come up, and only now did she realize how tired she was. She'd never been much of a night owl.

When Scott slowed after entering Memphis city limits, she tensed automatically. He turned his head halfway and opened his visor.

"I'm trying to find us a place to stay," he announced.

"Another house for sale?"

"No, I think I have a better idea." He motioned to a van driving in front of them.

She read the writing on the back. The van was an airport shuttle. "You want to go to an airport?"

He didn't answer and closed his visor again, while he cruised behind the van. When it turned into a driveway and stopped there, Scott continued driving. He stopped at the next intersection, took a left turn and stopped the motorcycle, but kept the engine running, his feet on the ground.

"What are we doing?"

He put his hand on her thigh. "Patience."

She followed his gaze as he looked to the left, back to where they'd come from. It took only a few minutes before the airport shuttle left the driveway, several passengers sitting in it now.

"Perfect," he said and turned the motorcycle around.

When the van disappeared in the distance, he put the bike back into gear and drove to the house from which the van had picked up the passengers.

She opened her visor. "Are you sure the house is empty?"

He turned his head halfway. "Two adults leaving with two teenagers. High probability it's vacant."

He pulled into the driveway, still under cover of darkness, though in a few minutes it would be light enough for the neighbors to see the motorcycle.

Scott pointed to a tall wooden gate next to the garage. "Open it."

Phoebe jumped off the motorcycle and walked to it. She reached over it, finding the latch on the inside and releasing it. In the meantime, Scott had turned off the engine and was pushing his Ducati toward her. She stepped aside and let him pass. When he and the bike were inside, she entered behind him and closed the gate again.

Scott parked the motorcycle next to the trashcans and motioned her to follow him.

As they walked into the backyard, Phoebe noticed the high wooden fence that surrounded the property and the high bushes and mature trees lining the perimeter. An alley ran along one side of the large lot. A wooden deck was attached to the back of the house. There was a barbeque, a table and chairs.

Scott walked ahead. She watched him take in his surroundings, though she suspected he saw more than she did. For the first time she now noticed how alert he was, how his eyes scanned the area outside the house with purpose and efficiency. As if he'd done this many times before. Like a professional. But what kind of professional?

He seemed to like what he saw, while she was still nervous, expecting at any moment a door to open and a grandparent or house sitter to appear from within the house. While she cast nervous looks over her shoulder, Scott approached the door leading from the house onto the deck and tested it. It was locked, which Phoebe had expected.

He pulled something from the inside of his jacket pocket and went to work on the lock, but his broad back blocked her view and she couldn't see what he was doing. By the time she'd crossed the deck and reached him, he was already pushing the door open. He hesitated for a moment, then stepped into the house. Phoebe followed him gingerly and looked around.

Scott took his helmet off and placed it on the clean kitchen counter. "You can take your helmet off now."

She removed the motorcycle helmet and shook her hair out, combing through it with her fingers. They felt sticky from the long ride. In fact, her entire body felt sticky.

"Stay here. I'll take a look around," Scott said. "Don't turn on any lights, and stay away from the windows."

Phoebe watched him leave the room and barely heard his footsteps as he walked into the hallway. She remained quiet, still fearful they weren't alone in the house. Meanwhile she let her gaze wander around the kitchen. Her look fell onto the large refrigerator. She approached and opened it.

It was practically bare, cleaned out of all perishable items such as milk or eggs. Only condiments and other longer lasting items were still inside. And water. She took a bottle and twisted its lid.

She drank a big gulp and instantly felt better.

"May I have some of that?"

Scott's voice behind her made her whirl around, her heart beating like a jackhammer. She hadn't heard him come back.

He reached for the bottle in her hand. "Didn't mean to startle you. Ingrained habit." He shrugged apologetically and set the bottle to his lips, gulping down half of it before handing it back to her. "Thanks."

"Is it safe here?"

He nodded. "We can rest here for a day or two."

"And then?"

"I'll figure something out." He must have noticed her worried look, because he stroked his knuckles over her cheek. "If you want to get cleaned up, there's a large master bath upstairs. Back of the house. I've drawn the shades everywhere. I'll check to see if I can find us some food in the meantime."

Phoebe pointed to the refrigerator. "Fridge is empty."

"There's a freezer, and if they are like every American family, they'll probably have another one out in the garage. I'll fix us something and then we'll need to sleep."

Phoebe nodded gratefully. Sleep was what she needed. And a shower. And food. Though she had no idea in which order. She walked out of the kitchen and took the back stairs leading to the second floor. To her surprise the house had two staircases, one in the front and one in the back. The house looked well maintained and comfortable. The thick carpet under her feet swallowed the sound of her footsteps when she walked along the upstairs corridor in search of the master bedroom. Double doors led into it. A massive king-sized bed dominated the room which had French doors leading to a balcony overlooking the backyard. Closets lined the walkway that led into the bathroom.

The shower was equipped with dual showerheads, a luxury she'd never enjoyed before. But what drew her attention was the large soaking tub. Yes, that was exactly what she needed now. A long soak in the tub to soothe her aching muscles which weren't accustomed to riding on a motorcycle for hours without a break.

Luckily the woman living in this home liked her baths too, if the variety of the various bath foams and salts was anything to go by. Phoebe picked a lavender-scented bath foam and filled the oversized tub with hot water while she undressed.

Minutes later, she sank into the heavenly liquid and closed her eyes. Time to relax and to think. So many questions swarmed in her head. She didn't even know where to start. She would have to make a mental list. And on the top of her list was the most important question: who was Scott?

Other questions followed easily from there: who was

he running from and why? Had he committed a heinous crime? Why had he saved the children and her? As the memory of the train collision surfaced again, she recalled the news report from Debbie Finch from WYAT News. She'd mentioned another, similar incident where a motorcyclist had saved the victim of a collision and had then disappeared before being identified. Had Scott anything to do with that? She shook her head. Impossible. It would be too much of a coincidence. After all, the odds of somebody happening upon an impending disaster like that and arriving in time to prevent it were huge. The odds of the same thing happening to the same person twice were astronomical.

Only somebody knowing of events like these in advance would be able to achieve this impossible feat. And she didn't believe that Scott had anything to do with the bus driver or the cab driver from the incident two years earlier. No, it had to be a coincidence. A very lucky coincidence.

Phoebe sighed and dipped the back of her head into the water, wetting her hair before sitting up again, her eyes still closed. She'd only switched on the light over the sink which bathed the room in an orange glow.

"You look comfortable. May I join you?"

Phoebe gasped and jerked up. Water sloshed over the side of the tub. She found Scott standing at the door, looking at her, his eyes unreadable.

"You have to stop sneaking up on me like that," she admonished.

"Apologies," he said and stepped into the room.

She ran her eyes over him. He'd taken off his leather jacket and boots, but was still wearing his black T-shirt and pants. Involuntarily she licked her lips and felt her nipples pebble. Suddenly she was fully aware of the fact that she was sitting up in the bathtub and the foam wasn't covering her breasts anymore.

"I take that as a yes."

Her throat dry now, Phoebe watched him undress. First he pulled his T-shirt over his head and tossed it onto the clothes hamper. Then he opened the button of his pants and pulled down the zipper.

Slowly she sank back into the water, her breasts now beneath the foam again. When Scott stepped out of his pants, her eyes zeroed in on his boxer briefs. The fabric stretched tightly over his groin. The moment his thumbs hooked underneath the waistband, she dropped her lids and looked away. God, she was ogling him like a star-struck teenager! It was positively shameless. Hadn't she cursed herself only yesterday morning for being so naïve and falling for his seduction? And now she was about to do the same: succumb to his sex appeal when what she should be doing was asking him questions.

"Don't tell me you're suddenly shy," Scott said and stepped into the tub.

When he remained standing, she looked up to him and stared right at his cock. It hung there, long and heavy, but relaxed.

"Are you gonna stand there forever?" she asked instead of an answer.

"May I get behind you?"

Phoebe scooted forward and he stepped around her to slide into the tub, sitting down behind her, his legs in a vee, his arms immediately pulling her against his chest. One hand slid to her stomach, resting there. The other lay across her breasts, though he was making no attempt to caress them.

"This feels good." Scott's breath blew against her nape.

She remained stiff in his arms, her head raised.

"What's wrong? Relax, Phoebe. Rest your head against my chest." When she finally did, his hand stroked leisurely over her stomach. "That's better."

"I need answers, Scott," she blurted before her courage could desert her. And this time she wouldn't stop until she'd gotten the answers she sought.

16

Scott sighed. He had the feeling this time he couldn't pacify Phoebe with a kiss like he'd done the night before. But no matter what she asked, *he* would be the one controlling what he told her. He wouldn't be cajoled into revealing his secrets, though he knew in order to keep Phoebe from mounting a mutiny, he'd have to give up some information.

"Why is this story so important to you?" he asked to buy himself some time.

"It's not really about this story." She hesitated. "Well, it is and it isn't."

"I'm not sure I understand."

Phoebe shifted, turning her head sideways. "The paper is in financial trouble, and they're letting people go. If I can't prove I'm somebody worth keeping, I'll be axed. And since the editor-in-chief's son was one of the kids on the bus, he's gotten it into his head to get your story."

"So that's why you followed me." For a moment he'd thought maybe she'd followed him because she'd felt spurned by him. And some women just needed to have the last word.

"Well, your insulting note didn't help. That's for sure."

He pressed her more firmly against his chest and dropped his head to hers. "I already explained why I wrote it." He planted a quick kiss on her temple. "But I'm afraid you'll have to tell your editor there's no story." Scott slid his mouth farther down and kissed her neck, but she pulled away, making it abundantly clear he couldn't butter her up this time. "Fine," he conceded. "I'll tell you about myself."

She turned her face to him, smiling, her mouth already opening, ready to ask her question, but he stopped her.

"But you can't print any of it. If the public finds out about it, I'm as good as dead."

Her face fell. "But there must be something I can give to Eriksson."

"Make something up. Isn't that what reporters do anyway?"

Outrage colored Phoebe's face. "That's not true! I only write the truth! I'm not some unethical gossip columnist writing for a worthless rag. I work for the Daily Messenger."

Scott lifted his hands in defense. "Nothing personal, but I know from experience that not even the Daily Messenger always prints the truth. And with this lie you would protect me. Unless of course you don't care what happens to me." He threw the bait out there, hoping she'd bite.

She did, but not without making her own demands. "Fine, but you'll tell me the truth."

"Good, but you'll never breathe a word of it to anybody. I'll give you the truth." Well, a sanitized version of it, anyway. Because Phoebe would never believe the entire truth, and it wasn't for him to divulge it. Too much was at stake. He couldn't risk the lives of other men like him, if some of them were indeed still alive and living in hiding like he was.

Scott pulled her back to lean against his chest and wrapped his arms around her again, one arm across her luscious breasts, one hand low on her stomach. So low that his fingertips were grazing the top of her mound, ready to take action if he needed to divert her attention when her questions went in a direction he didn't want to take.

"I spent the first eleven years of my life in an orphanage in Richmond, Virginia," he started. "I hated every moment of it. I didn't belong there. I didn't get along with the other kids. I was bullied. Well, back then, I guess they didn't call it that."

"What happened to your parents?"

"I don't know. Nobody knows who my parents were. They abandoned me. I was found as a baby in a trashcan, barely alive."

A shocked gasp came from Phoebe.

"I assume that my mother was a teenager and I was the result of an unwanted pregnancy."

"Did you ever try to find out? I mean, these days with DNA analysis and everything…"

He shook his head and closed his eyes. "I don't want to know who she is. She didn't want me. So why would I want her?" Scott wasn't bitter about it anymore. Because somebody else had given him the love he'd craved as a child. "I was adopted when I was eleven."

"A good family?"

"A single man who gave me the home I needed. He taught me everything. He was my father in everything but blood. We were so much alike."

"Could he have been your biological father? I mean, maybe he found out about you and came to claim you because he knew you were his son?"

Scott smiled wistfully. "No, he wasn't my biological father. But it didn't matter. I loved him and looked up to him."

"He's gone, isn't he?" she asked hesitantly, pity evident in her voice.

"Murdered."

"Murdered?" Phoebe echoed. "Oh my God!"

"I couldn't prevent it."

"Were you with him when it happened?"

"No. Had I been there, maybe I would have been able to save him. But they made sure they got him alone."

"Did the police find the killers?"

"There was never an investigation."

Phoebe spun around, staring at him in disbelief. "But for every murder there's a police investigation."

"The official story was that he died of a heart attack."

Her eyebrows knotted. "But…I don't get it. Are you sure he was murdered?"

Scott saw skepticism in her eyes now and couldn't really blame her. If somebody were telling him the story, maybe he'd be skeptical too. "I never saw his body, but I managed to access the unofficial report."

"Unofficial report?"

"They covered everything up, swept it under the rug."

"The police? But if they did that, you'll have to try to prove it. Go to the FBI, have them investigate. Or the government. There must be people who can help you."

"I'm not talking about the police, Phoebe. I'm

talking about the government. They are the ones who covered it up."

Phoebe's head went from side to side. "But why?"

"Because they can't afford for anybody to find out that one of their top secret CIA programs was compromised and its director murdered. They can't let anybody know the program even existed. And because of that, they've become accessories. I can't trust them."

"But don't you think that's—"

"Paranoid?" Scott finished her sentence.

"I was gonna say crazy, but paranoid works too."

"I'm alive. If that means I'm paranoid, then I'm paranoid."

Her forehead furrowed. "But why would they be after you too? Just because your father was the director of some super-secret government program? That makes no sense."

Scott took her chin in his hand and looked into her eyes. "Phoebe, I worked with my father. I was one of his agents. The people who killed my father are hunting me and everybody else connected to the program. And when they catch me they'll kill me unless I kill them first."

A shocked gasp came over Phoebe's lips. She swallowed. "What program were you in?"

"I can't tell you that. I've already told you more than I've ever told anybody else. Please don't ask anything else. The less you know, the safer you are."

Slowly, Phoebe nodded, then she turned fully and put her arms around his neck, pressing herself against him.

"What's that for?" he murmured, surprised at her sudden show of affection. He hadn't expected her to agree to his demand so readily.

"Thank you for telling me about you."

He didn't know what to say, suddenly feeling tongue-tied. And guilty. Because he hadn't told her the most important thing. He hadn't revealed to her that he'd had a premonition about her death. And the knowledge that he was the only thing that stood between her and her killer sent an ice-cold shiver down his spine and chilled him to the bone.

Scott shifted to sit up with Phoebe in his arms. "The water is getting cold. Let's dry off." He reached for the plug and pulled it, letting the water drain as he got out of the tub and helped Phoebe out of it.

He opened the large linen closet and pulled a bath towel from it, draped it over Phoebe's back and started to dry her off. When she took a step toward him, rubbing her still damp body against his, he was suddenly fully aware of her nakedness.

She lifted her head and met his gaze. "Scott," she murmured, her lips parting while her hands reached for his face and the towel slid from her shoulders.

Automatically, his hands went around her back, one capturing her behind to press her against his growing erection. Maybe that's what they needed right now—a reaffirmation of life, though Phoebe couldn't even guess the extent of the danger she was facing. "Can you feel what you're doing to me?"

A tantalizing smile crossed her lips. "Are you always aroused that easily?"

Scott arched an eyebrow. "Are you trying to seduce me?"

"Do I need to?" Her fingers trailed down his torso, heading for his groin. "Or are you going to give me what

I want voluntarily?"

"What is it that you want this time? More answers?"

She shook her head and licked her lips. Her hand now combed through the thatch of dark hair that surrounded his cock. When her fingertips made contact with his hard flesh, he hissed in a breath. Yes, making love to her would take the edge off. And after that he'd come up with a plan to prevent the event that could end Phoebe's life. The premonition had shown him that they were already onto him and he couldn't outrun them. It meant he had to fight them. Before they had a chance to force him into a corner.

"I think you know what I want," she said.

"I think I do too." Scott glanced around the bathroom, homing in on the spot where Phoebe had left her clothes and handbag. "Please tell me you have a condom in that purse."

"You're in luck. I always have one emergency condom on me."

Scott lowered his head to hers. "I think this qualifies as an emergency."

17

The moment Phoebe handed Scott the condom from the handbag, he lifted her into his arms and carried her into the master bedroom. A few seconds later, Phoebe found herself with her back on the bed, while Scott stood there, looking at her hungrily. Already during the night she'd spent in his bed she'd thought he was an extraordinary male specimen, but today he appeared even more so. There was a determination about him, an intensity she could only assume was caused by the fact that he was on the run and could be caught at any moment. Why else would he look at her like a man who needed to experience everything he could because this could be the last time he had the chance?

When she stretched her arms out to him, he ripped the condom open and slid it over his cock, his hands almost trembling. There would be no foreplay today, no slow caresses, no drawn-out kisses. This would be an intense coupling, a passionate union of their bodies.

Scott didn't say anything when he joined her on the bed and moved over her and used his knees to spread her thighs farther apart. Yet his gaze spoke volumes. He needed her. If only for this moment, this day, maybe this week.

When she felt the thick head of his cock at her sex,

she only had a split second to take a breath before he breached her portal and drove inside. Only a groan came over his lips, while he clenched his jaw. Then his mouth was on hers and his tongue mimicked the actions of his cock, stroking her tongue in the same rhythm as his cock thrust in and out of her.

His pelvis slammed against her sex with each movement, hard and relentless, while his hands on her body practically immobilized her. As if he needed to have absolute control. Had she not seen the tenderness he was capable of, the compassion and selflessness he'd shown her that first night, she would have been frightened by his dominance. But now this side of him only added to the complexity of his character. A man who craved love—she'd gathered that from what he'd told her about his adoptive father—yet was forced to demonstrate strength and control, supremacy and power. Scott was showing her both sides of himself: the vulnerable one and the powerful one. She was drawn to both—the man she could comfort, and the man she could submit to.

And right now, she submitted to him and adjusted her movements to his demands. She allowed him to take what he needed from her, to prove to her with his body that he was strong, that he would fight anybody who threatened them.

Phoebe locked her ankles behind his butt, forcing him deeper into her while her hands roamed his body, wanting to feel him, to touch him, to remember him. Her actions seemed to spur him on even more, and his thrusts turned more forceful and faster.

When she gasped for air, Scott released her lips for a short moment, breathing hard, before he slanted his mouth over hers again and continued kissing her. As if something bad would happen if he stopped.

Phoebe felt strangely safe in his arms. Oddly protected. But more than that, she felt desired. Wanted. Needed. Much more so than when he'd worshipped her body by making her come with his mouth. Because that night he'd been in control of himself. Today he wasn't. Something was driving him. And because of it, she saw the man beneath the mask, the man whose passion was raw and untamed, the man whose desires were unleashed. And he'd unleashed them on her.

Instinctively she knew this was a first for him. The first time he was letting himself go. The first time he wasn't holding back. She felt it in his kiss and the way his body tensed every time he plunged into her.

Her own body heated, caused not only by Scott's physical actions, but by the knowledge of what he was trying to tell her with them. She still had questions, even more than before he'd told her about his past, and she sensed there was so much more he was keeping to himself. But at the moment, none of that was important.

Only their lovemaking counted. And though Scott was neither tender nor gentle today, it was still lovemaking. Any outsider looking at them would have seen it as frantic sex where neither participant was looking for anything but his own pleasure. But the desperation with which Scott kissed her and the passion he poured into her proved to her this meant more than just physical release.

When Scott suddenly severed the kiss, she felt his cock jerk inside her. His face tensed and he cursed, before his body spasmed. For an instant she thought he'd have the same kind of seizure she'd watched him have the night before, but then she realized he was climaxing, and her body relaxed with relief.

Seconds later, he stilled and braced himself on his elbows to take his weight off her.

"I'm so sorry, Phoebe. You deserve better than me fucking you like an animal." He looked away, seemingly too ashamed to meet her eyes.

She took his chin and forced his head back to her. "Scott, look at me."

He opened his eyes.

"I enjoyed this."

He shook his head. "You didn't come. It was selfish of me."

Phoebe stroked his cheek. "You're not selfish. Or do I need to remind you of when you went down on me and made me come with your mouth?"

"How about I repeat that now?"

She laughed. "Oh, Scott, how about you just hold me in your arms for a while?"

"Is that all you want?"

"For now, that's more than enough."

~ ~ ~

At her words, Scott rose from the bed. After discarding the condom and cleaning himself off, he rejoined Phoebe in bed and slid under the covers with her. He pulled her against him, cradling her in the curve of his body like he'd done the night she'd spent in his bed.

He didn't understand what had come over him, fucking her like this. Pounding into her without taking care of her, without seeing to her pleasure. But he'd needed this. He'd needed to feel alive.

Even though Phoebe had said she only wanted to be held now, Scott couldn't accept that. He had to grant her the same pleasure he'd taken for himself. He knew she was aroused. Her sex had been warm and wet, and now, as he pressed his groin against her backside and slid his hand over her mound, he felt that same moist heat.

"What are you doing?" she murmured.

"What I should have done earlier."

"But we don't have any condoms left."

"I won't get inside you this time. And I won't come. This is just for you."

"You don't have to—"

He cut her protest off by rubbing his finger over her center of pleasure.

"Lift your leg a little," he coaxed. When she did, he guided his still semi-erect cock between her thighs and slid along her female folds. Her juices made the contact smooth.

"Now relax and let me take care of you."

With slow, circular movements he caressed her clit, while his cock rubbed along her sex, sliding back and forth without entering her. The soft petals felt intoxicating. So amazing, in fact, he knew he would climax again if he continued doing this for too long. He tried not to think of the sensations that touching her like this sent through his body and instead concentrated on Phoebe.

"You're so soft," he whispered into her ear and continued caressing her.

"Hmm."

His touch remained light and playful. Every so often he gathered moisture that oozed from her sex and bathed her clit in it, and every time he did so, Phoebe moaned softly. He wasn't rushing her. In truth, he was going to draw this out for as long as he could. Whenever he felt her breathing accelerate and her body tense, he stilled his finger and only continued thrusting his cock along her folds. He'd gotten hard as an iron bar again, but this time he would only use his cock for her pleasure and forgo his.

"Don't stop," Phoebe begged now.

"I'm not. I'm only making sure you don't come too quickly. I want this to last."

Slowly Scott resumed his gentle ministrations, drawing circles around her center of pleasure, teasing the engorged bundle of nerves until again she tensed. And again, he stilled his finger and only moved his erection back and forth, her plentiful juices coating it.

He pressed his lips to her neck, kissing her there, then nibbled on her earlobe. "I wish I could touch you like this all day and all night."

"Scott, please, you're killing me." She thrust her pelvis against his hand in an unmistakable demand that he rub his finger over her sensitive flesh again.

He complied with her demand and now caressed her with more pressure. She moaned out loud.

"Oh yes!"

"Not yet, baby," he cautioned and slowed again, then he slid his finger lower and pulled back his cock so he could thrust his finger into her.

Phoebe bucked against him, hissing out a breath.

It was a shame they didn't have any condoms left, because now that he felt her muscles clench around his finger, the urge to take her became overwhelming. But he'd have to exercise restraint. To distract himself, he pulled his finger from her and slid it higher, rubbing the moist digit over her engorged nub again.

This time, he didn't get a chance to remove it again, because Phoebe pressed her hand over his and imprisoned him there.

"All right, then," he conceded. "As you wish, baby."

Scott rubbed her clit, accelerating his tempo and increasing his pressure, while he thrust his cock back and forth in the same rhythm. When he felt Phoebe tense in his arms, her breath hitching in her throat, he doubled his efforts.

A relieved moan rolled off her lips and her sex spasmed underneath his hand. He felt the waves that traveled through her body reach his erection and bounce against it. The sensation nearly robbed him of his control. He clenched his jaw to fight back his orgasm.

Breathing hard, his hand stilled and he simply cupped her sex with it and pressed her to his heaving chest.

When she turned her head to him, he slanted his mouth over hers and kissed her tenderly. Then he looked into her eyes. "See? Much better than just holding you in my arms, don't you agree?"

"Well, if you put it that way."

Her cheeks were flushed, and he realized he liked that look on her. He liked it very much. "Why don't you sleep a bit while I take care of a few things?"

Instantly, an alarmed expression filled her eyes. "Take care of what?"

He brushed a strand of hair out of her face. "I'll be back soon. I promise. There's virtually nothing in the freezer. I'll have to get us something to eat."

She clasped his hand. "But you'll be back."

"Phoebe, do you really think I'd just abandon you after this?" This wasn't a one-night stand anymore. Phoebe meant something to him. What, he wasn't sure yet. But in any case, he couldn't leave her until he'd made sure he'd eliminated the threat against her. And even after that—well, he was getting ahead of himself.

First he'd have to put out his feelers to find out who was onto him. And there was one place to start.

18

Few people knew what the Deep Web—or Deepnet, as it was sometimes called—really was. Even fewer had ever accessed it. Scott knew it well. He'd used it many times during his time in the CIA. Though he had never been a true field agent—never been sent out on missions like the regular agents, because he was part of the Phoenix program—he'd received the same training as all other CIA agents. And he'd made contact with certain underground elements, people who didn't want to be identified but were happy to trade secrets, sell information or weapons, or cruise the job boards for him. However, for the jobs posted there, the resumes consisted of the number of kills one had under one's belt. And failing an assignment meant certain death.

When creating the Phoenix program, Sheppard had insisted on his agents being trained in all manners of combat and clandestine affairs, though their work didn't require it. Their training and later their work had consisted of having to watch news and current events, read articles and books on vast and various topics, view images and surf the Web with the idea that these images and input would stimulate the agent's precognitive gift and show him a premonition. Whenever an agent had a premonition, he had to report it to Sheppard, who would then analyze it and decide whether to act on it.

In the meantime, the men from Phoenix lived regular lives, worked regular jobs. Scott had always repaired motorcycles, a task that calmed him. Whenever he'd had a premonition, he'd reported it to Sheppard, just like he assumed the other Phoenix had done too. He'd had more contact with the CIA than he believed others of the program had, simply because Sheppard was his father.

Scott was glad now for the training he'd received at The Farm and later from his father. Had Sheppard known that his Phoenix would one day have to rely on this training to stay alive? Had he had a premonition about it?

After going through the closet in the teenager's bedroom, Scott picked an outfit he hoped would attract less attention than his motorcycle gear, and dressed quickly. When he stepped out on the street, he could have been mistaken for a college kid out for a run—a baseball cap obstructing half his face, running shoes, baggy shorts and a T-shirt completing the disguise. He didn't want to take the motorcycle out in plain daylight, concerned about any nosy neighbors being alerted. As a pedestrian he drew much less attention in this neighborhood.

He knew he wouldn't have to run far. There was a mall just two blocks down the road, and downtown was only a mile away. The house wasn't in the suburbs, where he would have been more concerned with neighbors knowing their neighbors and therefore watching out for anything unusual while a family was on vacation. While he knew he still had to be careful, there was a certain anonymity in a neighborhood this close to downtown and the mall. The fact that there was an apartment building on the end of the block and another one on the next cross street told him there was enough turnover in this neighborhood that he would blend in easily.

Scott ran past the mall and continued toward the city center, keeping his head down while scanning the streets from the corner of his eyes. He didn't have to look for long. Next to a laundromat there was an internet café. He could, of course, have used the computer and internet at the house he'd broken into, but he didn't like to take unnecessary risks. Sure, supposedly IP addresses couldn't be traced on the Deep Web, but he preferred to be paranoid rather than dead. Having seen the kind of technology the CIA had at their disposal, about which the general public didn't have the faintest clue, he had to suspect the people hunting him had access to the same technology. Besides, he'd been out of the game for over three years, and three years was an eternity when it came to technology. Who knew what they'd developed in the meantime?

Scott entered the internet café and ordered an iced tea plus one hour of internet access, paying cash and leaving the amount of tip on the iced tea he figured a college kid would have left. He chose a computer in a corner, where he could have his back to the wall and monitor the front door. He took a sip from the tea, feeling warm from his leisurely run in the late morning heat, and went to work.

Navigating the Deep Web was difficult if you didn't know where to start. Luckily, Scott did. He didn't waste time and logged into a private area message board, searching for one of his previous contacts. None of them was online, but it didn't matter. He knew some of them were monitoring the message board under user names he didn't know. Once he posted his message and used the right phrases and trigger words, the right contact would log in and respond to him. He just had to be patient.

While he waited for a reply, he navigated to the job board and scanned the listings. The way they were phrased was subtle, but Scott knew the codes for assassination, for kidnapping, and other heinous crimes. He shuddered at the number of jobs posted. Once the orders were matched to a taker, lives would be impacted. Families would be destroyed, loved ones would be lost. He didn't want to think about it.

There was a movement in the corner of the screen. He widened the window. A user had logged off. In its place another user's name now showed. His contact.

Moments later, a window popped up. The cursor moved, and a message appeared.

Assignment? Scott read.

Tail suspected, confirm signs of breach, Scott typed back.

Tracing now.

The cursor blinked. Scott tapped his fingers on the wooden surface of the table and sipped from his drink, his eyes drifting away from the screen and gliding over the few customers in the café. Nobody looked at him. Everybody was busy staring at their respective monitors.

The seconds stretched to minutes, while the cursor kept blinking, the last message still on the screen. His contact was a skilled hacker, one who knew how to find if somebody had made inquiries about others.

A movement on the screen made Scott snap his head back to it. His contact had an answer for him. One Scott didn't like.

Confirmed. Multiple breaches detected.

A list of acronyms followed. Scott had no difficulty deciphering them: somebody had found his apartment and ransacked it. His new license plate had been entered into an online database and was now compromised. Somebody was onto him.

The last acronym, though, confirmed his worst suspicion: there was a contract out on Scott, and somebody had accepted it.

Location of last known breach? Scott typed.

Missouri.

"Shit!" The assassin was closer than Scott had suspected.

Identity of subject?

Subjects unidentified, the response came.

Scott stared more closely at the screen.

Subjects? Plural?

Positive.

Scott ran a hand through his hair. Exactly how many people were after him? But why? Nobody sent two assassins out on the same job.

Action to take? his contact now asked.

For a moment, Scott paused. If the assassin was already on his tail, there was only one thing he could do: face him head-on, but on his own terms. Scott composed a message to his contact to set out the bait. He hit enter and waited.

Price: fifteen, was the reply.

Fifteen. He wasn't in the mood to haggle.

Transfer.

In ten; execute at 6pm, Scott replied.

Execute order at 6pm. In the next line, a skull appeared. His contact had always had a flair for the macabre.

Then the small window closed by itself. His contact had accepted the job he'd posted.

Scott shut down the browser window and logged into a different area of the Web, completing the transfer in less than three minutes, before downing the remainder of the iced tea and clearing the browser history from the computer.

Then he rose without haste and walked to the exit.

Once his contact planted the bait for Scott's enemy, it wouldn't take long until whoever was chasing him would be led into the trap he was about to set.

At the mall he stopped off to buy food and a few other supplies, before returning to the house. When he reached his motorcycle he used some of the supplies to alter the license plate. It took ten minutes, some electrical tape, colored markers, and clear plastic film to create an entirely new license plate number. Satisfied with his work, he went into the house.

Phoebe was asleep when he entered the bedroom, but stirred when she heard him undress.

"Scott?" she asked with a sleepy voice.

He set the alarm of his watch to four p.m. and slid under the covers. This would give him enough time to get prepared before his contact set out the bait.

"I'm here, baby." He put his arms around Phoebe and closed his eyes.

Soon he would have to be fully alert again, but right now he needed to garner his strength to be ready for the coming fight.

19

"You're going to send me away?"

Phoebe tensed involuntarily and dropped her fork back onto the nearly empty plate. Across from her at the kitchen table, Scott looked at her.

"It's not for long. Just a few hours."

"But why can't I stay here? Didn't you say just last night that I have to stay with you to be safe? I believed you."

Scott reached across the table and captured her hand in his. "I promise you that you'll be safe. But you won't be if you stay here with me."

"Why?"

He sighed. "You're not just going to take my word for it, are you?"

She shook her head.

"I've put events in motion to draw out the person who's after me."

"But, that's—"

"Crazy? No. Crazy would be to let him chase us all over the States. I have a better chance at defeating him if I get to choose where and when I encounter him. I'll be on the offensive and have the element of surprise on my side."

Phoebe rose from the table. "But you don't even

know that he's after you. You said yourself you've been careful."

"I know he's coming," Scott insisted.

She placed her plate in the sink and turned back to him. "No, you can't know that. You're just paranoid."

Scott stood and walked toward her, his gait calm and determined. He stopped a few feet from her. "I saw him."

Her breath hitched in her throat and involuntarily her eyes darted to the kitchen window. The blinds were drawn, just like in the rest of the house. "Oh my God, where? Why didn't you tell me?" Panic slithered down her back like a snake, making her shiver.

"I didn't tell you because you'll have a very hard time believing what I'm going to say now. I want you to keep an open mind. And I want you to trust me."

His words made her take a step back until she felt the sink press into her lower back. "What are you saying?"

"I have a gift, Phoebe." He cupped her shoulders. "The gift of foresight. People call it premonitions. Second sight. A precognitive skill. But whatever you want to call it, I can see events in the future. And I've seen the assassin. He's coming."

Phoebe felt her head go from side to side as if by this motion she could erase the strange words that had come out of Scott's mouth. "You're a psychic?" Her eyes narrowed. "Of all the rotten things to try to pacify me, this one takes the cake."

He smirked. "I believe you also said that when I left you that note in my apartment."

Phoebe pulled free of his grip and tried to squeeze past him, but he blocked her with his body. She glared at him. "After all that's happened between us, I didn't expect you to lie to me so blatantly. Well, that just goes to show that it didn't mean anything to you."

Before she could sidestep him, Scott's hands were clamping around her biceps, pulling her closer so her chest pressed against his.

"It meant something," Scott gritted out. "More than I wanted it to mean. Damn it, Phoebe, I care about you. I find myself thinking about you, about what could be if circumstances were different. I find myself wanting a…"

She stared at his lips, waiting for his next words. Did he really care about her?

"…a relationship," he continued and looked away. "Even though I know it's impossible."

Stunned by his words, she was speechless for a moment. "Why is it impossible?"

Slowly he turned his head back to her and faced her inquisitive gaze. "Because of what I am and what I do. What I used to do," he corrected himself. "I told you I was a member of a top secret program at the CIA. The group my father was spearheading. Somebody didn't want the program to exist. That's why they killed my father. The rest of us scattered. We went underground. But what I didn't tell you is what we really are. What I am. We were all selected because we have a form of ESP, extrasensory perception. We see things. We have visions of events that will occur in the future."

Phoebe's chin dropped.

"That's how I knew the school bus would get hit by the train. That's how I was able to save you and the kids. I had a premonition about it that same morning."

Her head spun. CIA. Top secret program. ESP. Visions. Premonitions. The words bounced around in her head like a bullet ricocheting in a confined space. The things he was telling her were impossible, but she couldn't help but look at one piece of irrefutable evidence: Scott had saved her and the kids. He'd known what was going to happen and he'd acted accordingly. Barring any lucky coincidences, only a man with advance knowledge would have been able to do what Scott had done.

"This wasn't the first time, was it?"

Scott shook his head.

Phoebe remembered the news report from a few days earlier. "Two years ago, a motorcyclist saved a man out of a taxi before a truck—"

"I know."

She didn't need to ask him. His face said everything. "It was you."

"I was lucky back then. Nobody took a photo with their iPhone. I got away before anybody could plaster my face all over the news."

Phoebe found herself nodding. Scott was telling the truth. She knew it. In fact, she felt it.

"Please, will you trust me?"

"I trust you."

He released her. "Then let me take you to a safe place."

She reached for his arm. "But there's so much I don't know yet. How do these premonitions happen? How early do you know? How many do you get? Where did you see the person who's after you?"

"There's no time, Phoebe. I will tell you everything when this is over. But right now you'll need to trust me. I'm doing this to keep you safe. To keep us both safe."

It appeared as if he wanted to add something, but he

fell silent. Nevertheless she knew what he couldn't say: he was trying to keep her safe so they could be together. Or at least that was what she wanted him to say. And for now, she was going to hold on to that belief.

"Okay," Phoebe finally agreed. "But you'd better not get killed."

A weary smile curled his lips upward. "Trust me. I only need two or three hours to set everything up, and once that assassin shows up here, he's toast."

Phoebe shivered at the thought that Scott would put himself in harm's way.

"Promise me something," Scott added.

"What?"

"If something goes wrong, you won't come back to this house. You won't mention it to anybody. Nobody can know you were ever here or that you have any connection to me. If you don't hear from me within twenty-four hours, leave Memphis and go to wherever you feel safe. I'll find you, no matter what."

Then he pulled her into his arms and kissed her. She clung to him, kissing him back with a desperation and need she surprised herself with. Too soon, Scott severed the kiss.

"Scott, promise me you'll come back," she pleaded.

"I promise, baby. I promise."

20

With a heavy heart, Scott deposited Phoebe in a motel. He hated having to leave her alone, but he trusted she would be cautious and not do anything to draw any attention to her.

Phoebe would be safe for the next few hours. The premonition he'd had about the attack on her had given him enough clues to figure out the location where it would occur: Nashville. And they were about four hours' drive from Nashville. If he took down the assassin here in Memphis, he'd change the future and therefore the premonition wouldn't come true. Just like the kids hadn't died in the school bus. He could do it again. He could change the course of history. Fulfill his purpose to use his premonitions for the good of society.

He hadn't told Phoebe about the premonition where he'd seen her die. It would have scared her even more. But he was glad she'd finally accepted what he'd revealed to her. Though he should feel worried now that an outsider knew his deepest secret, he only felt relief that he didn't have to lie to her anymore. He recalled the moment of their first embrace on the side of the railroad and how even back then he'd gotten the sense he could tell her everything. His intuition hadn't failed him. Just like he hoped it wouldn't fail him now.

Scott parked his motorcycle outside a busy diner where numerous other motorcycles stood and walked the six blocks back toward the house. He'd bought various things at the supermarket and together with items found in any garage, kitchen, and bathroom, he'd be able to turn the house into a veritable powder keg. He was no novice when it came to improvising. His father and the CIA had taught him well. Once the assassin entered the house, he would be at Scott's mercy.

But Scott wouldn't exercise mercy. He would deal death. Once and for all.

Scott was approaching the house when he felt an odd prickling sensation at his nape. He tensed, every cell in his body instantly alert. Without making any quick movements, he scanned the area ahead of him with his eyes. There was nothing amiss. At the next property, he stopped and lifted his foot up to the concrete socket of the fence and proceeded to retie his boot. From the corner of this eye he looked in the direction he'd come from.

A sedan was slowly driving past, a pretty woman with short blond hair at the wheel. She didn't look at him, but kept driving. On the opposite side of the street, a teenager on a skateboard was trying out a maneuver and promptly landed on his ass. His frustrated curse echoed in the otherwise empty street.

Maybe Phoebe was right, and he was getting a little paranoid. After all, according to his watch, his contact in the Deep Web hadn't even posted the bait yet which would alert the assassin to his location. It was fifteen minutes too early for it.

Scott shook off the strange feeling and walked into the small alley next to the house, then waited there for a few long moments, looking back to the main street. Nobody passed by. He let a minute elapse for good measure before he continued and reached the back of the property. He vaulted himself over the four-foot-high fence and landed in the soft grass.

Carefully scanning the backyard, he approached the door to the kitchen and knelt down, his eyes zeroing in on the lock. The hair he'd stuck over the gap between door and frame was still in place, indicating nobody had entered the property via the backyard.

He opened the door and slipped inside. The shades were still drawn, and the house was dark. Everything was quiet.

Scott breathed a sigh of relief and opened the cabinet under the sink, grabbing a bottle of bleach, some rags, and a bucket. He carried the items to the dining room table and switched on a standing lamp that gave just enough light so he would be able to work at the table. The bag of things he'd bought already lay on a chair nearby.

Scott marched up the narrow back stairs to head for the bathroom. There were a few things he would need from there. When his feet hit the soft carpet on the landing on the second floor, a faint sound drifted to his ears. His heart stopped and he held his breath, waiting for the sound to repeat. It didn't.

The guy was good, Scott had to give him that. How the assassin had found the place already was anybody's guess, but one thing was crystal clear: he'd just entered the house—at least an hour ahead of schedule. Scott's idea of booby-trapping the property and letting the assassin walk into it wouldn't come to pass. It appeared this would turn into a bloody hand-to-hand combat.

Scott slipped his hand into the inside pocket of his leather jacket and gripped the handle of his knife. He gritted his teeth, ready for it. His skin started to prickle again. Oddly enough, the feeling reminded him of being near his father. He'd always been able to sense when Sheppard was near. It was almost like a sixth sense. But this had to be something else, because his mentor was dead. Pushing the unnerving sensation aside, he concentrated on his other senses, trying to figure out the assassin's plan.

Scott glanced down the upper floor hallway. The main staircase was in the front of the house. If Scott could reach the first floor from there, there was a chance he could surprise the assassin. Scott silently snuck toward the main staircase, then turned and looked back. His eyes fell on the sideboard where a few knickknacks were displayed. He snatched a carving of a tiny mouse, no larger than his thumb, and tossed it toward the back staircase. The sound it made as it hit the carpet wasn't loud, but it was audible. Anything louder and the assassin would realize it was a diversionary tactic. But this faint sound would rouse no suspicion in him.

Scott turned to the front stairs and set one foot onto the first step, descending slowly, his eyes scanning the area in front of him, peering into the dim foyer. He reached the last step and held his breath. The wall obstructed his view into the living area. He was about to take the last step when a prickling sensation raced over his skin once more.

Shit!

Knife in hand, Scott rounded the corner and pounced. The assassin was right there, waiting for him. He hadn't fallen for the diversion.

The intruder was as tall and well-built as Scott, his sandy brown hair in stark contrast to his dark clothes. Scott tackled him. They both lost their balance and landed on the ground, kicking a lamp over. As it crashed on the hardwood floor, Scott aimed his knife at the assassin's head, but the guy was fast and blocked him by jerking his elbow up. With his other hand he twisted Scott's wrist, making him lose his hold on the knife. It tumbled to the floor and slid out of his reach.

"Scott! No! Phoenix r—"

Scott landed a right hook under the guy's chin, cutting him off. If the assassin's shout was meant to distract Scott, it didn't work. Of course the man would know his name and that he was a Phoenix. After all, he'd come to kill Scott.

Before Scott could land another blow, his attacker kicked his knee up and managed to thrust Scott to the side, slamming him against the sofa.

"Stop, Scott!" the stranger ground out, jumping up. "I'm not your enemy! I'm—"

Scott was already on his feet again and launched himself at the assassin once more. "Could've fooled me," he hissed from between clenched teeth as he delivered a roundhouse kick then followed it up with a blow to the guy's temple.

But the assassin was no willing punching bag, defending himself by blocking the next punch and sidestepping the kick that followed.

"Fuck, Scott! I'm not here to harm you!"

Scott let out a bitter laugh, but for the first time noticed the assassin didn't seem to be armed. Had he come without a gun or a knife to finish Scott off? "Fuck you!"

Scott slammed his fist into the guy's stomach, making him fold in half for a second. Time enough for Scott to dive for the knife that had landed at the edge of the carpet. He stretched, reaching for it, his fingers already feeling the handle when he was jerked back. He rolled onto his back and kicked his legs at the attacker, thrusting him back. But he kept coming. This time he landed with such force, the impact made Scott slide on the waxed wooden floor, bringing him closer to the knife.

Scott reached above his head, and without looking at it, his fingers found purchase and gripped the handle. Scott twisted onto his side and hauled himself onto his attacker, swinging his arm forward to aim the knife at the assassin's neck.

"That's payback for killing Sheppard!"

The assassin's eyes went wide as the knife veered toward him. "Phoenix rise! Phoenix rise!"

The command made Scott's heart beat into his throat. He froze. Nobody but the members of the Phoenix program knew the command. It was meant as identification in emergencies only. And Scott knew from Sheppard that this particular command had never been put to paper. It wasn't in the files or the official records of the program. Only another Phoenix would know it.

The assassin breathed hard, still staring at the knife that had stopped less than an inch from his carotid artery. "I'm Zephyr. I'm Phoenix, just like you."

Scott's breath rushed from his lungs in erratic pants. "Shit!" He stared at the man who'd called himself Zephyr, a codename from the list Sheppard had made him memorize. There was no menace in the man's eyes as he met Scott's gaze. Still holding the knife, he sat back on his knees, taking some of the pressure off his captive.

"Why the fuck didn't you use the emergency code immediately?"

"I was trying, but you kept cutting me off with those vicious hooks." He rubbed his chin. "Nice work, buddy."

"Cut the crap and tell me what you want!" He was still on the edge, still not sure whether the stranger was who he said he was. Involuntarily, he rubbed his nape with his free hand, as if he could rid himself of the strange prickling sensation by doing so.

Zephyr motioned to Scott's neck. "The tingling you're feeling is a sign of like recognizing like."

Stunned, Scott dropped his hand. "How did you—"

"I feel it too. That's why I had to sneak up on you. I needed to be sure before I made myself known to you. My skill of sensing another of my kind isn't very strong. I have to be physically close to someone to feel it. It was the only way for me to confirm that you're a Phoenix."

Scott rocked back onto his heels and rose, nodding to Zephyr, who followed his lead and got to his feet. "That still doesn't explain how you found me and what you want."

"Our enemy is on the move. An assassin came after me in Seattle not too long ago. And whoever sent him is going to come for the others too. You might be next."

"What happened to the one who came after you?"

"I killed him."

"But you think there are more?"

"Yes. Whoever destroyed the Phoenix program and killed Sheppard isn't done. Or he wouldn't have sent an assassin after me."

"Phoenix is done, finished. We don't even know

who's still alive. For all we know, it's just you and me."

"I don't believe that. I don't *want* to believe that."

"Well, we don't always get what we want. Guess what? This wasn't how I wanted my father to leave me, by sending me a message. Phoenix down," Scott spat, remembering the mental message he'd received from Sheppard.

Zephyr's chin dropped. "You're the one. You're Sheppard's son. It was rumored that he had a boy. So it's true. You're that boy."

Scott remained silent, unable to find the right words to respond. Finally, he said, "I'm Ace."

Zephyr offered his hand. "My real name is Ethan. It's good to finally meet you."

Scott suddenly realized he was still holding his knife. He sheathed it then shook Ethan's hand. "How did you find me?"

"Your premonition. You acted upon it. When I saw the news about that train colliding with the school bus, I knew you had to be a Phoenix. I followed the clues about your motorcycle and then that reporter who was on the bus. It wasn't too hard to follow you to St. Louis. That reporter was practically leaving a trail of breadcrumbs behind."

Scott snorted. He was glad he'd destroyed Phoebe's car and phone outside of St. Louis.

"But then it got harder. However, I got lucky."

"How so?"

"Your Ducati is a nice piece of machinery. People notice it. I was able to figure out where you were heading. But I lost the trail until just now, when I saw you park the bike outside that diner. I followed you."

"I didn't see you, and believe me, I looked."

Ethan chuckled. "I know. That's why I made Tori follow you. She draws way less suspicion on her than I do."

Scott raised an eyebrow. "I didn't know there were female Phoenix members."

"She's not a Phoenix. She's my girlfriend." He reached for his pocket.

Instantly Scott tensed.

"Sorry," Ethan said apologetically. "I'm just going to call her." He swiped his iPhone and initiated a call. A moment later, he said, "Hey, Tori. Coast is clear. You can come in. Use the back entrance." He disconnected the call and shoved the phone back in his pocket.

"Your girlfriend knows who you are?"

Ethan nodded. "I trust her with my life."

Scott heard the words and realized that he too knew somebody he trusted with his life: Phoebe.

Moments later, there was a sound at the door to the kitchen. Ethan walked ahead, and Scott followed him. A young blond woman stood in the kitchen, and the moment Ethan reached her, she wrapped her arms around him. He recognized her instantly. She was the woman who'd driven past him when he'd tied his shoe.

"I was so worried," she murmured.

"Everything's all right, babe." He turned his head to Scott. "Right, Scott?"

"Apart from the fact that I'm getting ready for the assassin to show." He glanced at his wristwatch.

"How do you know he's coming?"

"I put out some bait via the Deep Web."

Ethan motioned in the direction of the dining room. "So that's what you were planning on doing with the stuff on the table."

Scott nodded. "Had you come a little later, you would have gone up in smoke."

"Lucky me that I'm an early bird. Want a hand?"

"Sure thing." Then Scott nodded to Tori. "Nice to meet you, Tori. But I don't think this is a good place for you right now."

Ethan stroked his knuckles over Tori's cheek. "He's right, Tori. You should go to a safe place."

"I'd rather not be alone."

"It's better that way."

Scott took a step toward her. "You won't have to be alone. You should go where Phoebe is waiting for me."

Ethan's forehead furrowed. "Phoebe? Are you talking about the reporter from Chicago?"

Scott nodded.

"She's still here? You didn't ditch her? But what if she—"

"She won't betray me."

For a moment, Ethan said nothing, only looked at him. "How would you know that?"

"What's between us…it's special. I trust her with my life."

Ethan let out a breath. "Well, I hope that's not your dick talking."

"It's not any different from you telling your girlfriend all our secrets," Scott countered.

"I bet you I've known Tori a hell of a lot longer than you've known this Phoebe person."

"What are you implying?"

"Shut up, both of you!" Tori yelled, bracing her hands at her hips. "This is not a competition about who trusts his girlfriend more." Then she turned to Scott. "So where do I find her?"

"I'll write it down for you." He grabbed a pad from the kitchen counter and started scribbling. Then he looked up and handed the piece of paper to Tori. When Tori turned, he stopped her. "Wait. I need to write a note to her first. I've given her instructions not to trust anybody. She'll have to know I sent you."

He scribbled a few lines on a piece of paper and signed it, before handing it to Tori. She glanced at it, then looked at him quizzically.

"Scott '*you wouldn't understand*' Thompson?"

He shrugged. "It's an inside joke. She'll get it." After all, he'd told her in his first note that she wouldn't understand, and he hoped Phoebe would make the connection and know this note was legitimate.

After Ethan and Tori said their goodbyes, Scott walked into the living room. Ethan followed him.

Ethan rubbed his hands together. "So, let's make a few nice firecrackers for our guest. At least this is going to be one explosion I'm not going to have to prevent."

Scott cast him a sideways glance. "What do you mean?"

"Do you sometimes get premonitions that keep repeating again and again?"

One premonition instantly came to mind. A premonition that only ever came to him in his dreams, not like the others that he got when fully awake. "Yeah. And there's nothing I can do about it. Some things we just can't prevent from happening."

"I can't accept that," Ethan said, suddenly agitated. "I just can't. Too many lives are at stake. Every time it happens, every time I see it, it shakes me to the core. The explosion…it's so powerful, it knocks me on my ass. I can feel the heat, the burning, my skin melting."

Scott's heartbeat accelerated. He braced himself on the table, nausea hitting him out of nowhere. "Shit!"

"What?" There was a twinge of panic in Ethan's voice while his eyes darted around the room as if sensing danger.

Scott searched his fellow Phoenix's eyes. "I see myself running toward the explosion. I see the six Marines carrying the coffin. They get incinerated. I can't stop them."

"Six Marines? I don't see those."

"But you see the explosion."

Ethan nodded. "Yeah, but there are nine black diplomatic vehicles. A caravan. They drive across a desert road. I can't stop them. And then the explosion hits."

"Nine cars?"

"SUVs. It must mean something."

"There are no SUVs in my premonition. Only the explosion and the six Marines carrying the coffin draped with an American flag."

"But it still looks like it's the same event. Maybe we see it from a different angle?" Ethan mused.

Scott put his hand on his forearm, stopping him. "But it's not the same. I don't see the SUVs."

"But you see everything else. It's still the same premonition, only we both see different parts."

For a moment Scott let the revelation sink in. Why would both he and Ethan see the same future event? He stared at his fellow Phoenix, a thought suddenly piercing his mind. "Do you think the other Phoenix see the same?"

"It's a possibility."

Scott nodded. "I've never been able to figure out

when and where this event will take place. It's been haunting me not to be able to do anything about it."

"Are you thinking what I'm thinking?"

"We have to find the others. Maybe they can help us figure out what we're meant to prevent."

Ethan smiled. "Once we've smoked the asshole who's after you, we'll search for the others."

"Deal."

21

Scott had brought her to the motel only an hour earlier, and already Phoebe was pacing nervously. He hadn't elaborated on what he was trying to set up. And now she wished she had insisted on Scott telling her how he was planning to draw the assassin out and defeat him. Not knowing made her edgy.

She needed something to calm herself down. She needed to talk to somebody—not to talk about Scott or what was happening, but simply to hear another person's voice. And there was one person who could always calm her down: her father.

Phoebe sat down on the bed and reached for the phone on the nightstand. She knew her father's cell phone number by heart, but she knew she couldn't call it. She'd watched enough thrillers and suspense movies to know that if somebody was really using her to get to Scott, they would by now have figured out who her family was, and tapped the phones. Considering that Scott was ex-CIA, she had to assume his enemies had all kinds of resources at their disposal to find her.

She was still trying to take it all in: Scott having precognitive skills and having been part of a secret CIA program. She believed it, because it explained so many things. But the whole situation made her nervous—and afraid for Scott's life. To think that he was living in danger for his life every single day made her heart bleed. And to realize that she had contributed to making it easier for his enemies to find him by putting that stupid GPS tracker on his motorbike flooded her with regret.

But there was one thing she couldn't regret: the times they'd made love. She felt a closeness to him, a connection that seemed impossible, given that they'd only known each other for such a short time. Yet it was there, and she knew she was falling for him. At the same time she knew instinctively that their relationship had no future. He was on the run. Scott didn't need her slowing him down.

With a sigh, she called information and got the number she wanted. She dialed it.

"Nashville PD, how may I direct your call?" a woman's voice answered.

"Christopher Chadwick, please." There was a click in the line, and she waited. She knew it was safe to call her father's workplace and go through the switchboard rather than dial his extension. Nobody would be able to find out who she'd called, and there was no way somebody would be able to tap the police department's phones.

"I'm sorry, ma'am, Mr. Chadwick already left for the day. Would you like his voicemail?"

"No, thanks. That's fine." She disconnected the call, disappointed but not surprised at all. Her father wasn't a police officer; he was the PR and press liaison person who'd been brought in because of his connections to the press. He'd been hired to improve the image of the police department, and worked a nine-to-five job.

Well, maybe it was better that she hadn't reached

him. After all, her father would probably ask her where she was and what was going on. Maybe he'd already tried her cell phone and realized that something was wrong.

A knock at the door tore her from her musings and made her jump up. Her heart beat into her throat. She'd pulled the shades, so nobody would be able to look into the room, but she nevertheless suddenly felt watched.

Who was at the door?

On tiptoes she stalked to it and brought her eye to the peephole.

Phoebe instantly jerked back. Outside the door to her motel room stood a police officer dressed in a black uniform.

Shit!

Her hands trembled. Should she open the door? Or should she pretend she wasn't in?

Another knock accompanied by a male voice nearly robbed her of her breath. "Miss Chadwick? Memphis PD, please open the door."

He knew who she was. *Oh God!* Something was wrong.

Her hand was damp when she turned the doorknob and pulled the door open halfway. "Yes?"

The police officer nodded politely. "I'm sorry to bother you, ma'am. Are you Miss Phoebe Chadwick?"

She nodded hesitantly.

"I'm Officer Grant. May I come in?"

Phoebe glanced at the name on his uniform, but kept blocking the door. "What is this about?"

"I'm afraid I have bad news." He looked to his left and then his right. "I'd rather not do this out here. I think it would be better if you sat down for this." A regretful smile crossed his face.

Her heart instantly clenched. She stumbled backward while Officer Grant entered and closed the door behind him. He glanced around the room.

"Are you alone, Miss Chadwick?"

She nodded numbly.

"Please, why don't you take a seat?" His voice was calm and kind.

"I'll stand. Please just tell me what's wrong." Her hand gripped the backrest of the chair for balance.

"Ma'am, I'm sorry to be the one to have to tell you this, but there's been an accident. Do you know a man named Scott Thompson?"

Her heart stopped, refusing to pump blood through her veins, while a cold shiver raced down her spine. Her lips trembled, and no words issued from her suddenly dry mouth.

"Ma'am?" he prompted.

Phoebe simply nodded.

"I'm afraid Mr. Thompson was involved in an accident. The paramedics confirmed that he died instantly."

A sob tore from her chest. She slammed her hand over her mouth to hold in the scream that was building inside her. Tears shot to her eyes. "No! No!"

The police officer took her arm and nudged her toward the bed, making her sit down. "I'm so sorry. He obviously meant a lot to you."

Phoebe gasped for air, but all it did was produce more sobs. "How?" she choked out, looking up at him. How could Scott be dead? He'd been alive only an hour earlier.

Officer Grant pulled out a small black notebook and a pen. "That's where things get complicated. I'm sorry to have to do this at a time like this, but in order to know what we're dealing with, we need to find out exactly what happened before the accident. That's why I'll have to ask you some questions."

Her forehead furrowed. "What questions?"

"We need to know the exact timeline. Can you tell me what happened when you last saw Mr. Thompson? Don't leave anything out, please. It might be crucial to our investigation."

Phoebe shook her head in disbelief. "I was with him earlier today. I can't believe he's dead. No, it can't be him. Maybe it's not him."

He put a calming hand on her shoulder. "I'm sorry, Miss Chadwick. I know how hard this must be on you."

She dropped her head. Another sob escaped and she rubbed her eyes with her hand, wiping away the tears. She stared at the floor, the police officer standing only half a foot away from her. The white of his shoes almost blinded her and she lifted her eyes to his black pants, the color soothing her eyes. But before she could raise her gaze back to his face and answer his question, her eyes veered back to his feet without her doing.

White shoes; white sneakers, in fact. Phoebe knew enough about police uniforms to know that they didn't come with white sports shoes.

Her heartbeat accelerated. This man wasn't a police officer. And now that she raised her eyes to run them up over his legs and his torso, she noticed his pants were a bit too tight, as if they were a size too small.

Shit!

Two thoughts collided in her mind. One was comforting, the other frightening: Scott was alive, but the man who stood before her now was the assassin who was after him.

"Miss Chadwick?" he prompted once more, his voice still kind. But she knew now that it was all a ruse to get her to reveal where Scott was hiding.

Phoebe lifted her head and took all her courage to respond to him. "Would it be okay if I came down to the station later and answered your questions then? I'm sorry. I'm just such a mess right now."

The stranger's eyes narrowed, then he looked down to the floor. When his gaze landed on her again, his demeanor had changed. The kindness in his regard had made way for a coldness she wasn't prepared for.

"You are one perceptive woman, aren't you?" He pointed to his white sneakers. "I'm afraid the guy's shoes were a couple of sizes too small."

Before she could respond, he jumped and pinned her to the mattress. Air rushed from her lungs.

"So you'd better talk or you'll meet the same fate as Officer Grant."

Cold fear gripped her. She knew instinctively that the policeman was dead. Killed in cold blood by the man who was restraining her. And for what? Just so he could take his uniform and trick her.

"Where is Scott Thompson?" he gritted out from between clenched teeth.

"I don't know!" she lied.

He slapped the back of his hand across her face, whipping her head to the side. The pain stung and sent new tears into her eyes.

"He left me here. He didn't want me around anymore."

"Lying bitch!"

She wouldn't give Scott's hiding place away. Only an

hour had passed since he'd dropped her at the motel. And according to Scott's own words, he would need two to three hours to get ready for the assassin. If her attacker showed up at the house too early, for all she knew, he'd surprise an unprepared Scott. No, she couldn't risk that. She owned him too much. She had to stall this man. "How did you find me?"

"That's irrelevant!" he answered and pressed harder onto her chest, his entire weight now squeezing the air out of her lungs. "Where is he?"

Phoebe pressed her lips together.

"Fine! Have it your way."

He jumped up and flipped her onto her stomach so fast that she couldn't put up a fight. When she felt the cold steel of the handcuffs around her wrists and the corresponding click as he locked them, she kicked her legs out, trying to escape, but it was to no avail.

"Well, let's see," she heard him say and turned her head sideways.

She watched him rummage through her bag then tossed the contents onto the bed, grunting to himself but finding nothing of value.

"No cell phone?" he asked, narrowing his eyes again. Then he glanced past her at the nightstand.

He stalked to it and lifted the receiver. "I thought I heard you talk to somebody before I knocked. Well, let's see who you were chatting with, shall we?"

He pressed the redial button and waited.

Panicked, Phoebe breathed hard. When he put the receiver down a moment later, he glared at her. "Who's in Nashville? Why were you calling the police there?"

"Nobody." She wouldn't drag her father into this.

"It's him, isn't it? Scott went to Nashville."

"No!"

"Well, guess where you and I are going now?"

"No!" She had to stay here. She couldn't allow this man to drag her to Nashville. She only needed to stall him long enough so Scott would be ready to fight him. "Scott is not in Nashville. He's here. In Memphis. I'll tell you where." She would make him drive around the city for an hour, before she'd lead him to the house where she and Scott had been staying.

A bitter laugh came from the assassin. "Sure you will." He pulled her up by the handcuffs. "Once we're in Nashville."

Phoebe stumbled over her own feet as he dragged her to the door. She tried to escape and crashed into the chair, toppling it. He jerked her back, snarling at her.

"No! Please, you're making a mistake. Scott is here. He's in Memphis."

"Bitch!"

His fist came toward her face so fast she had no way of evading the blow. The impact knocked her head sideways, but she barely felt the pain because darkness descended on her.

Noooo!

But her scream never left her throat.

22

Scott looked at the IEDs that lay on the dining room table. "That went a lot quicker than I'd hoped. Thanks for the help."

Ethan smirked. "Anything for a good cause."

"Let's get this show on the road."

Scott was reaching for one of the homemade explosive devices when Ethan's phone rang.

Ethan pulled it from his pocket and looked at the display. Frowning, he answered it. "Tori? Something wrong?"

Immediately, Scott froze and watched as Ethan listened intently.

"Shit!" Ethan cursed and met Scott's inquisitive gaze.

Unease crept up Scott's spine. "What?"

Ethan held up his hand, then said to Tori, "Come back immediately. Make sure nobody's following you." He hung up.

"What's going on? Why is she coming back?"

"Tori got to the motel. She found the door to Phoebe's room open."

Scott's heart stopped.

"The room was empty. There was evidence of a struggle. And her handbag was emptied out on the bed."

An icy hand wrapped around his heart and cut off his air supply. "Shit! He's got Phoebe. The assassin has got Phoebe." Scott ran a shaky hand through his hair, his mind working overtime, searching for a solution.

"You can't know that," Ethan said, trying to calm him.

Scott glared at him. "But I *do* know! I saw it coming. I saw his hands around her neck."

"Ah, shit! You had a premonition? Then why did you leave her alone?"

"I left her because I thought she was safe in Memphis. This wasn't supposed to happen here. That's why I put out the bait to trap him here. So he'd never have a chance to get to her. I was trying to stop the premonition from coming true."

"You know where it's supposed to happen?"

Scott nodded. "He's taking her to Nashville. And once he realizes I'm not there, and Phoebe won't tell him where to find me, he's going to strangle her." The thought chilled him to the bone. He met Ethan's eyes. "This is my fault. She's in danger because of me. I have to get to her before he kills her."

"Nashville?" Ethan asked.

"Yes, why?"

"Tori pressed the redial button of the phone in Phoebe's room. It went to the Nashville Police Department."

"Shit, do you think the assassin was trying to call somebody there?"

Ethan shook his head. "He would have used a burner phone. More likely Phoebe tried to call somebody there. Does she know anybody in Nashville?"

"I don't know. She never mentioned anything."

"Don't worry. I'll make inquiries while we're on the road. Let's get going."

~ ~ ~

By the time Tori returned with the car, Scott and Ethan had packed up all incriminating materials, including the homemade bombs. Moments later, they'd piled in the car and Tori dropped Scott off at the diner where he'd parked his motorcycle. Scott sped off, ignoring all rules of traffic, while Tori and Ethan followed by car.

It was almost midnight when they reached Nashville. At a gas station, Scott pulled over and waited for Tori and Ethan to stop beside him. Tori was driving, and Ethan lowered the window. He balanced a laptop connected to his cell phone on his legs.

"What did you find?" Scott asked, praying that the information he'd given Ethan before they'd left had borne fruit. He'd given him the details of the surroundings he'd glimpsed in his vision so Ethan could find the place where the assassin was holding Phoebe prisoner.

"I scanned Google Maps. I think I found something that matches your description," he said.

"Show it to me." Scott leaned his head closer, and Ethan tilted the screen so Scott could see it through the open window.

"Here." Ethan pointed to a spot on the street view of a Google Map. "You said you saw a tower with AT&T on it. There are numerous angles from which you can see it. It's downtown. Does this look familiar?"

Scott perused the scene on the monitor. With his

finger, he swiped over the touchpad, moving the images so he was able to get a 360 degree view of the area. "He must be somewhere near the Convention Center. Possibly on Broadway or Commerce Street. He was on an upper floor, maybe fourth or fifth. Perhaps a hotel. Anything else about who Phoebe might know in Nashville?"

Ethan nodded. "She grew up here. And guess what? Her father works for the police."

"He's a police officer?"

Ethan shook his head. "No, he's some PR guy the police hired. He works out of the downtown precinct, a station on Broadway. It looks like Phoebe was trying to reach him there."

"The assassin must think she was trying to reach me."

"It's odd, but it's a possibility. Particularly because it looks like your message to the Deep Web didn't post in time."

Scott stared at Ethan in disbelief. "What?"

"Yeah, I checked an hour ago, and it posted at 6pm *Pacific Time*, not Central Time. I think your guy screwed up."

"Shit, no wonder the assassin didn't show up at the house." He cursed. "Let's go. Can you try to see if you can reach Phoebe's father?"

"Will do."

"Just don't—"

Ethan lifted his hand. "No worries. I know the drill. I'll make sure he doesn't suspect anything."

"Thanks. Follow me."

Scott turned the handlebar and sped away. He'd been to Nashville once before and knew how to get downtown. The assassin couldn't have more than an hour head start, if that much. After all, they'd gunned it all the way from Memphis and made it in record time.

~ ~ ~

Phoebe groaned. Her face ached from the blow the assassin had knocked her out with, but otherwise she was unhurt. However, there was no chance of escape. She was still handcuffed. On top of it, she sat in the back of a police car. She had to admit the assassin was clever. Even if she tried to draw attention to herself by gesturing to any passersby as they drove through Nashville, nobody would lift a finger to help her. After all, they probably thought she was a criminal. Why else would she be in the back of a police car?

She remained quiet, contemplating her next course of action, when a cell phone rang. The assassin answered it.

"Yes?"

A short pause, then he replied, "I've got the reporter… No, but I'll have him shortly. He's in Nashville… Don't worry, he'll be dead soon, just like you ordered… Yes, the woman too. No loose ends."

A chill went through her bones but she pushed it away, knowing she had to stay strong if she wanted to survive.

Her abductor disconnected the call and put his phone back into his jacket pocket. She made a note of it. Maybe later she would have an opportunity to steal it and call for help. Phoebe stared out the window. Downtown was hopping with tourists enjoying the nightlife.

A moment later, her kidnapper turned off busy Broadway and entered a side street. A block farther, he pulled into a parking garage and drove up to the fifth level. He pulled into the first empty parking spot and killed the engine.

He turned around to glance at her before exiting the car. For a moment, she wondered if he was going to leave her locked in the police car, but she wasn't that lucky. He opened the door and reached for her, pulling her out. Not being able to use her hands for balance, she stumbled over her own feet and fell forward. He grabbed her and jerked her up.

"Let's go!" he ground out. "One wrong word out of you, and you're dead. Are we clear on that?"

She could only nod. Judging by the evil glint in his eyes, there was no doubt he would make good on his threat.

"Good." He turned her around, uncuffing her, only to cuff her hands again, this time in the front. Then he pulled his cell phone from his jacket and shoved it at her. "Call him! Tell him you need to see him!"

Phoebe stared at the phone in her hands, hesitating. She didn't have Scott's number. He'd never given it to her. In fact, she'd never seen him use a cell phone.

The assassin brought his face close to hers, glaring at her. "Don't think I'm stupid! I know he's somewhere in this town. And you're going to bring him to me. Now!"

"Where do you want him to go?" she stalled.

He dragged her to the edge of the building, where a light breeze blew past the concrete columns holding up the structure, and pointed down to the street level. "Have him go to the roof bar of Tootsies."

Phoebe looked to the street corner. The roof of a

two-story building was hopping with activity. At least three or four dozen partiers were celebrating. From where she and the assassin stood, they had a clear line of sight to it. Any sharpshooter worth his salt would hit his target at this range.

Trembling, she dialed the number for the Nashville Police Department. Before the call connected, he hit the speaker button, his eyes narrowing suspiciously.

"Nashville Police Department, how may I direct your call?" a woman's voice answered.

"Officer Thompson, please." Phoebe crossed her fingers, hoping that Scott's last name was just common enough for there to be an Officer Thompson in the Nashville Police Department.

"One moment, please."

The assassin glared at her. "Remember, one false word." The threat was clear.

Her heart bled; guilt crept up from her gut. She was going to send an innocent man into harm's way.

"Thompson," a man answered.

"Scott, listen, it's me, Phoebe. I need to see you right away."

"Excuse me? I'm not S—"

"Please don't say anything; I know you can't talk freely. Just listen. Come to the rooftop bar of—"

A blow to her face cut off her last word while the line went dead.

"You fucking bitch! That wasn't Scott! That was an old man." He glared at her, his eyes nearly bulging out of his head. "I'll find him myself, you fucking bitch! I won't need you any longer!"

He slammed her onto the hood of the police car and dove after her.

Fear paralyzed her. She would die here, alone, in a dark parking garage.

~ ~ ~

Scott brought the Ducati to a stop in the middle of the block and looked around. They were near Broadway, and despite the late hour the streets were busy with tourists and locals who hopped from one bar to the next.

The area looked familiar. His eyes drifted up. He scanned one building after another, trying to find what he'd seen in his premonition. Behind him, Tori and Ethan had parked and were waiting for his lead.

Suddenly the side of a building drew his attention. *Tootsies*, it said there. He lifted his gaze. A roof terrace bar. He'd seen it before. Frantically he shifted on the bike, looking over his shoulder to find the right angle from where he'd seen it. Somewhere from high up.

It was dark back there, but he could make out the top of a building peeking from behind another one. A parking structure. That had to be it.

He turned his bike around, not waiting for Tori to make a U-turn with the car, and sped toward the building. When he spotted the entrance to the parking garage, he drove in and raced from floor to floor.

At each parking level he stopped for a split second, finding the view of the rooftop bar, but all the way up to the forth level another building was blocking the view. He sped up to the fifth level, hoping in his heart that his hunch was right, and that he'd found the correct place.

Silhouetted against the dim light in the garage, a police officer was hunching over the hood of a police car, his torso obstructed by the car itself. Scott skidded to a halt when the man lifted his head and whirled in Scott's direction.

The moment they met eyes, Scott knew he'd found his man. Though he'd not seen the assassin's face in his vision, he recognized when somebody was caught in a heinous act. And now, he also saw the legs that kicked out from underneath the policeman. Phoebe! She was struggling to free herself.

"Phoebe!" Scott screamed, but knew his helmet muffled the sound. He revved up the engine and raced toward the police car.

Just short of it, he swerved and made the Ducati slither to the ground while he jumped off. As he rolled between the police car and another parked car, he saw the assassin release his hold on Phoebe and pull his gun from the holster.

A shot echoed in the garage, hitting a car.

Scott's helmet obstructed his view and hindered his movement, so he jerked it off and let it roll out from his hiding place. The assassin fired another shot, hitting the helmet, making it slide farther.

Scott drew his Glock from the holster he'd put on before heading into Nashville. Tonight it wasn't about killing silently, but about killing swiftly.

"I have your girlfriend, Thompson!" the assassin warned.

A shriek from Phoebe confirmed the statement.

Scott spied under the car and watched as Phoebe's feet touched the ground, the assassin's feet behind her. He was dragging her in front of him, using her as a shield now as he moved toward the lane beyond the parked cars.

"Come out, Thompson, or I'll kill her."

"What guarantee do I have that you won't kill her anyway?"

The assassin chuckled coldly. "None."

Scott had figured as much.

"Toss your weapon this way."

No fucking way!

Both he and Phoebe would be as good as dead if he did. Instead, Scott unsheathed his knife and tossed it out, using the couple of seconds it took the assassin's eyes to spot the item to silently creep toward the hood of the police car which was only about two feet away from the wall of the building.

"Bad move, Thompson!"

There was a click. The assassin had cocked his gun.

Knowing he had only a split second, Scott dove to the other side of the car and aimed. The assassin stood sideways with Phoebe pressed to his front.

Before Scott could fire his weapon, a car sped up to the fifth level and its bright headlights shone right at the assassin. The assassin twisted and tossed Phoebe toward the oncoming car, his gun aimed at her back.

Scott pulled the trigger. His shot hit the assassin in the back. As car tires screeched to a halt, the assassin just stood there. Afraid that he might still manage to fire a shot at Phoebe, Scott aimed higher. Blood splattered as the bullet hit the assassin in the back of the head.

He tumbled to the ground.

A ragged breath tore from Scott. He jumped up and raced toward Phoebe, horrified when he saw her lying on the ground in front of Ethan's car, drops of blood on the back of her shirt.

Tori and Ethan were already jumping out of the vehicle, but Scott reached her first. He pulled Phoebe into his arms and turned her to face him.

"Phoebe!" he cried out. "Phoebe!"

He searched her body for injuries, when she suddenly stirred and opened her eyes.

"Phoebe, baby! Are you all right?"

"Scott, you came."

Hearing her voice, though a little feeble, restarted his own heart which had stopped the moment the assassin had aimed his gun at her.

Scott pulled her to his chest and pressed kisses to her face and head. "I promised you, didn't I? I promised I'd find you."

He slanted his lips over hers and kissed her softly, afraid of robbing her of oxygen. He hadn't missed the redness on her neck, evidence the assassin had tried to strangle her.

"She okay?" Ethan asked.

Scott looked up at him and Tori, and felt Phoebe shudder in his arms. He gently stroked her back. "These are my friends, Ethan and Tori. They helped me find you."

Phoebe raised her eyes to them. "I'm so grateful."

"Scott is exaggerating. He found you all by himself. We just came along for the ride." Ethan slid his arm around Tori's waist. "Isn't that right, Tori?"

Phoebe gazed back at Scott, smiling now. "Thank you." She leaned in for a kiss, and he welcomed her open show of affection.

But he knew they didn't have the luxury of staying here for long. He severed the kiss, and only now he realized she was handcuffed. "Let's get these off you."

He motioned to Ethan, who understood immediately and searched the dead man's pockets for the key.

"Got it," he announced a moment later and uncuffed Phoebe.

She rubbed her wrists. "Thank you."

"We'd better leave before somebody alerts the police," Scott suggested and helped Phoebe up.

"Wait!" Phoebe stopped him and pointed at the body. "Take his cell phone. He got a call from whoever hired him shortly before we got to Nashville."

While Ethan rummaged through the dead man's pockets and pulled out the cell phone, Scott cupped Phoebe's shoulders. "What did he say?"

"Not much. Only that he would find you soon and get rid of you. And me. He didn't want any loose ends. It must have been the person who hired him."

"That was all?"

She nodded. "I'm afraid so. How do you think he even found me?"

Scott exchanged a quick look with Ethan, who was scrolling through the display of the phone. "Anything?"

"It's a burner phone, like I expected." Ethan's gaze moved to Phoebe. "No stored numbers, no call history, nothing."

"Leave it, then," Scott advised and locked eyes with Phoebe again. "As to your question—I don't know how he found you. He shouldn't have. He traced me. I got confirmation of it via the Deep Web, but he couldn't know where you would be once I dropped you off at the motel. He didn't follow me, otherwise he would have come to the house and tried to kill me there."

"Then I don't understand." Phoebe looked up at him, confusion in her eyes.

"I don't either. But we'll get to the bottom of it. We'll

find the source of his information." Maybe not today or tomorrow, but Scott knew eventually he'd find out how his enemy knew things he couldn't possibly know.

Ethan interrupted his musings. "Where to now?"

"My father owned a cabin in the woods of West Virginia. Nobody knows about it."

Ethan nodded in agreement. "Let's go, then."

23

The drive to the remote mountain area in West Virginia took over nine hours. Scott had insisted on Phoebe riding with Ethan and Tori in their car, while he was following on the Ducati. It would have been too strenuous for Phoebe to ride on the bike with him, particularly after what she'd been through. At least she could sleep in the backseat of the car, though Scott had to admit he missed feeling her body pressed to his and her arms wrapped around his torso.

In Grafton, Scott took over the lead and guided Ethan and his passengers through remote mountain roads ever deeper into the woods, until they were driving only on unmarked paths that could barely be considered roads. There were no street names, no power lines, no signs of civilization. But Scott knew where he was heading. Sheppard had made him memorize every bend in the road, every tree, and every creek. Although he'd not visited the place in several years, he was confident he'd find it with his eyes closed.

When he finally saw the familiar structure peek from between mature trees and thick shrubbery, Scott sighed with relief. Finally, they could all rest.

He slowed the Ducati to a crawl and raised his hand to give Ethan behind him a sign to stop. Then he parked the motorbike in the middle of the dirt path and got off. He walked the few steps back to where Ethan's car idled. His fellow Phoenix had already opened the driver's side window.

"That it?"

Scott nodded. "Sheppard must have known one day we'd need a place like this."

"You sure it's safe?"

"We'll know in a minute. Wait here." He glanced into the back of the car, locking eyes with Phoebe for a short moment. She gave him a hopeful smile.

Marching back to his motorcycle, he unlocked one of the side cases and rummaged through the contents. He found what he was looking for and pulled the small handheld device from it. It was square and a little larger than a cell phone, though its screen was much smaller, and there was a number pad below it. Scott pressed the on button and allowed the device to boot up.

In the meantime, he pulled a spray can from the case and crouched down to the ground. He released the gas from the container, pointing it low on the ground toward the house. As it dispersed, red laser beams crisscrossing the area leading up to the property became visible. The booby trap Sheppard had set up was still intact.

Scott looked back at the device in his hand. When a green light flashed on the tiny screen, he typed a ten-digit number into it, then pressed enter. A moment later, he sprayed more gas toward the laser field, but it was gone.

He rose to his feet and placed the can and the device back in his side case and mounted his motorcycle. He turned to wave to Ethan to follow him.

Moments later, they were both parked in a wood shed next to the house. Scott watched as Ethan and his passengers opened the doors. When Phoebe stepped out of the car, Scott took her hand and pulled her to him. "You okay?"

"Much better now," she replied.

"Good." He pressed a quick kiss to her lips and turned to Ethan and Tori. "Let's go inside."

Ethan took Tori's hand and walked to the front door, then motioned toward the area they'd just passed. "Laser field?"

Scott nodded. "In case anybody finds this place and approaches, the person would blow up."

Tori tossed him a curious look. "What about the animals around here?"

Scott smiled involuntarily. "The system is pretty sophisticated. It can distinguish between human and animal."

Ethan clicked his tongue. "Looks like Sheppard had a few aces up his sleeve, excuse the pun."

"He did, but it didn't save him in the end."

He exchanged a look with his fellow Phoenix. Ethan's estranged father had met with the same fate, killed by the assassin in Ethan's tail. While at the house in Memphis, Ethan had revealed everything that had happened.

Phoebe squeezed his hand. "Maybe it wasn't meant to save him, but all of you. The Phoenix."

Arrived at the front door, Scott unlocked it and entered. The interior smelled stale. Nobody had opened a window here in years. The house consisted of a large living area with adjacent kitchen, a bathroom and a bedroom. It was comfortably furnished, but not luxurious.

Scott invited the others to enter then closed the door

behind them. He flipped the light switch, and the living area was suddenly bathed in warm light.

"I didn't see any electrical lines in the area," Ethan commented.

"Solar energy from panels a few miles away, and a backup generator running on diesel," Scott explained.

Ethan pointed to the sink in the kitchen. "And the water and sewer?"

"A private well and a leach field."

"And nobody's ever found this place?"

Scott shook his head. "Sheppard made sure it can't be seen from the air. That's why it's surrounded by mature evergreens. They provide a thick canopy. And that's why he put the solar panels off site."

"Smart man."

"We're staying here for the night?" Tori asked.

"Yes. You guys can take the fold-out couch. It's pretty comfortable. I slept there when I was a child." Scott motioned to the door leading to the bedroom. "Phoebe and I will take the bedroom. But first, I think we need to sit down so Ethan and I can work out a plan of action."

Ethan nodded in agreement. "Yes. Tomorrow Tori and I will leave and get to work."

"So soon?" Phoebe asked. "Why?"

"It's best if we split up. We can get more done that way. Not that I don't like this charming retreat, but I doubt Scott meant for us to move in." Ethan grinned.

"I don't want to seem inhospitable, but Ethan is right," Scott agreed with a smirk. Then he turned serious again. "Let me just get us all settled." He looked at Phoebe and Tori. "Are you hungry?" They'd stopped for some food hours ago.

"Now that you mention it, a bit," Phoebe admitted. She looked around. "I doubt there's anything here. We should have gone shopping first."

"No worries. There's a cellar."

Scott walked to the kitchen and crouched down next to the wall. He pulled away the rug and reached for the latch, lifting the large trap door and revealing a wooden staircase into the darkness. He reached inside and flipped a switch, illuminating the cellar.

Behind him, Phoebe let out a breath. "Impressive. What's down there?"

Scott turned his head to her. "A couple of large freezers, some dry goods, and a hell of a lot of canned food to survive the apocalypse."

Phoebe exchanged a look with Tori. "Guess we won't starve."

"As long as one person here can cook," Tori agreed and sat down on the loveseat in the living room.

Ethan joined her.

Scott pulled a notepad from the small desk that stood at one wall and sat down on the couch facing Ethan.

"Looks like you have a plan," Ethan started.

"I do. I had a lot of time to think while driving."

"Let me hear it, then."

From the corner of his eye he noticed Phoebe standing next to the sofa. He glanced at her and reached his hand out to her in invitation. She sat down next to him, and knowing that she was here with him, alive and well, soothed him. He gave her a warm smile then looked back at Ethan.

"We know there are others like us," Scott started.

"Yeah, but we don't know who, how many, and

where they are. Sheppard kept that information to himself."

"Well, not all of it. He gave me a list of the codenames of all members of the Phoenix program."

"Where is the list? Let me see it."

Scott tapped his temple. "In here." He put a pen to paper. "I'll share the list with you." He started writing down the names, starting with Ace, his own codename, and ending with Zephyr, Ethan's codename. Then he handed the list to Ethan. "Memorize it. Then burn it."

Ethan ran his eyes over the piece of paper. "That's quite a lot of agents. You wouldn't by chance know their real names?"

"I'm afraid Sheppard thought it would be too dangerous for me to know."

"Well, we can cross two names off, you and me. Which leaves us with what, a couple dozen others to figure out?"

"Right."

"Looks quite impossible from where I'm standing."

"I know. But we need them. If we're right, and each of us has the same premonition, then something big is going down. Something we need to prevent. But we can't do it alone, nor can we figure it out on our own. Everybody seems to have one piece of information. And only if we can get our hands on all the pieces will we see the big picture."

Ethan hummed to himself. "I agree, but it won't be easy to draw the others out. They're hiding, just like we are. They must assume anybody wanting to find them is doing it in order to destroy them. They'll be careful."

"I wouldn't expect them not to use caution. But we have to use methods that will tell them we're their allies.

Something that will identify us to them as Phoenix, while making sure we won't give our positions away to our enemies."

"Do you trust your contact in the Deep Web?"

Scott raised his eyebrows. "You mean despite the fuck-up about the time? Yes."

"We might be able to use him to put out a few feelers for us." Ethan tossed a glance around the room. "Do you have internet access here?"

"I have a secure satellite system I can hook into when I need to."

"Good. I'm assuming there's no phone out here."

"No. But I have a secure cell you'll be able to reach me on. And there's more equipment buried underneath the shed outside. We have everything we need to set up a command center here. It's as safe as we'll ever get it."

"Good. Let's do that. We might be able to find others that way."

"Good idea. But there're other ways too. You were alerted to me because I acted on my premonition. We have to assume the other Phoenix will eventually act on theirs. We need to monitor the news."

"I can help you with that," Phoebe said from beside him.

Scott and Ethan turned their heads to her.

"You don't need to get involved in this," Scott said.

"I already am. You might as well let me use my skills. I'm in this too. That jerk was going to kill me!"

Scott felt a cold shudder race down his spine at the memory of Phoebe in the hands of the assassin.

Ethan chuckled. "My suggestion is to give in." He glanced at Tori. "I've learned that once a woman has made up her mind, all resistance is futile."

Scott locked eyes with Phoebe. "We'll talk about it later." Then he gave Ethan a sideways glance. "And I thought as a fellow Phoenix you'd be on my side."

"I *am* on your side."

"Why is it called the Phoenix program, anyway? Seems an odd name for some agents with premonitions," Phoebe commented.

Scott took her hand in his. "Have you ever heard of the Stargate program?"

Lines formed on Phoebe's forehead as she visibly searched her memory. "The name sounds vaguely familiar. But I can't place it."

"I remember hearing about it," Ethan said. "Got declassified sometime in the 90s, right?"

Scott nodded. "Yes, the Stargate program was a top secret CIA program the government started in 1975. They were trying to train a select group of agents in remote viewing and extrasensory perception. However, the results were disappointing. The CIA shut it down in 1995. Sheppard was involved in Stargate. It hit him hard when it didn't succeed."

"But you have ESP. You have premonitions. So it must have worked," Phoebe insisted.

"Because Sheppard made sure the program was resurrected—in secret. He made it his mission in life to find people like him, people who possessed the gift of premonitions. He knew they existed, because he found me five years before Stargate was shut down. When I turned eighteen, he used his influence to get me into the CIA training program and in secret, he created the Phoenix program with me and him as the first two agents. He called it Phoenix, because the program rose from the ashes of Stargate. He believed in this. And he was proven right. The Phoenix had a gift. And it's real."

"I never knew that about Sheppard," Ethan admitted.

Scott looked at him. "He was dedicated to his work. It's time for the Phoenix to rise again."

Ethan smiled. "Where do we start?"

"We'll have to monitor the news. We know our enemy is doing the same. That's how whoever hired the assassin must have been alerted to me. We have to be faster than he is."

Ethan nodded. "We know what we're looking for. We know how the others think, how they were trained. You of all people can run this. That's why Sheppard gave you that list. He wanted you to take over should anything happen to him. He wanted the program to survive. I think we owe him that."

"This time nobody will be able to stop us," Scott prophesized. "Because this time we'll work together, not in isolation. That was the only flaw in Sheppard's thinking. He kept us separate from each other, thinking we'd be too powerful if we worked together."

But together they could prevent the impending disaster that both Scott and Ethan had seen in their visions, and fulfill their destiny.

24

Phoebe watched as Scott entered the bedroom, his hair still damp from the shower. He wore pajama bottoms, but no top. The sight of his virile body made her feel better instantly. The anxiety caused by her ordeal at the hands of an assassin was finally seeping from her and making way for more pleasant sensations. She was safe now. Safe with Scott, and because of him.

"You tired?" His rich melodic voice sank deep into her body as he walked to the bed.

She shook her head. "Not that tired." She pushed the duvet lower, exposing her naked torso.

Scott's lips curved upward, turning into a smile. "I'd hoped for that." He loosened the knot that held his pajama pants up and let them drop to the floor.

Instantly Phoebe feasted her eyes on his nakedness. His cock hung heavy between his legs, thick and long…and rising with every step he made toward her.

When he lifted the duvet and slid underneath it, her mouth went dry. It felt like an eternity since he'd made love to her, and only now did she realize the extent of her need to feel him inside her. But this would have to wait for a few minutes, until she'd said what was on her mind.

Scott reached for her.

Before her courage could desert her, she said, "I've decided to move in with you."

Scott froze in his movement. "Phoebe—"

"No, please hear me out," she interrupted him and clamped her hand around his wrist. "About what I said to you and Ethan today, I meant it. I can help you. I know how to get the news before the general public does. I have contacts. I can find out stuff that you and Ethan won't have access to. Please!"

He sighed. "Phoebe…"

"You need me. And you know as well as I do that I can't go back to my old life. Whoever sent the assassin will send somebody else, and then they'll force me to give up your hiding place. And I can't stand much pain. I'm going to crack. That's why I'll to have to live with you."

A chuckle broke from Scott's lips.

Surprised, she glared at him. "What's so funny about that?"

"You, making a case for why you want to live with me."

"But those are all valid reasons."

He shook his head. "There's only one valid reason why I'd let you move in with me." He freed his wrist from her grip and slid his hand to her nape, pulling her face closer to his. "So, are you gonna give me the right reason, or do I have to torture it out of you?"

Her eyes searched his, and her mind went blank. One valid reason? What was he talking about?

"Phoebe, I'm waiting." There was no menace in his voice. Rather, he sounded amused.

"I…I…I'm thinking." Still, her mind remained blank. Maybe she didn't do as well under pressure as she'd previously thought.

"Oh, Phoebe, is it really that hard? Maybe I should tell you the reason why I was going to ask you tonight if you wanted to stay with me."

"*You* wanted to ask *me?*"

"Yeah, but I guess your mouth works a little faster than mine. I suppose since you're a reporter, that's to be expected." He chuckled. "Though it seems you're a little tongue-tied right now. Maybe I should use this opportunity to say what I have to say." He stroked her jaw with his thumb. "I've fallen in love with you, Phoebe. I don't know how it happened, but it did. When I saw the assassin's hands around your neck, it felt like he was choking me instead of you. I never want to feel like that again. You see, that's why you need to move in with me. Because I can't live not knowing whether you're safe. And the only way to make sure you are is to have you by my side."

Her mouth dropped open and her eyes welled up with tears. Scott loved her.

"So, how about you tell me now why you really want to move in with me, hmm?" he murmured, his breath ghosting over her lips. "Preferably before I throw you under me and make love to you all night."

"I love you." The words suddenly burst from her.

"Now was that so hard?"

Scott's lips descended on hers and robbed her of her breath. His mouth was warm and his tongue demanding as he kissed her. His hands on her skin wiped away the last of her tiredness, arousing her body and her mind.

He pressed her into the sheets, and she welcomed his warm and hard body and let herself fall. His hands explored her, caressed her heated skin, touched her naked breasts and squeezed them gently, almost reverently. As if he worshipped her. She wrapped her arms around him and slid her hand to his nape, caressing him there.

Phoebe greeted the visible shiver that raced over his back with female satisfaction. She clearly wasn't the only one who was out of control.

Scott drew his head back and looked at her. "I need you, baby."

Phoebe felt a smile tug at her lips. "You have me, body and soul."

Lust and passion shone from his eyes. "Then you won't mind if I take what I need, will you?" His hand moved down her front and slid between her legs, cupping her sex.

Her breath hitched, and she licked her lips. "Anything you want."

"Anything?" The glint in his eyes turned wicked.

Her heart rate increased. She laid her hand over his and pressed against one of his fingers, pushing it into her. Her back arched away from the mattress as she felt the invasion. Slowly, Scott began to thrust his finger in and out of her.

"I take that as a yes."

Phoebe hummed her acquiescence and closed her eyes, luxuriating in his touch. But her pleasure was short-lived when he suddenly pulled his finger from her. Before she could protest, he'd rolled her onto her stomach. A moment later, his hand was back between her legs, and he was bathing his fingers in her wetness.

Instinctively, she spread her legs, and he slipped into the space she'd made for him. Then his hands gripped her hips and he pulled her onto her knees, so her backside pointed up. She should feel exposed in this position, vulnerable, but all she could think of was having Scott inside her. She braced herself on her elbows.

"I'm sorry there won't be any foreplay tonight, Phoebe. But if I don't take you now, I'm going to burst. You understand that, don't you?"

Already she felt the tip of his cock at her sex. Then he plunged into her without preamble, seating himself to the hilt. The power of the impact made her lose her balance and drop her face into the pillow. Her surprised gasp was swallowed by it before she was able to lift her head again.

The contact of flesh on flesh felt intoxicating. She'd never experienced a thrill like this, and she instantly realized why: Scott wasn't using a condom. But before she could react, he was thrusting harder and faster, extinguishing any sane thought from her mind. Moans came over her lips, sounds of pleasure she couldn't keep inside her, then his name.

"Scott! Oh God!"

Her words seemed to spur him on even more. His heavy breathing filled the room, and his moans and grunts bounced off the walls. His cock was iron-hard and relentless. And impossible to resist. Scott had never been so wild before. Passionate, yes, but not so out of control. Instinctively she knew why: they'd faced death together and triumphed, but the narrow escape from danger had made them both realize how precious life was.

Phoebe welcomed Scott's wildness. It felt as if he wanted to imprint himself on her, to leave his mark, to brand her. As if to show the world she was his, and anybody who hurt her would be dealt with swiftly, and with deadly force.

As she moved in sync with him, she felt their emotional connection too. This was no frantic fucking, no mindless coupling, but a melding of body and soul. Despite the apparent dominance in the position Scott had chosen, she didn't feel subservient or weak. She felt like an equal partner, one who could drive her man wild with desire.

"Oh fuck, Phoebe!" he groaned between hard thrusts. "I'm coming!"

Scott took one hand off her hip and slipped it to her front, bringing it to her sex, moistening his fingers. Then he rubbed over her clit while he continued to thrust into her from behind.

"Come with me, baby!"

With more pressure his finger continued to rub over her center of pleasure, adding to the pleasure she gained from his thrusting cock. Her heartbeat accelerated and she panted, her body preparing itself now, knowing what was coming. She tensed. A moment later, a wave of pleasure washed over her and a moan burst over her lips.

Behind her, Scott groaned and his cock suddenly jerked inside her. She felt the warm spray of his semen fill her and his thrusts slow until he finally stilled, before he collapsed and rolled off her. Immediately, he pulled her to him, cradling her against his heaving chest, nuzzling his face in the crook of her neck.

"Oh God, Phoebe, that was amazing."

She sighed contentedly and squeezed his hand, but there was something that concerned her nevertheless. "Scott, we didn't use a condom."

"Yeah, about that." He hesitated. "I had another

premonition."

Instantly alarmed, Phoebe turned her head and pinned him with her eyes. Was he trying to tell her that an assassin would get her in the end, and that's why there was no need to be concerned about a pregnancy? Her heart raced uncontrollably. "About what?"

"Our future…our family."

"Our family?"

Scott moved his head to bring his lips to hover over hers. "I saw a little boy on a sleigh. I was giving him a push down a hill, and you were waiting for him at the bottom of it. You looked a few years older than now, and your winter coat was showing a big bump. You were pregnant again." He rubbed his palm over her flat stomach.

Relief and surprise collided inside her. She would live? And she and Scott would have children together? A future? A home? Overwhelmed by this news, she couldn't utter a single word.

Scott pressed his still semi-erect cock against her and grinned. "So why don't we continue practicing now?"

Phoebe stroked his thigh, before slipping her hand onto his cock, making him hiss in a breath. "Yeah, why don't we?"

~ * ~

ABOUT THE AUTHOR

TINA FOLSOM was born in Germany and has been living in English speaking countries for almost her entire adult life.

Tina has always been a bit of a globe trotter: she lived in Germany, Switzerland, England, worked on a cruise ship in the Mediterranean, studied drama and acting at the American Academy of Dramatic Arts in New York and screenwriting in Los Angeles, before meeting the man of her life and following him to San Francisco.

She now lives in an old Victorian in San Francisco with her husband and spends her days writing and translating her own books.

She's always loved vampires, Gods, and other alpha heroes. She has written over 25 books, many of which are available in German, French, and Spanish.

For more about Tina Folsom:

www.tinawritesromance.com

tina@tinawritesromance.com

Twitter: @Tina_Folsom

www.facebook.com/TinaFolsomFans

www.facebook.com/PhoenixCodeSeries

Look for the next heart-stopping
PHOENIX CODE SERIES
romantic adventure

SPRING 2015

Releasing in ebook, trade paperback and
unabridged audiobook editions.

For more information on the series, visit:
www.PhoenixCodeSeries.com

Never miss a new book from

LARA ADRIAN or TINA FOLSOM!

Sign up for their email newsletters at

www.LaraAdrian.com

www.TinaWritesRomance.com

www.PhoenixCodeSeries.com

Be the first to get notified of new releases and be
eligible for special subscribers-only exclusive content
and giveaways.

Sign up today!

CPSIA information can be obtained at www.ICGtesting.com
Printed in the USA
LVOW12s1557041214

417193LV00006B/782/P